FEELERS

FEELERS

BRIAN M. WIPRUD

MINOTAUR BOOKS ⚇ NEW YORK

FEELERS. Copyright © 2009 by Brian M. Wiprud. All rights reserved. Printed in the United States of America. For information, address St. Martin's Press, 175 Fifth Avenue, New York, N.Y. 10010.

www.minotaurbooks.com

Library of Congress Cataloging-in-Publication Data

Wiprud, Brian M.
    Feelers / Brian M. Wiprud.—1st ed.
        p. cm.
    ISBN-13: 978-0-312-38861-4
    ISBN-10: 0-312-38861-6
    1. Junk trade—Fiction.   2. Buried treasure—Fiction.   3. Criminals—
Fiction.   4. New York (N.Y.)—Fiction.   I. Title.
PS3623.I73 F44 2009
813'.6—dc22

                                                                    2008034161

First Edition: March 2009

10 9 8 7 6 5 4 3 2 1

For all you conquistadores out there

ACKNOWLEDGMENTS

I'd like to thank Alex Glass, my agent, for the tenacity and guidance of Cortés. I'm also indebted to my editor, Michael Homler, truly a Pizarro of editorial sagacity. Last but not least, my thanks to the Ponce de León of friends, Jeff Parker.

Every man is as heaven made him, and sometimes a great deal worse.

—Miguel de Cervantes (1547–1616)

FEELERS

Father Gomez Entropica
Nuestra Señora de Cortés
La Paz, BAJA CALIFORNIA SUR 23000
MEXICO

Dear Father Gomez:

As you will see, this letter is attached to two packages. One is an explanation. Of course, I know it is more like a book than an explanation, and more like a confession than a book, but that is just the way it came out once I got started. I went to mass as a kid, not much, but I think confession is somehow good when one has been through an ordeal such as mine. Especially when the confession is to someone who is honor bound by his God to keep his mouth shut, such as yourself. I am not an idiot, I know confession is usually done in person, but I did not think you wanted me to try to explain all this in a confessional booth. I think we would both get claustrophobic, and if I had to kneel the whole time, my knees would surely blister. To be brutally honest, I felt the second, larger package needed an explanation so that you would understand its meaning. As a spiritual person, it must be plain to you that life is all about meaning, whether or not something illegal happened.

And I ask that you excuse my occasional portrayals of weaknesses of the flesh, Father. I guess it wouldn't be much of a confession without some of that. Yes?

Very truly yours,

M. Martinez

ONE

A SQUAD OF DAY LABORERS lifted the sofa. There on the wooden floor—where the couch had been—were thirty-two tight ones. An invasion of little cylindrical money robots that lived under the sofa.

I'm sure, Father Gomez, you are asking, "Yes, but what is a tight one? And why were thirty-two of them under the couch?" I will tell you.

A tight one is a short can—usually a Planters nut tin—with a roll of cash squeezed "tightly" into it. Some would have you believe that such a can of money is called a tight one because it sort of resembles . . . well, an asshole. It is what they call a play on words.

This may sound unusual, to find a tight one under a couch, much less thirty-two tight ones. Not so. Old people believe a sofa is somehow more secure than Citibank. They do this because they do not trust banks, because many of them remember the Great Depression, a time before ATMs and credit cards, a time when cold hard green cash was king, and so it is that these old people hoard cash. A nut can is a little taller than the bills are wide, but low enough to fit under most of the cheap-ass couches you're liable to find in one of these places.

This is not to say they don't hide money other places. I have found old people's money built into drapery valances. I have found cash in hollow Bibles. I have found cash in mattresses, taped under dressers, built into the underside of Barcaloungers, and in a wall cavity behind a bathroom medicine cabinet. You have to be clever to find a geezer's money, and you have to have a feeling, or sense, that the money is there in the house. Like people who find water in the ground with sticks, certain people have a talent for finding cash. I am one of them. It is in the blood of my ancestors.

Within the industry of estate liquidation, I am called a "feeler." It is not because I have a feeling about money being in a house. The name suggests that we feel up the furniture looking for hidden money.

It does not surprise me you have not heard of feelers, unless maybe a parent died with a house full of crap that needed to go away. Nothing of obvious value, usually, just a kitchen full of dented saucepans, scratched glassware, soiled mattresses, a sagging sofa, and perhaps a curio cabinet choked with Lillian Vernon trinkets. It all goes to the dump, and it is feelers that are hired to load the junk into a container and haul it away. In the Brooklyn yellow pages, you would not find me under FEELERS but under HOME CONTENT REMOVAL, if I was actually listed. Dedicated feelers don't advertise. Work comes to us mostly by referrals from estate lawyers, funeral homes, movers, real estate agents, what have you. I hire the day workers, arrange for the Dumpster, salvage and sell what I can, and make it go fast.

When called for a job, I take a look at the house, walk through and try to imagine where the money is, or if there are any antiques that could bring some money. The clients, relatives of the deceased, have removed anything they think is valuable from the house—that they know of, anyway. Sometimes I am not sole sourced, and the client is taking bids from different feelers. In those cases, I have to have a very keen sense about what loot the house might contain to make a good bid on the work. And a keen sense about possible tight ones, of course. If it looks likely that there may be some return on the furniture, and I get the feeling the place might have hidden treasure, I might even barter our labor, clean the place for free.

No matter what, I have the client sign the complete release of all contents to me. All signed and legal. I explain to the client that this is to ensure that they have removed everything they want and that I am free to dump the whole lot. What this means to me is that any valuables I find, I get, even thirty-two tight ones.

At this particular house on Vanderhoosen Drive, I wasted no time in directing my day laborers to the greasy floral-print, sagging, stinking, crumb-laden couch and motioning them to lift it. What did I hope to find? One or two, maybe four or five, tight ones. Perhaps none at all. But thirty-two? There wasn't room for many more under there. I about shit myself.

Especially since I narrowly beat out other feelers for the work. Including a feeler they call Pete the Prick. After I won the job and he didn't, he shouted to me across the bar at Oscar's Grille: "Good luck finding any tight ones in that shack, asshole spic motherfucker!" You see how Pete got his unfortunate name? From his unfortunate disposition.

How much was there in those cans? I could not know. If it were all Georges, Lincs, and Hams (ones, fives, and tens), nothing to write home about. Jacks? Now we're talking. If the cans were loaded with Grants or Bens . . . there could be a million or more squeezed into those peanut tins. Routine procedure, no matter how many tins there are, is to make them vanish. You don't want the client to stumble in and see all that cash because they may balk and try to back out of the contract, call lawyers, the police. It gets ugly. Also, as a general rule, you want to limit the number of people who see you carrying large sums of mazuma, especially anybody from the government. You didn't imagine that this was declared income, did you? So I grabbed a black construction bag from the pile of supplies, opened it, and motioned for the laborers to throw the cans inside. My foreman, Speedy, directed them in Spanish. Even though I am part Spanish and grew up in a Hispanic neighborhood, I speak Spanish poorly. So Gonzales speaks for me, in a variety of different South and Central American dialects. He also listens to what the workers are saying to make sure there's no stealing on their part. I thumbed a wad of bills in one of the cans—twenties and fifties—and handed it to Speedy, for him to distribute to the workers at the end of the day, and to take his cut of whatever is inside. I share the wealth a little when I find loot. Good karma, they say, and worth every penny. Besides, you have to pay something in the hopes that the laborers will keep their mouths shut, at least for a little while.

I took the bag down the cracked brick steps along the overgrown lawn to my car. It was an old beater, a white Camaro with rusty patches and MARTINEZ HOUSE CLEANING printed on the doors in black stick-on letters that were almost completely straight. It was parked behind the truck-sized Dumpster. With the bag in the passenger seat, I drove carefully home to my apartment. You don't want to get pulled over with a lot of cash. The cops can smell money. Whether they want some, or just to break your balls, you know they're going to ask questions. Yes, the money was legally mine. But I would just as soon not have the police involved in anything I do. Most people are this way, I think.

I mentioned the Brooklyn yellow pages before because Brooklyn is where I lived and had always lived. Nobody has any control over where they grow up, and East Brooklyn is not too bad. The neighborhood is bordered on the east by Rockaway Bay, the west by a slanting parkway, the north by a canal, and the south by a shopping center. There is a boulevard and an avenue that cross, and each is commercial. The avenue is shopping centers and one-story brick businesses like car washes, diners, auto repair, and convenience stores. The boulevard is more village-like with two- to four-story brick buildings in a variety of styles and colors. The first floors are commercial, and the upper floors are residential, so it is where people who live in East Brooklyn go to shop for daily life. Side streets are tree-lined, with runs of unremarkable brick two- and three-story buildings set just far enough apart to park an unremarkable car. Midblock, there are often alleys, which are very old and historical with names of the original settlers. Yes, our neighborhood goes way back, but the past has been paved over and all that is left are the street names. These alleys cut through blocks at slants for two or three blocks and then stop. They tell me these alleys sometimes slant because it is how cows and pigs used to move with the contour of the land. I cannot tell you if this is true. Contours of the land are now roads and buildings.

In fact, I drove through an alley on my way home and parked on the street near the front of my four-story redbrick building. Bag over my shoulder, I keyed my way into the foyer and almost didn't check my mail. You would think with a bag bulging with tight ones over my shoulder, I would let the mail wait, but I had been expecting an important envelope. And there it was! Crammed into the little box was a big white envelope from Genealogy Consultants LLC. This was turning into quite a day.

I climbed the steps to my apartment in what seemed only a few strides. I live on the fourth floor of a postwar redbrick twelve-unit building on the avenue. My apartment is nothing special. Just a place to lay my bones at night after a run to the dump. In fact, it's so plain, I once walked into my neighbor's place while he was taking a shower and watched the first period of a basketball game before I realized the remote had the mute button in the wrong place. I just don't care about where I live—now. I have my dreams, though, my destiny. I've been saving the tight ones. Just not under the sofa.

Two hours after arriving home I was looking at eight hundred thousand and forty dollars in mostly Grants in stacks of ten thousand—ten rows by eight—on my living room floor. (I put the extra forty in my pocket—everybody likes a round number.) They had been curled so long that I needed eighty weights to hold them flat. I don't keep that many weights around my place; nobody expects to find that many tight ones. So I used anything I could put my hands on. My collection of Spanish history books, shoes, boots, a flashlight—my shelves and cupboards were bare by the time I was done.

Hands on my hips, I surveyed the money with the amazed wonder of a conquistador before an Incan treasure. I glanced at the white envelope from Genealogy Consultants LLC on the table next to the front door. I hadn't opened it, but I didn't need to now. What lay before me was proof positive. The blood of Spanish explorers burned in my chest. Could the name Cortés or Pizarro be in the white envelope? I am not an idiot. I know, I hunt money in old houses, and do not conquer foreign lands for treasure, but the compulsion to look, to look every day, it must be the same as dropping anchor at an uncharted land.

Where had this wondrous pile of greenbacks come from? Is it possible old Mr. Trux had hoarded so much? Had he stolen it?

Of course, there was no way to tell where it all came from originally, so I stopped asking myself this ridiculous question. The important thing was to get it to a safe place where nobody could take it away. I knew I couldn't keep it on my floor, but I needed to flatten out the bills, you know? Got to store it flat.

So I went to the closet and found a suitcase, an old thing I never use because I never go anywhere. It was cloth and plastic and had a blue-and-green plaid design on the side like it was Scottish, probably because it was cheap like a Scotsman. I had not used it since my honeymoon. Marta was long gone, and good riddance, so being rid of this reminder of her was a good thing, too.

One by one I pushed the stacks of bills in, and though they kept curling, the weight of the money itself started to hold the rest down. When I finally zipped it closed, the suitcase was bulging like a pregnant bagpiper, and it was heavy, perhaps twenty or thirty pounds.

So I ask you—where would you put a large sum of cash like that? Everywhere you turn, you imagine what could go wrong. There wasn't much time, either. How long before word trickled through the day laborers and got around?

The closet? What if the house burns down? What if my place is robbed?

The car? What if I have an accident? What if some junkie pries open the trunk?

I don't have an office; I work out of my car. I don't have a basement, or an attic. A safe deposit box isn't big enough.

I snapped my fingers: self-storage. There's a place off the boulevard.

I looked out my front window to make sure there was nothing suspicious on the street, and then looked out my peephole. I opened the door a crack. I looked both ways. Hey, you can't be too careful. I wouldn't put it past Pete to send some guys around to take it away.

With the Genealogy Consultants LLC envelope under my arm, I left and locked the apartment, the floor still covered with most of my belongings. I took my time down the four flights of stairs, looking over the banister, listening. When I made it to the ground floor, I was almost to the building foyer.

"Where you going?" The voice—like that of a chain-smoking three-hundred-pound toad—was behind me. I recognized it and felt the hair on my arms stand up. It was the voice no person wants to hear when you have a lot of cash, or usually any other time. It is the voice of one of Brooklyn's most reviled inhabitants, one without a soul, conscience, or scruples. Nobody likes them; most fear them.

Turning slowly, I heard the sandals flip-flop toward me. I beheld those black, untrusting eyes, the scowl, the brown gnashing teeth of . . . my landlord.

"Going on a trip, Morty?" It was like he knew something, like he suspected, like he could smell the cash, the greedy man-beast.

I tried not to show fear, standing taller, and as I did so, so did he. I am taller than he, six foot, and he was too fat to go to his toes, so I was looking down on him when I smiled my big white teeth, like the smile I make for the girls. I gestured to the bag with a wave of my hand and said, "Ah. Because I have a suitcase, you think I am traveling?"

This landlord, he only squints and says nothing, as though what I had said was stupid. I continued.

"Shirts. I am taking shirts to the cleaner."

"In a suitcase?" he snarled.

"But of course, and why not, yes? This way they don't get as wrinkled."

"But they're going to press the shirts anyway, *yes*?"

"If they are less wrinkled, my cleaner charges me less."

Now the landlord monster toad is looking more curious. "What cleaner you take them to?"

"What cleaner?"

"Chinks down the block?"

If I say yes, he will check. Why does he care? Why would he do this? Because he is a landlord, and they live to snoop.

"Nnnno. I take them to . . . New Jersey." Even he wouldn't go all the way to New Jersey to check on a cleaner to see if I was charged less for shirts that were wrinkled less.

His eyes went wide. "Well, that would explain it." For many Brooklynites, New Jersey is the object of suspicion and general disdain, like it was one large insane asylum. It doesn't help that the state is host to towns with names like Weehawken and Hoboken and Piscataway—could they be towns where elves live? Anyway, as a rule of thumb, anybody who lived outside of Brooklyn, much less New York City, was clearly out of their mind and capable of anything, even charging to clean shirts by how many wrinkles they have.

"You go all the way to . . . why d'you go all the way . . ."

"My girlfriend—she lives there."

"What the hell is wrong with you, Morty? We got girls here in Brooklyn you can fuck. Lotta spic girls, too. You don't need to go to . . ." he couldn't even bring himself to say the state's name, just jerked a thumb westward.

I began moving to the front door, having thwarted my landlord like the conniving troll that he was. He was now thinking about the girl and not the suitcase.

"They say you cannot pick your woman. *She picks you.*"

"TED!"

This was the voice—not a voice, because like a banshee, she never spoke—the choleric shriek of the landlord's wife. It came from the gloom beyond his open apartment door. She was even more horrible than he, and he feared her like we fear landlords. She was so large she could not even leave their grotto. The woman's howl made him cringe, and he eyed me sadly as he turned to retreat to his cave, as if to say, "You got that right, buster."

Olé! I was out the door with my money, and an hour later the eight hundred thousand in the Scottish suitcase was safely sealed in a storage locker. As you can imagine, I was flying. I'd scored the money free and clear.

I could write my own ticket. I could accelerate my plans for the future, to reclaim my birthright.

But like Pizarro with the wealth of Peru at his feet, I would be lucky to escape with my skin. He did not.

I AM NOT A FORTUNE-TELLER, but if I were a gypsy,
I might have foreseen what was happening thirty miles up the
Hudson River at a state correctional facility. The date and facts
are a matter of record, and as we know records make a dull
story, and sometimes no story at all, really just a list of dates and
times. I can only imagine the full series of events based on the
facts as I know them now. But I will be brutally honest, Father
Gomez: This is what happened in my life, my explanation, my
confession, so I will paint you the full picture of Danny Kessel.
Of what happened. Of how it all started.

Danny was a model prisoner. In fact, they called him Mr.
Manners. When the guards opened his cell for him to go in or
out, he said thank you. When they served him slop in the dining facility, he said thank you. When he slid a shiv into the
neck of a fellow prisoner who stole his cigarettes, he said sorry.
A man has to do unspeakable things to survive in prison, to
position himself so that he is not abused. Danny proved to be
talented with a shiv—you know, a slim homemade dagger—and
he became a hired killer. He had a reputation for being quick,

decisive, unpredictable, and precise. And, of course, deceptively polite.

Yes, they have hit men in prison, too. Sometimes a prisoner is being tormented by another and wishes to wreak vengeance. Sometimes a gang leader is sent to solitary and needs someone outside the gang to punish the prisoner who sent him there.

Yet Danny did not start out as what people think of as a hardened criminal. He was the driver for an armored car heist. He and four others knocked over an Atlas Security truck collecting cash from supermarkets in Queens. They got away, too, but of course made mistakes and the cops came and shot them all up in a gun battle on the Coney Island boardwalk.

All except Mr. Manners.

They sent him away for fifteen years, and he was smart enough to claim he didn't know where the money was. I say "smart" because he did know where the money was, and the others who did were all dead. No sense in losing fifteen years of your life for nothing, is there?

Even as I was driving the Scottish suitcase full of money to the storage locker, this darkly handsome man was being led through the drab institutional hallways to the place where they process parolees. See, they did not know the bad but polite things he had done so expertly with his shiv. Only the other prisoners knew. Of course, Danny knew, and if you looked closely you could see it in his cold blue eyes. The same eyes that from the prison bus windows scanned all the strange SUVs on the highway, the billboards for Web sites, ads for cell phones, and fast food chains he had never heard of. You would not have known he was just a little bit afraid to be out. You would not have known when he stepped from the bus and entered the subway that he was confused by the fare card machine—he still had some tokens that were now worthless. He just walked right back out of the subway and began walking, eyeing police cars as though they might screech up alongside, throw him in the back, and take him back to Sing Sing. They would have, had they known what he was thinking.

His first stop was probably a hardware or home store, perhaps some little mom-and-pop place on Queens Boulevard.

"Can I help you?"

Danny would smile at the store owner. A smile like that of a child, really. You know the kind—like everything was new and pleasant. Probably because it was. Nobody knew he had just gotten out of prison. Nobody knew he was a killer. Nobody was treating him like scum.

Why would the owner suspect? Danny was wearing the suit and turtleneck he wore in court fifteen years ago. Never mind that the suit was a little tight around the shoulders, the lapels long, the belt bunching the pants around his waist.

"Thank you, I could use some help. Could you tell me where you have the kitchen stuff?"

"Housewares?"

"Thank you."

"Anything in particular?"

"No."

At this point, I imagine the store owner paused, sensing something, but not knowing what, before leading the parolee to the spatulas, meat thermometers, and turkey basters.

"Here y'go."

"Thank you."

Probably a few minutes went by before Danny appeared at the

register. It would not have taken long, because Mr. Manners knew exactly what he wanted, even though he told the store owner no.

The owner looked a little uneasily at the assembled products. He thought about asking what Danny was making for dinner that would require three ice picks, a meat hammer, and boot laces.

Small plastic shopping bag in hand, Danny began walking south, against the shadows of parking meters and hydrants toward Brooklyn again. He needed some privacy. But not for very long.

So he probably stopped in a bar, which on a hot spring day was likely to be empty except for pensioners nursing beers while watching the latest from Pimlico on cable TV. He put a ten-dollar bill on the bar and ordered a cola, no ice. If it was a barmaid, she probably put a hand to her hair, maybe batted her eyelashes at the tall dark stranger.

In the bathroom, he removed his jacket and struggled with the plastic packaging to open his purchases. The boot laces were threaded through holes he poked in the lining of his jacket at the shoulders, dropping the ends down the sleeves. These ends he tied to the handles of the ice picks. When he put his jacket back on, the ice picks hung down the inside of his sleeves to his forearms, hidden. But all he had to do was shrug a certain way on one side or the other and the ice pick slid down to where he could grab it. He could not grab both at the same time, but how often does one need two ice picks to kill someone?

The other boot lace he looped through the hole in the handle of the meat hammer. The loop was big enough to go over his wrist. This weapon he tucked in his belt, at his side.

Then there was the third ice pick. He tried tying it to his leg, but it was too uncomfortable, so he just put it in his inside breast

jacket pocket. Why so many ice picks? Probably an impulse purchase. Presented with a bounty of well-made shivs, and at such a
low price compared to prison, I think he could not resist stocking
up. They say you cannot have enough weapons handy in the
lockup. Especially if you're a prison hit man.

Exiting the bathroom, he walked down the bar, picked up his
change, and said thank you to the barmaid before walking back
out into the bright sun. The barmaid shrugged and dumped his
untouched cola in the sink.

Sun. There was so much of it—he had forgotten. He stopped at
a bargain store where they have the racks of cheap sunglasses
out front. He was a little frustrated by all the stupid sunglasses
they sold, ones with strangely tinted lenses, and many looked
more like goggles.

I have to wonder if the clerk asked Danny if he was buying the
sunglasses for his wife, because he purchased some giant black
counterfeit Donna Karans. But how was he to know?

Somewhere along his walk, I like to think he had to pass a cop
standing on the sidewalk. Maybe just as he was exiting the bargain store. Maybe it was as he turned a corner. The ice picks in
his sleeves must have felt like they bulged, and the meat hammer
in his belt must have felt like it weighed ten pounds, but from
life in prison, Danny was practiced at walking normally with a
four-inch shiv up his rectum. By comparison this was a cake-
walk. And why should a cop suspect him of anything? Every
prisoner was suspect. Now he was John Q. Public.

Did the cop look at Danny as he passed? Did he look at the man
in the woman's sunglasses and a turtleneck on a hot May afternoon? Did the cop sense anything at all? You know, many cops
can almost smell a bad guy, having sniffed so many. But probably
the cop just thought Danny was a little strange, or the cop was

distracted, because obviously nobody stopped Danny and frisked him and took him in and got him back where he belonged, caged and bound in chains like the homicidal monster that he was.

I only wish they had.

THREE

REMEMBER WHEN I SAID BEFORE that I was not an idiot? Well, sometimes I wonder. What do you do when you come into a shitload of money? Well, some people with white picket fences, a minivan in the driveway, a wife, and a squad of bratty kids would pay down some of their loans. Others would seek investment counseling from their local banker.

Feelers are fiercely competitive, and I told you how Pete the Prick had been busting my shoes about there being no tight ones in that house on Vanderhoosen Drive.

And there is no denying: I was in a festive mood.

Do you win the lottery and not tell anyone?

Do you inherit a fortune and go home and watch a ball game?

Do you win on the long shot at Aqueduct and not crow?

So after checking to make sure my workers had finished loading and securing the Dumpster at the job site, I found myself strutting into Oscar's Grille on the boulevard.

The usual characters were there. Louie "Frog" Franco, a fellow feeler with long blond hair and loud shirts. He specializes in apartments, the quick buck. Hugo—I don't know his last name—Frog's foreman, a big man with a small voice like a cartoon squirrel. Buddy, the old-timer, was in his usual seat by the door and the pay phone, his OTB slips in a pile next to his racing form. His daughter, who looked as old as he was but dressed like a biker and who people called Buddy Dyke. The two of them were feelers that specialized in commercial properties and dealt in used office furniture. Slim Jim was at the digital jukebox—his name was a joke as he was like a human bowling ball, but also he was a repo man who broke into cars and stole them legally, often with a device known as a Slim Jim. Mim was a skinny old bird with oversized glasses and a bee-hive wig. I do not think she had ever been a feeler, just was part of the bar. She held down the opposite end of the bar from Buddy, like they each had their turf. She surrounded herself not with racing forms but with the daily tabloids and could be found at Oscar's from opening to closing every day sipping Canadian and cola. Finally, at his table in the corner was Pete the Prick, back to the wall, a scotch and grapefruit highball in his hand. At his elbows were a couple of his heavy-lifting boys drinking pints. Not big but powerful, these were the ones we simply called the Balkan Boys who never wore anything but denim bib overalls, crew cuts, and scowls. I had no doubt that it would have been these two Pete would have sent to take the thirty-two tight ones from me had the Prick got wind of it soon enough. Those two looked like they just got out of prison and were not afraid of going back.

"Ooo," Buddy said as I came in.

You will notice that in Brooklyn, people often say "Ooo." Depending on how it is said, it can mean many things. Buddy said his "Ooo" up and then down, which I took to mean he knew about the tight ones.

I smiled, but just a little, like I was remembering something from the funny papers. "Hello, Buddy."

"We hear good things." Buddy planted his fist on the bar, waiting for a reply.

Like a ripple down the bar, each patron turned to look my direction.

"Yes?" I tried not to look at anyone but Buddy and Buddy Dyke sitting next to him.

"*Yes,*" says Buddy Dyke, her black T-shirt bulging with muscles and tits like battleships.

Oscar approached from behind the bar, nodding. His face and bald head was like something carved from stone. It looked like it had been around for a million years. "Hiya, Morty. Ginger and cognac?"

"Sure."

"So?" Buddy was waiting.

I shrugged, and he looked exasperated.

"*Tight ones?*" Buddy Dyke rolled a finger in the air. "We hear you found a hundred of 'em."

"A hundred?" I shook my head, but I was smiling. "That is crazy. I never found a hundred tight ones."

Now Slim Jim rolled over to join the interrogation, his piglike eyes sparkling with curiosity under his Mets cap. "So how many was it?"

I looked at the ceiling as if I were indulging children. "Look, my friends, I almost always find a *little* something extra. It is no big deal." That was more for the Prick's benefit. I could feel him squirming over there in the corner, but I would not meet his eye.

"But we heard—"

"I do not care what you heard, Slim," I said, laughing lightly, the way I imagine people do at cocktail parties. "People hear all sorts of things. Rumors."

Oscar's boulder of a head leaned across the bar as he set my drink in front of me. "Over at the chica bar some of your boys are throwing money around."

"They just got paid. I gave them a little extra. Does it surprise you that they are spending it?" I shrugged, real cool customer, enjoying my secret. There was no way I was going to tell them anything more than I had already. Besides, they already knew I had scored big. Was I to tell them it was eight hundred grand?

"Forget it, morons!" Mim crowed from across the bar, running an arm across her mouth to mop up the spittle. "Youse think he's gonna tell you if he scored big? Why should he?"

"Ooo. Who asked *you*?" Buddy and his daughter said in unison.

Mim belched. "'Cause I'm tryin' tah read over here the papers."

"Morty?" Frog was gesturing for me to join him and Hugo. "Let us buy you a drink. Come on."

So I went farther down the bar and took a stool just down from Frog and several up from Mim. Frog was wearing a Hawaiian shirt with big pineapples on it. His blond hair was slicked back, and he smelled like aftershave. A lot of aftershave.

Oscar set us up, and Frog raised his glass for a toast. "To good fortune. May it smile on us all!"

"Amen," Hugo squeaked. It was cruel of God to give a man the body of a rhinoceros and the voice of a dog toy. His pants and T-shirt could have made a circus tent. Two bar stools were necessary to support him, and I felt a little safer drinking with Hugo what with the Prick and his pals eyeing me from the corner.

I grinned, clinking glasses, locking eyes with Frog. His eyes said he knew I scored big, but they also said he didn't begrudge me my luck.

"So it was the place over on Vanderhoosen, eh?" Frog cocked his head.

"We cleaned it out in one day, worked hard, made an honest dollar."

Frog laughed and elbowed Hugo, who didn't seem to notice he was being nudged any more than a hippo knows a bird is perched on his back.

"I did the place next door a couple weeks back, for High Class Realtors. Bid on that place you did myself. What a dump. Smelled like old man piss. Didn't look like there was nothing to salvage."

There was a pause.

"Well," I began, but more for the Prick's benefit than for Frog's, "sometimes you have a feeling about a place. Yes?"

"*Yes.* I know." Frog threw back his drink, clunked the glass on the bar, and raised his hands as if surrendering. "Sometimes you have a feeling about a place, that you might find something. It's that feeling that'll put you ahead in this game. I've scored my share of tight ones on a hunch. But the smell of old man piss . . . I never find anything in a place where they can't hold their piss."

Hugo shifted on his stools and eyed me in the mirror behind the bar. His neck was so thick he had trouble turning his head. "Well, I guess there are exceptions to every rule. Am I right?" It was as if there were a helium leak just where Hugo sat.

"It's a tricky business, that's for sure." I was not sure what Hugo meant, but in the spirit of the moment I raised my glass, and they both clinked it.

Three chairs behind us screeched on the linoleum floor, and I braced for a confrontation with the Prick. I relaxed as I saw the three of them exit Oscar's open doorway, arms swinging.

I exchanged glances with Frog and Hugo—and the three of us began to laugh. They were enjoying the Prick's displeasure almost as much as I was.

Then the laughter stopped almost as soon as it started. The bar's doorway darkened, and I watched Frog's pupils dilate as he beheld whoever was entering Oscar's. I sensed danger and turned slowly to look.

Was it the Balkan Boys returning to work me over? Surely not with Hugo there. The cops?

I squinted at the bright doorway, my eyes adjusting to the shape, which came into better focus as it entered the bar. It moved oddly, as if it were limping and swaying. I had been expecting one thing and was surprised to see something completely different.

It was a woman.

And what a woman. She was not thin but what they call curvy, and in all the right places. Her short skirt betrayed long legs and thighs a man could sink his teeth into like a ham. OK, maybe not a ham, but you understand, Father. You may be a priest, but you are a man just the same. She was delectable and tall for a woman, a few inches shorter than me. Her hair was long, dark, and naturally curly; her breasts were cruelly imprisoned in a tight blouse.

As she moved down the bar toward me, I could swear to you I heard bongos. Then congas. Then timbales as she stopped and took the stool just down from mine. There was daylight on her face from the doorway, and she had a proud nose—that is, it was not small, but not a honker either, sort of regal. Full lips parted as she asked Oscar for a sangria.

Then her eyes met mine. The dark lashes fanned at me coyly. The scent of jasmine landed on my nose like a butterfly. It was a heroic effort not to let my gaze leave hers to ravage her body.

I stood, sliding a twenty at Oscar, and waved at the bottle of Yago he delivered to her.

"Allow me to buy the lady a drink?"

I was standing above her, looking down, with the smile I reserve for the ladies—the one I sometimes use on my landlord to make him feel small. To the women, it makes me look like a gallant Spaniard.

She looked up at me from under those lashes, and when she brought the bottle to her lips, her velvety, glistening, serpentine, sensual pink tongue came out to meet it.

I did not feel like an idiot at that moment.

FOUR

SOME MEN SEE THE ACT of love as baseball, where there
are bases to be rounded in a hurry to reach home.

For me, the act of love is like *el toreo,* or bullfighting. For
those who have not seen a bullfight, it is important to note that
like baseball, it has four stages, or *tercios,* required for scoring.
In the first stage, the matador confronts the bull and observes
its behavior to see how it reacts to the cape. In the second, lanc-
ers enter and maneuver so that they can stab the bull in the
neck to partially disarm the beast, lower its blood pressure so
that it can be conquered. In the third, the *banderillas* enter the
ring with barbed sticks with which they impale the flanks of
the animal to further break its resolve. In the fourth, the matador enters alone, with just his cape and sword. He tempts the
bull with the cape, making it charge repeatedly. When the bull
is sufficiently weakened, the matador outmaneuvers the bull,
thrusts his sword, and the animal succumbs. I know all this
because I TiVo *toreo* from one of the cable channels.

I trust I do not have to explain how *toreo* is like the act of seduction and sex. Or why it is superior to dashing for the bases
and perhaps being tagged out.

And there is something about a naked exhausted woman sprawled on your bed that is not too unlike a conquered animal. Yes? Well, it is your misfortune as an ordained man not to know, but I ask that you trust me on this.

Her name was Fanny, and she worked at Tangles, a hair salon down the boulevard about fifteen blocks. I, of course, was fascinated by this profession, which I have always respected and admired. Well, at least from the moment she told me she was a hairdresser.

In the initial stages of seduction, it is important to introduce humor. Making a girl laugh loosens her up. As she was brunette, I thought a blonde joke might be good, and I happened to know one that involved a hairdresser.

A blonde, she walks into Tangles, and Fanny asks: "What would you like done today?"

The blonde says to Fanny: "I wanna to get my hair permed."

Fanny says: "Well, you must remove those headphones first." The blonde was wearing those white earphones everybody wears these days.

"But I can't! My parents said that if I ever take them off, I'll die!" the blonde answers.

Fanny says: "I am going to get the stuff for the perm, and when I return you must have the earphones removed so I can do the perm."

Fanny comes back into the room and finds that the blonde is on the floor—flat on her back! Quickly, Fanny takes the poor girl's pulse, and there is none. Then Fanny tries to revive her, but it is no good. That's when Fanny picks up the earphones. There is still sound coming from them, and so Fanny listens and hears a recorded voice:

"Breathe in, Breathe out, Breathe in, Breathe out, Breathe in, Breathe out."

This joke went over very well indeed, enough so that the timing was right to ask her if she would like to go somewhere else. I was not entirely comfortable working on Fanny with an audience of people I know. Frog was making the occasional groan over the obviousness of my attentions. But why keep my intentions secret? This was no time for subtleties. You must engage the woman, flatter her, throw a little money around.

The classy places to drink in outer Brooklyn tend to be clubs, all with slinky names like Enigma or Mystique or Rendezvous, but they were not yet open at that time of day. This means you must go to a restaurant to find a bar without deadbeats like Buddy and Mim and Frog and Hugo and Pete and Slim Jim hanging around. Yes, they are my friends. Well, more like coworkers, who are not usually friends, more like perpetual acquaintances. Either way, let's face it: You do not want friends or coworker acquaintances around when you are working a girl. Why? Because they suddenly cease to become friends and acquaintances and will almost always do things to trip you up or somehow make you look foolish. They think it is funny to see you fail with a woman. I do not know why, Father, but this is true.

As soon as I knew we were going to a restaurant bar, I knew this would mean that I would have to spring for dinner to make my conquest. But what was I thinking? Old habits, they say, live a long time. Sitting on eight hundred grand, I could take four girls to dinner all at once at the nicest place around and not think twice. So I suggested heading down to Grinaldo's Lobster Pot, which is on the creek near the marina.

So we ate lobsters and drank champagne. Then we went disco dancing at Octavio. Then we went back to my place and opened a bottle of cold duck, and the matador took to the arena with just his cape and sword for the finale.

They say a man is at his best with women when he is confident.

With eight hundred grand in my pocket, I was very, very confident.

FIVE

I ASK YOU NOT TO give me a hard time about playing gypsy again, Father Gomez. It is the only way I know how to tell you this story so that you understand everything that happened. I am a romantic and therefore have certain privileges, and one of them is to imagine freely. If you just read the newspaper clippings you would not get the whole story, and it is much more entertaining to paint the picture for you rather than describe painting the picture. Yes?

So I must tell you about another player in this drama, one behind the curtain that I could not as yet see, so I can only imagine how he prepared to enter the stage that was my life.

What do retired people do, anyway? Most do not seem to know what to do, and so they do not do much at all. Maybe they sit on a park bench feeding pigeons, or playing cards with other old people with nothing to do, or maybe they watch television. Mostly I think they do the last one, because the houses I clean always have well-worn furniture right in front of the TV while reading chairs and other furniture seem not to have been used at all except on Easter Sunday when people came to visit.

The advertisers on television show us happy old couples walking hand in hand on the beach with a golden retriever bounding along beside them. They show them playing golf, in tracksuits exercising, and sailing boats. Is it just me, or is it Brooklyn? I never see any old people like this in real life. Maybe in California they are like this, I do not know.

Then again, you have someone like Charlie Binder, a small man with short wiry ginger hair like you find on certain orange terriers, I forget which ones. I mean that—it was not just on his head, you could see it went down his neck and came spilling out at his chest and cascaded down under his shorts, carpeting his legs all the way down to his sandals. There was no mistaking he was obsessed with sailing and sailboats. The windbreaker, shorts, deck shoes, and nautical sport shirt—what I call sailing togs—gave it away.

Yet he was one of those people who look angry all the time, with wisps of hair shooting out their ears like jets of steam. This effect was probably because he had a heavy brow and a forthright manner from thirty years on the force, the last twenty as a detective in Brooklyn. He had been shot once in the leg, stabbed once in the ear, and hit once by a car in the line of duty. So he figured that was enough and retired at fifty-two, and it had been ten years since then, so he was not that old. His wife had died from smoking a few years back, and that hardship and the void it left in his life made him feel older. That is when he bought a big-ass vintage sailboat to fill his life. I understand it was almost a yacht or something, the kind you have to wear white pants and a blue blazer to look right owning it. So this project of fixing up this giant boat meant he spent much of his time at the marina scraping and sanding his sailboat in dry dock, his retirement project. How this sort of drudgery is supposed to be fun I do not know. It is like buying a busted TV and spending years fixing it so you can finally watch it.

For reasons you will soon understand, Charlie was under the impression that a windfall was coming, and had been for years, which is why he bought a big-ass vintage boat that he planned to sail around the world or something in search of his tropical paradise. Which is also why the name on the back of the boat read *Windfall*.

Perhaps Charlie looked angry because he felt angry. As I have heard people say about fixing up boats, the boat owns you, you do not own the boat, and many in this predicament are not happy about this arrangement. In this case, it was even worse than that. The boat project had cost him a fortune between the teak repairs, rigging, hull rot, and new masts, much of which had to be specially fabricated. It would have been cheaper to buy a new boat, or build one from scratch, but once you start investing money in something like this, it takes on a life of its own—and like a life, it is filled with debt. Charlie owed almost two hundred thousand dollars, much of which he was having great difficulty paying while still needing to buy more things for his boat. His phone mailbox was constantly filled with calls from debtors and suppliers looking for their money.

So even as the matador was awakening to find the slain bull in bed beside him, Charlie was sanding the hull of his boat. His phone rang.

Charlie had to put down the sander and put on his reading glasses to look at his cell phone and see who it was. His eyes peered at the number suspiciously. Was this someone he owed money? Or his daughter? She was always calling to make sure he took his heart medicine, which he did, sometimes.

By the time Charlie had studied the number, he had missed the call, so he found the appropriate button and called his messages. He listened and then called the person back.

"AJ, this is Charlie. You called me?"

"Charlie! It's AJ. Howareyah? How's the boat?"

Charlie scanned the hull of his sailboat before answering. Was that dark spot more rot?

"Coming along. Almost finished. How's Heather and the twins?"

"Good. Heather is still with the judo—I think she could beat the crap outta me, you know? And the kids, well, you know kids. Whadda they know, am I right? Nothing. Feh. Let 'em make their own mistakes, I say."

"Uh huhn." Charlie was getting a little tingly. He got that way every time AJ called over the last fifteen years, but now especially, because it had been fifteen years.

"But I called you this morning to tell you he's out."

"Out?"

"That's right, I just heard. Yesterday. Last they saw him was going into the subway in Queens."

Some people who retire are waiting for death, while others are pretending it isn't just around the corner.

Charlie? He was waiting for Danny to get out of prison.

CHAPTER
SIX

I KNOW YOU CANNOT WAIT to see what happens in my bed when the bull awakens next to the matador. Then again, maybe you can. Anyway, I must elaborate more on Danny so you understand what happens later.

Danny found his way into the gang that knocked over the Atlas armored car almost by accident. As his good manners suggested, he was as clean a Brooklyn kid as you could hope for. His parents: devout, hardworking, loving. His grandparents: always around and involved with the grandkids, helping put them on the straight and narrow, aimed at a virtuous and happy life. Jesus, I only half wish I had been brought up like that, maybe I would have even gone to college—which is where Danny was headed. In fact he had been accepted into Yale and was going to become a lawyer. No shit.

You have to understand about Brooklyn and college. It is not that a lot of kids here do not go to college when they graduate from high school. It is more a matter of what college and for how long. There are a lot of fine institutions of higher learning in Brooklyn. Well, not a lot, really, but some anyway, and there are also a lot of vocational schools. When someone here says they are going to college, it sounds lofty, but often it only means that they are in some sort of crappy half-assed two-year college. Often the next time you talk to them they have dropped out and are enrolled in a vocational school. And often the next time after that you see them they are working for their uncle at his warehouse or delivering pizza because their girlfriend is pregnant and they need money. Well, that is what I see around East Brooklyn, anyway. Maybe it is not that way out west in Brooklyn Heights, or in California.

So Danny was the shining star of his family, bound for glory in Connecticut, where he would no doubt wear ascots and play polo and go sailing and do all sorts of things unimaginable here in Brooklyn. Going to a place like Yale was like going to the moon, like the Brooklyn laws of physics did not apply and you were lighter than air in New Haven.

Fate is a bitch, they say. Which was exactly the case for Danny; fate took the form of a manipulative woman. This often happens just as a man is on the verge of success. I think this is because a shrewd and calculating woman senses a man's potential and wants to cash in on it, so she puts the hooks in him. Danny grew up in the same neighborhood with Delores, a wild redhead, who came from a family of wild redheads who were always in trouble. They lived on the same block as his Uncle Cuddy. Danny's girlfriend had just dumped him, and Delores swooped in when he was weak. You can see where this is going—she knew her four brothers were doing the holdup and wanted a piece of the money herself but not the risk. So she gets Danny to participate, and in the safest possible role, as the driver.

It sounds impossible that Danny—who was headed to the moon—could veer so wildly in the wrong direction and crash-land in Sing Sing. Ah, but there are two very different kinds of love.

There is the good love that endures and makes people happy for life. Then there is the bad love, the one that burns hot and insatiable, consuming your soul in its flames. Such was Danny's unhappy fate.

One of the gang's neighbors was an Atlas Security guard in the truck, the one who became the inside man. On the selected day, the gang of redheads and Danny were waiting for it in the Pathmark parking lot. The plan was to box the truck in as it was driving up one of the lanes of parked cars. One car would pull out in front, the other in back. From between cars, others of the gang would rush forward and douse the truck in gasoline and set it on fire, then wait for the occupants to exit to keep from being burned alive.

I know what you are thinking, Father Gomez. Once the gang had the truck where they wanted it, they no longer needed the inside man, and by burning him in the truck, they would no longer have to give him his share of the money.

Doused in flames, the truck doors flew open, and the guards emerged, guns drawn, and the brothers shot them down and grabbed the money. In the process, one of the brothers caught himself on fire and ran off across the parking lot like a rocket sled trailing smoke.

It is anybody's guess how such a ridiculous plan could succeed. The fast-burning fuel did not even set the truck on fire, so the guards did not need to come out and get wounded or killed at all.

I think it is interesting, though, how many good plans do not work when dumb ones do. How untalented people excel, lazy sons of bitches get rich, and bad people often win. I would say this in itself makes a good case for the impish hand of fate touching our lives. Perhaps that is not a very Christian thing to say, and I hope it does not offend you, Father. Unless that imp is the devil, yes?

Anyway, Danny was in a plumbing van parked just up the lot, and the brothers hustled in with the canvas bags and their smoldering brother, who was badly injured and needed medical attention.

So they drove away to their chosen safe house down on the edge of the salt marsh near Flatlands Avenue. It was a shabby weather-beaten bungalow, just the type of place where you would expect to find a gang of criminals, with mattresses strewn on the floor and piles of cheap food and beer for them to hold up for a while.

At first the burned brother was sort of in shock and tried to shrug off his injuries—his hair was all gone, and when they peeled his shirt off his skin came off, too. Disgusting, I know. So they went to the pharmacy and bought a pile of ointments and lathered it all over their brother like jam on burnt toast. But the pain set in, as did an infection, and they needed professional help for their brother.

That is how they ended up in Coney Island, on the boardwalk. They had heard that the Russians there were very secretive, that you could go to them for things you did not want the police to know about. They fished around bars and restaurants for a discreet doctor, and as so often happens, this got back to the police. What they did not understand was that the Russians could be very secretive with other Russians, but these three redheads were as foreign to them as the police. Next thing you know, they all come to meet and transport this doctor to their injured brother. The cops swoop in. Guns are drawn, lives are lost. In the pocket of one of the brothers is the address of the safe house.

And there is poor Danny at the safe house icing down the torched brother, who is screaming his head off from the agony of his wounds. The police waltz in and arrest them both. The burned brother died a week later. Delores went to prison as an accessory and after only three weeks was killed in a knife fight. Danny went to prison in a deal with the prosecutor, where he stayed for fifteen years.

The money had, of course, been moved from the safe house to the home of Danny's Uncle Cuddy on Vanderhoosen Drive.

SEVEN

WHEN I AWOKE AND WENT to the bathroom is when I saw Fanny sprawled facedown on the bed, twisted in the sheets like she was in the grasp of a white octopus's tentacle. She had a beautiful back—and I don't mean her behind. I would like to think men appreciate many of the curvaceous and delicate features of a woman's body beyond the more obvious charms, and that we are not adequately credited for doing so. A wide, tapering back with velvety sloping shoulders is as alluring as swelling breasts. The nape is another part of a woman you do not hear much about, the slender delicious contour of the neck to the shoulder. The indentation at the small of the lower back is another excellent spot on a woman's body. It promises the delights of what is below, and is sometimes covered in a very light hair that is sensuous and tantalizing to the touch. And one must not overlook the navel, which is like some small beckoning and delectable fruit.

By the time I got back from my pee, she was sitting up, clutching her knees with the sheets pulled around her. At first she was frowning, and I was worried that she had regrets about coming home with me.

"Good morning, *querida*," I purred, sitting gently next to her. There are some Spanish words that are indispensable—the endearments.

Her full lips betrayed a quizzical smile. "*Querida?*"

"It means lovely."

Hugging her knees tighter, she said, "Do you have to go to work?"

I brushed some of the dark curls from her round face. "Not today. I have a few calls to make, but . . ."

"I have to be at Tangles at nine. Will you drive me?"

"Of course, yes. But you have time, let me make us some coffee."

She pouted slightly, slipping back into thoughts that looked like regret. "I betcha think I'm a little . . . I mean, the first night . . ."

"It was meant to be, our union. Was there any sense in delay?"

She looked around my Spartan room. The empty champagne glasses. The cold duck bottle on the dresser. She heaved a great sigh.

"It doesn't look like you've lived here very long. Or that you're staying."

I shrugged. "I appreciate simplicity. Life is more adaptable that way."

"Adaptable?"

"If my landlord is a huge pain in the ass, I rent a van and move, it is that simple. There are no dining room tables, china cabinets, and other cumbersome furnishings that would inhibit me to consider a move. But I have lived here seven years. Come, let us have coffee."

With the white sheet wrapped around her like the toga on a

Greek goddess, she followed me into the living room and perched on a stool at the breakfast bar. I set about preparing the coffee as she continued to interrogate me.

"Why are all those things on the floor? Looks like there was an earthquake."

Of course, I had not had time to return all my belongings, the ones used to flatten the tight ones, back to the shelves and cabinets. I wasn't about to tell her the truth. I didn't know her well enough to tell her I was sitting on a large sum of cash.

"Or," she continued, "it looks like someone tossed the place looking for something."

I flashed a toothy smile. "I was going to clean the shelves when I realized I did not have anything to clean the shelves with. Then I got wrapped up in business . . ."

"The house you cleaned on Vanderhoosen?"

"Yes. And then I decided the cleaning could wait when I stopped to have a drink with some associates at Oscar's. I have never seen you there before, and was frankly surprised that such a beautiful woman would come to such a place."

Her big brown eyes met mine briefly. "I don't know why, either. Maybe you're right, it was meant to be or something."

I placed a carton of milk and a bowl of sugar on the bar, then reached across and took her chin gently in my hand. "*Querida,* why the worried face?"

She bit her lip. "I never did something like this before. I'm afraid."

"I used a condom. What is to fear?"

"Ooo, not that, Morty, jeese. I mean . . . this is kinda sudden. I don't even know you."

"Me? I am the man making you coffee and driving you to work. Now, what does that tell you?"

Fanny squirmed uncertainly. "Dunno."

"Is it the kind of man who doesn't have a heart? I could say I had to go to work and let you take a bus. I could have rushed you out of my apartment. Yes?"

"You sure you were cleaning your shelves?"

Women amaze me. Their minds work on so many levels at once.

"Why else would all those things be on the floor? Why else would I take everything off the shelves except to clean them?"

"Mmm."

"Well, what sinister reason do you think there might be for all my belongings to be on the floor?"

"I dunno, but I don't like things thrown around like that. It looks wrong. It looks like you're leaving."

"Fanny, listen to me." I clasped her hand across the bar. "Unless you decide otherwise, I would very much like to see you again."

"When?"

"Tonight, tomorrow night . . ."

"Can we clean up your place tonight?"

What in the name of God was this woman on about? (I'm not really asking you, Father Gomez, even though you may have an idea.) But I am an accommodating man. I know the female has many peculiarities that must sometimes be humored. And if she was so intent on helping me clean up, why not? This was probably a domestic impulse. So I laughed and waved a hand across my dwelling.

"If that would please you . . . of course." I poured her a cup of coffee. "Milk? Sugar?"

Now she seemed less uneasy and picked up her coffee with the first real smile of the day. "Black is good, with an ice cube. And yes, it would please me. You know, Morty, you have a funny way of talking, even for a Latino. It's like you're not from Brooklyn at all."

I was not sure what she meant, or if it was an insult, so my sunny mood wavered. I dropped an ice cube in her coffee. Why the ice cube? I have found it is better to relish rather than question a woman's adorable eccentricities. "How do you mean?"

As she sipped her coffee, her eyes looked up into mine from under the long sultry lashes. "You're cute."

"Cute?" I must say, it is my belief that no man wants to be "cute." It suggests he is like a small rabbit or fluffy yellow baby duck—a threat to no one, incapable of self-defense. Is there such a thing as a *cute* matador? Again, I tried to smile because I knew it meant she liked me.

She stood and swayed toward the bedroom with her coffee mug. At the bedroom doorway, she paused, and the sheet slipped down her back all the way to the fuzzy spot that is sensuous and tantalizing to the touch. Half turning, her slender delicious nape curved seductively, she almost looked at me. Instead she smiled to herself and moved slowly out of view.

I followed, and I was not cute.

EIGHT

NOW LET ME TELL YOU how I first saw Danny in person after driving Fanny to Tangles. To explain this, I must explain how he came to be in East Brooklyn, trying to accustom himself to the outside world. It began, as you know, the very morning I found the tight ones, continuing through the previous day to when Fanny was sitting at my breakfast bar draped in a sheet like a Greek goddess.

Danny walked all the way from Queens to Brooklyn. Why would he do such a thing? I guess if you had been in prison for fifteen years, a long walk in one direction without fences or walls would seem a luxury. And so it was for Danny.

Along the way, he noticed a lot of people talking into cell phones. He had no idea that so many people actually had them. From watching TV in Sing Sing, he thought maybe this might be so in California. Some people even had ones that plugged into their heads, and they just talked as if they were crazy and muttering to themselves. Danny could not imagine what all these people could be talking about so continuously.

He needed to call his sister for a place to stay, and the pay phones he tried were all either broken or expensive or so confusing that he didn't know how to make them work. So he stopped in at a store that said they sold cell phones.

"Good afternoon. I need a cellular phone."

The clerk was in chinos and red sport shirt, like any of the legions of people selling cell phones at malls across America. Except this one had dreadlocks and a gold tooth and a lip ring. Danny thought he'd fit in nicely at Sing Sing.

"Sure. You have one now?"

"No, this would be my first."

The clerk snorted. "Yow. OK, this one here is a good one, it's new, you know?"

"How much is it?"

The clerk went on for about five minutes on all the features, multimedia, messaging . . . Danny didn't understand any of it, so finally interrupted.

"Thank you for the information, but I just need a phone, and a phone only."

"Bargain basement, huhn?" The clerk snorted again. "Then you might as well take one of these bubble pack phones."

"I'll need you to demonstrate it, please."

"Damn. Ain't you even used a cell phone before?"

Danny stared into the middle distance. "I've been out of town."

The clerk began clearing his throat. He knew what that meant and saw the ex-con glaze in Danny's eye. "OK, that's cool, don't worry about it, man, I'll show you how it works, it's real easy, nothing to worry about."

"I'm sorry, do I look worried?"

Now Danny's ice blue eyes were trained on him.

"No, man, no. I was jus' sayin', since you never used a cell phone before and all, that, you know, there's no reason you can't easily learn how to use one in just a few minutes." The clerk struggled with the bubble package but finally opened it and showed Danny how the phone worked and sent him on his way.

On the sidewalk in front of the store, Danny carefully dialed his sister's number.

"Hello?" It was a nasally male voice.

"It's Danny," he said uncertainly. "Is Clara in?"

"Who is this?"

"This is Danny. Who am I speaking to?"

"Who did you want to speak to?"

"Clara. She's my sister."

"Why you calling here?"

"This is her number."

"Something wrong with you?"

Danny was getting impatient, and repeated the number he dialed. "Did I misdial?"

"That's this number, my number."

There was a pause.

"I'm sorry. Then she must have changed numbers?"

"What're you, a fucking idiot? This is my number."

"Do you live at 901 East 109th Street?"

"This is also my house. Get off my phone."

The man hung up, and it took a moment for Danny to realize it—until he looked at the tiny screen and saw that the phone said DISCONNECTED.

Danny slid the phone into his inside jacket pocket, next to ice pick number three. He walked down the block and around the corner onto 109th Street, and in five minutes he was at the door to 901 East 109th Street.

A man in thick glasses, a sleeveless T-shirt, and several days' beard stubble came to the screen door suspiciously. "Who the hell are you?"

"I'm sorry to disturb you, but I just called. My sister Clara used to live here, and I'm wondering if you know where she may have moved to."

The man stepped up to the screen. "What am I, the goddamn yellow pages? Get the fuck out of here, creep."

At first the owner of 901 East 109th Street thought that the stranger had punched him in the chest through the screen. As he staggered back, he looked down and saw blood soaking his T-shirt. When he lifted his hand from his chest, he saw the blood pumping out.

"Fuck! You stabbed me!" His vision swam as he dropped to the floor, more from alarm than the wound. He didn't know what else to say to the retreating stranger other than: "Asshole!"

Danny looked back. "Sorry." He had been conditioned not to allow himself to be talked down. In prison, where status is everything, it can amount to a demotion, especially by someone of a lower standing, like the rude man who lived in his sister's house. If you let yourself be talked down, the prisoners sense weakness and take advantage. Take food. Take you.

As he walked back to the avenue, Danny knew he should not have killed the man. Then again, there was no reason the man at 901 East 109th Street had to be so rude and hostile. Well, there was nothing to do about it, and probably no consequences. The man didn't know him, he didn't know the man, and Danny knew he'd got a good shot in, right into the aorta, the major artery sticking down from the heart. Rude Man would be dead in a minute or so. Danny dropped ice pick number three down a drainage basin.

The sun was getting low. Danny needed a place to stay, so he walked over near the highway where he knew there used to be a motel on the service road. It was still there, a bump and thump called the Luna Motel. They call this kind of motel a bump and thump because those are the sounds you hear through the wall from the other rooms. I'm told some call them Motel No-tell. So the desk clerk was not surprised that Danny had no luggage, just that there was no woman in tow.

The place was cleaner than Danny remembered. Yes, he'd been there with the woman who ruined him, with Delores, and even the girlfriend before that. In Brooklyn, most kids live in pretty close quarters with their family in row houses, apartments, or small houses with several kids to a room. It's hard to make love to your woman with any privacy, and it becomes tiresome doing it in the park on the picnic tables. So once in a while you spring for a bump and thump.

The clerk was actually a polite teenager with close-shaven scalp who looked like he was chewing an entire pack of gum.

"OK, Mr. Roberts, here you go." He handed Danny a plastic card. "Down there, up one flight, make a right, five or six doors on your left."

"Thank you." Danny held up the card. "What about a key?"

"That is the key, sir. Just slide it in the slot on the door."

"Thank you."

Danny managed to get into his room with the card. Then he called the front desk and said he wanted pizza and beer, and the nice kid at the desk dialed the number for him.

Pizza and beer. Danny had dreamed of it for fifteen years as though it were pure ambrosia. When it came, it was.

It was nice to flip the channels by himself and watch anything on TV that he wanted. After drinking all six beers, he slowly reclined on the bed and dozed.

Mostly, though, Danny lay awake, listening to the bumps and thumps, remembering the times he'd been there before. Remembering sex, the female kind. And it struck him how those muted sounds were not much different from those in prison, where he'd been just the night before, unable to sleep. In Sing Sing, there are all sorts of subtle sounds at night of men doing things they shouldn't, just like at the bump and thump. At times Danny could not be sure he was not still in Sing Sing and would reach out to touch the pizza box, just to be sure. One program after the other flashed on the TV, and Danny was happy just to have the companionship. A TV can be a companion to someone who is isolated. Popular culture is sitting there talking to you, including you.

The early years in prison, his family of course came to visit—but eventually his mother died, his father became frail, and gradually, like the sun setting lower and lower each autumn day, winter set in and they stopped coming entirely. They stopped responding to his mail. It was almost better that way. There was no reminder that there was any existence other than the daily routine at Sing Sing. And if you are to survive the ordeal of prison, you must embrace the routine and ride it out.

The motel room windows brightened, and the morning shows came on. The hosts on these shows were very friendly and inclusive, and he enjoyed them more than he ever expected he could. Danny had forgotten about these shows—the prisoners only got to watch TV in the evenings in Sing Sing.

Switching off the TV, Danny felt refreshed, more human, less like a prisoner and criminal, and he patted the cell phone in his pocket for reassurance.

Then, of course, he also felt the missing ice pick and was reminded of what he'd done to the man at 901 East 109th Street. Rude Man.

He left the motel at around nine and found himself standing in front of Uncle Cuddy's house. It was empty, with a Realtor's FOR SALE sign out front.

That's the exact moment I drove by, after dropping Fanny at Tangles.

Tall, in his dark suit and turtleneck, Danny stood staring at the house and sign, hands down at his sides. I took note of him because he looked out of place, and I wondered then if he was somehow thinking of buying the house on Vanderhoosen Drive.

NINE

THEN I DROVE ON WITHOUT another thought about the tall, out-of-place man on Vanderhoosen Drive. My thoughts were still on my good fortune, both in money and in love. Truly, the fates were shining favorably upon me, and I was intent on seeing how these new fortunes would develop and what my next move would be.

First, I had a few bits of business to take care of. The carting company was first, and I had to pay them in cash.

New York's solid waste removal industry has had a somewhat unsavory history. The legacy of the Mafia years was that the carting companies still liked being paid in cash and gave a discount for doing so. Either that or they charged twenty percent more for not paying in cash, depending on how you looked at it.

Carting companies are the ones who make commercial refuse vanish. They come by and place large Dumpsters for me and my men to fill with all the crappy furniture, appliances, and belongings I am asked to clear out. Then they come with a large truck, upload the Dumpster, and drive it to a disposal site, usually somewhere out of state. I do not ask; I do not care. So I dropped by their offices, handed over the envelope, and got my receipt—which had the twenty percent larger figure for me to use to inflate my business expenses come April 14.

Next, I stopped by my post office box that I use for business, and then on to the real estate agent office that had brokered the house cleaning. The owner pays the agent, they take seven and a half percent, and I get mine—it is that simple, and it is how I scooped the other feelers to win the bid. Perhaps "broker" is too nice a word for it. I paid the real estate agent an extra two and a half percent to let me win, is what I did. They do not like Pete the Prick any more than I do—he is too pushy, and often unreliable. Frog is too naive to think to bribe them the extra two and a half percent. Not all real estate offices will play this game, but Mary knows how to butter her bread.

I parked in front of the Upscale Realty storefront off the boulevard and walked in. Not a very upscale place, just rows of desks, bulletin boards full of listings, files stacked atop filing cabinets. The place was a disaster, and how they managed to keep their properties straight I could never imagine. All the agents were out except Mary.

"Mary—how are you today!" I approached the woman at the desk in the rear. She looked over her reading glasses at me.

"Ooo. Morty. Good. How did it go?" She struggled to her feet. Regrettably, Mary was not a small woman, and gravity was taking its toll on her knees. I tried not to look at her legs beneath her shorts—fat hung down on them, and they were dimpled and veiny and generally made one consider giving up eating meat. Lord knew what the rest of her looked like under the T-shirt, and let the Lord be the only one. An elaborate eyeglass chain hung around her neck, and she let her glasses fall to her waist, right about where her breasts ended.

"It went well."

"So I hear," she said, gasping from the exertion of just standing. Her sweaty eyes beheld me mischievously from under her bushy eyebrows.

I had hoped that maybe, just maybe, the rumors had not reached her. Why? Because it was also my custom to "tip" her if I found tight ones. As a businessman, I have to grease the wheels of industry to make them turn in my favor. So I was ready.

"There was some extra." She took the envelope from my hand and peered inside at the cash bonus—ten one-hundred-dollar bills—and ten percent check covering her cut.

Mary grunted with satisfaction. "Nice."

"But not as nice as rumor may have it. At Oscar's last night they told me I had scored a hundred tight ones. Crazy. The workers got drunk after I paid them and they exaggerated. You know how it is."

She smirked. "So how many were there?"

I put a hand on her shoulder and laughed softly. "How long have we been friends?"

Chuckling, she said, "Long enough to know you'd never tell me the truth, were it one or fifty. Was it fifty?"

I put a hand on my heart. "I can honestly say it was not fifty."

"More?"

"Or less." I shrugged. "I have profited, and you have profited, yes?"

"*Yes.*" Waddling back to her desk, she heaved into her poor chair, unlocked a desk drawer, and placed a strongbox on the desk. From a string around her neck she took a key that had been nestled in her bosom and unlocked the box. Flipping through a pile of paper, she found a check and handed it up to me. Then she dropped the envelope I gave her into the box and returned it to the drawer.

I glanced at the check for accuracy, folded it, and slid it into my wallet.

"Look, Morty, youse better be careful." Her look was ominous, and I wasn't sure if it was because she did not feel well or it was genuine concern.

I merely cocked an eyebrow, awaiting an explanation.

"If youse found the mother lode, the Prick'll be after you, know what I mean? I hear he's got his panties in a twist over this."

"Do I begrudge him when he finds good fortune? Besides, what is he really going to do?"

"You don't have it in your apartment, do you?"

"I never keep accounts anyplace but in the bank or somewhere safe. Not good business."

"Because I'll bet he's going to toss your place."

"Mary, I am counting on him doing just that. I didn't fasten the top lock before I left to make it easier for the Balkan Boys to get in. There's nothing there for them to find. And when they do not find what they are looking for, what will they do? Capture and torture me, try to make me talk? Pete is a prick, to be sure, but I really do not think he would go that far. Do you?"

"So you did find the mother lode."

"Mary, my friend, it does not matter if I did or did not. What matters is that there is a rumor that I did. They will believe the rumor—not me. So what can I do? I can let them look."

"And your car?"

"Nothing there, either. I will leave it unlocked until this rumor dies."

Mary grumbled something I couldn't hear and then added, "Well, be careful, willyah? I hate to see bad things happen to good people."

"I am taking all precautions."

"Ooo." She began rummaging through a pile of paper. "Where the hell did it get to? The guy was just here this morning."

"Who was here?"

"Some guy. Like a cop, you know?"

"*Like* a cop?"

"He smelled of cop. Or a detective. He was looking for a guy."

"I don't understand. What has this to do with me?"

"He was asking about the house you cleaned on Vander-hoosen."

I put a thoughtful hand to my chin. "Yes?"

"*Yes.* He wanted to know if somebody had come around asking about the owner of the house. Aha." She slid a crumpled piece of paper at me. "He said he'd reward anybody who could help him find this guy. Did anybody like that come by the house while you were cleaning it?"

"You didn't tell him I was the—"

"What? Am I an idiot? If you have seen the guy, I want ten percent of this reward."

It was a photocopy, with a grainy mug shot of a dark-haired young man. Below was a full description—height, weight, age—but no name. "It says this man is my age, thirty-three. This picture does not look like—"

"Morty, didja see him or din't you?"

I shook my head. "Nobody came by as we were cleaning."

"Sure?"

"Positive." The man I saw standing in front of the house on Vanderhoosen Drive was not eighteen years old and did not look like the mug shot to me. I had no reason to connect the two.

Mary looked unhappy.

"You could ask Frog. He was working in the neighborhood, at

the place next door. Maybe he saw this man, and you could get the ten percent from him?"

"Hmm. Long shot, but . . ."

"Worth a try. Look, I better be going. We haven't seen you over at Oscar's. I owe you a drink."

"A drink? Probably a hundred drinks is what you owe me, Morty, you lucky bastard. Get out of here."

As I went out the door I heard her call after me, "And for Christ's sake, be fucking careful, willyah? I hate to see bad things happen to good people."

TEN

IT COULD NOT HAVE BEEN long after I left when
Danny walked into Upscale Realty. Mary was still alone. It was
maybe ten in the morning.

She probably smiled at him—she liked the tall, dark, handsome ones, like me, like Danny.

"Can I help you, sir?"

"Yes, thank you. I'm interested in the house on Vanderhoosen
Street."

"You have good timing, my friend." Mary would have struggled to her feet, her glasses dropping to her belly. She was not
comfortable talking to people sitting down, especially potential
clients. "We just cleaned it out and put the sign up yesterday."

"Cleaned out, huhn? Not moved?"

"Died a month or so back. People pile up a lot of stuff in a life-
time, kids can't take it all in, so the rest has to be cleaned out.
Would you like me to have one of our agents show you the place?"

"Any available now? I was just passing by, not sure when I'll
be back around here."

"Ooo." I can picture Mary chewing a lip in thought. "Let me
see if I can raise one."

"Or if I could have the key, I could just take a look myself, and if I'm, you know, interested, I'll come back for another look."

"Well, we wouldn't want you to miss any of the features of the house."

"There's nothing to steal, right? Promise I'll bring the key back. Just around the corner."

"We trust you, it's not *that* . . . my name is Mary, by the way."

"Tom."

"Let me find the key . . ."

He watched as she tugged the keys from her boobs and opened a cabinet on the wall next to her desk. Then she fumbled with the ornamental chain around her neck and got her glasses on her face so she could read the little labels. The inside of the key box, like the rest of the place, was a mess.

"If you'll just bear with me, Tom, there are a lot of keys . . ."

The flyer with Danny's picture was probably still on the top of her desk, staring up at her, while he stared at her from across the room. I had not recognized him from the mug shot, so it is not a surprise that Mary did not, either. The mug shot showed a man in an open-necked white shirt with a look of restrained panic slapped onto his face. The customer in the turtleneck was cool and polite and fifteen years older.

"Can I help?" Danny approached, hands folded behind his back, the ice picks up his sleeves pressing into his forearms. He stood next to her, both of them squinting into the box, while his own mug shot looked up at them from the desk. I guess with all the rest of the stuff strewn on the desk, he might have been hard-pressed to pick it out from the rest of the papers, but the image was a familiar one. Too familiar.

Danny was unable to read anything on the scribbled tags in

the key box and so turned away. He was probably thinking he might as well just bust into the place on his own and look around. Scanning the premises of Upscale Realty, he was probably not reassured that she would ever find the key. He began to notice that there were keys dotted all over the place. On a stack of files on the desk, in an empty coffee cup on a desk, in an ashtray on a desk over there, hanging from a clip on the edge of a lamp shade. Even her desk . . .

"Ooo!" Mary came up with the key and plunked down in her chair with a gasp. "Now, let me just get your name and number." She found a pad of paper and dropped it on top of his mug shot.

"Tom Roberts." He had heard many times in prison that the best aliases were a combination of two first names. People had a hard time remembering them, got the names mixed up. Then he gave her the phone number of where he grew up.

She stared at the number. "So you live not far from here?"

"Excuse me?"

"This exchange, it's local."

She held up the pad, pointing the pen at the number. "It's a local exchange."

Danny blinked. He realized that he was behind on popular technologies, so lying about things having to do with phones made him nervous. As he looked at the pad in her hand, beyond it would have been his mug shot. Now he was looking directly into his own eyes from fifteen years before—but his eyes shifted and focused on Mary's instead of his own.

"That's for messages," he blurted.

"Oh, a message service."

"A message service." He nodded a little uncertainly. Even though they existed before he went to prison, he did not really know what a message service was.

"OK, well, here's the key. Back here within the hour? I don't want to have to call the police."

Danny froze, key dangling from his hand.

She looked up at him, focusing on his face, noticing the restrained panic.

"Tom, I'm just joking. I trust you. You have an honest face." People usually say that sort of thing when they aren't sure, and by way of warning.

"Right." Danny exhaled and tried to smile. Those smiling muscles hadn't been exercised in a long time, so it was more of a lopsided grin. "I'll be back soon with the keys."

"If nobody is here, just drop them in the mail slot in the front door."

"Thank you." He headed for the exit, his hand adjusting the meat hammer in his belt.

Mary looked for someplace to put his name and address, muttering to herself about the mess, and picked up the mug shot to put it somewhere. Suddenly it hit her.

"Ooo! Tom!"

He stood in the open doorway and looked back across the room at her.

"Yes, Mary?"

"You may have to jiggle the lock and give the door a shove."

"Thank you."

ELEVEN

WHILE DANNY WAS GETTING THE key to the place on Vanderhoosen from Mary, I was depositing the check she gave me at the neighborhood Ponce de León bank. Yes, believe it or not, Father, we have banks in New York with this name. The storage place was not far away, and I was tempted to go visit my money. It was still hard to believe, and I wanted to refresh my mind to the fact that I was now almost rich. Let us be brutally honest: You would have a hard time finding someone who did not enjoy looking at a big pile of cash that belonged to them.

As Mary suggested, though, I had to be careful. Very careful. Perhaps I was being followed, and I did not want to lead them to the cash. What worried me even more was what to do with the key to the locker. It had a bright orange plastic handle with the number of the locker on it and the name of the storage place. I had been keeping it temporarily under the floor mat in the rear of my car, but as I said before, I was not comfortable leaving things in my car, knowing that it was likely to be searched—even as I hoped that the Prick was searching my apartment at that moment, getting it over with.

I considered burying the key in the park, or putting it in a tree. But what if the grounds workers somehow stumbled upon it?

After much thought, I decided to hide it in plain sight and to remove the plastic handle. In the parking lot of a White Castle, I found a hammer in my trunk and smashed the orange plastic, reducing the key to just an ordinary-looking key. I slid this key onto my key ring between my car keys and apartment keys. I was sure the people at the storage place would not be happy with my decision to alter their key. Considering the options, though, I did not really care—let them charge me twenty bucks for my wanton destruction of their key. If someone stole my keys, they would have no idea where in Brooklyn to look for the locker, if they even thought that I had a locker.

The paperwork for the locker was another matter. If I threw it away, I would have no backup in case the key were lost, and if someone found the rental agreement, they would know which locker to bust into. So I slid it into a sandwich bag and placed it under the battery in my car. This is an old trick from my foreman, Speedy. His father in Central America somewhere used to keep the family's meager savings under the battery of a Ford Fairlane.

My mind turned toward more pleasant thoughts: Fanny. Ah, what a gem, and to stumble upon her the same day I discovered the thirty-two tight ones.

You may be wondering just how I felt about her—was love, marriage, and domestic glee a shimmering mirage in the distance?

I will tell you, the thought had crossed my mind. She was beautiful and, with a little gentle encouragement and training in certain departments, a superb lover. Fanny certainly had all the right parts in the right places, but Fanny posed a complica-

tion as well as a delight. How she would fit in with my plans . . .
it was early yet. You see, now that my ship had come in, I felt I
had sufficient resources to realize my dream of moving away
from Brooklyn, of leaving the feeler business.

As I was in this frame of mind, I left the White Castle parking
lot and drove to the library to go online.

I guess you would have to say that my dream to move away
came from my father. He claimed that we were descended from
the conquistadors who founded La Paz, where you are, Father, on
the Baja peninsula. He told me he was raised there, and he would
tell me stories of this tropical paradise, of the cool breezes, blue
waters, majestic mountains, and the beautiful hacienda where he
grew up. His stated mission in life was to buy that hacienda—Casa
Martinez—and regain what he called "our birthright." I remember asking him what that meant, and he said that as the descendants of conquistadors, we come from noble blood that does not
thin through generations and is bound to history, and thus to certain places, like Casa Martinez.

My mother did not really like my father, and I have no idea
how they ever came to be married. She said we were never going
to leave Brooklyn, that my father was a fool, and that my father
was never in Mexico, that he grew up in Jersey City. But how
could he have such detailed memories if it were not true? I am
not an idiot, I know the stories he told me may have been exaggerated. He was, after all, a very passionate and romantic man.
As am I. So even if he did grow up in Jersey City, and Casa Martinez only existed in his mind . . . so be it. Now it exists in my
mind, or as he would have said, in my blood, and it is my mission to voyage out from Brooklyn and return to the home of my
conquistador ancestors.

To La Paz, "the Peace."

Obviously, my father never achieved his dream. He was an auto mechanic. The money necessary to realize his dream was not going to come from doing brake jobs. So he gambled. This plan did not go well, and he was into bad people for big money. When I was twelve he was crushed and killed by one of the cars he was working on. It was said that local mobsters did it because he couldn't pay. My mother never forgave him. She died a very bitter woman ten years after him. She slipped on an icy stoop and tumbled headfirst down the brick stairs.

At the library, I had studied La Paz on the computers and discovered that the Baja peninsula was visited many times by conquistadors. As my father told it to me, our bloodlines went back to one of Cortés's compatriots, Hernando Martinez de Salvatierra, who established the Martinez home in La Paz. Subsequently, he left, intending to return, but was killed while seeking gold in South America. His descendants felt what my father and I felt—the need to connect with this place, and they returned, only to lose the home again when the family fortune was lost in a failed financial venture. My father left to come to America to find work. I have been unable on the Web to establish all this as fact. Except that there was an obscure conquistador named Hernando Martinez de Salvatierra.

For a few years, I had been on the library computers trying to locate Casa Martinez in La Paz, and I had found more than one. As you probably know, Father, Martinez is as common a name there as it is here, and the people in La Paz often name their houses after themselves rather than after the previous occupant. My ancestral home might have another name. So I had to search for the hacienda based on my father's description. It was walled, like a compound, with a white stucco and red tile mission house that had a central courtyard with a fountain. According to my

father, the three-tiered fountain was brought to La Paz by Hernando Martinez de Salvatierra from the Basque region of Spain
in the sixteenth century. On the side of this fountain is the Martinez coat of arms, which is very complicated but has a tree in
the center surrounded by eight stars. Of course, I knew it was
possible that the fountain had been removed and sold, as it could
be quite valuable.

I searched real estate sites on the Web and communicated by
e-mail with La Paz real estate agents. They would send me listings of houses like the one my father described. How would I
know the house when I saw it, if the fountain had been removed?
I can only tell you, Father, that I felt that the hand of fate would
guide me. I guess I hoped that the fates would bring me the
house at the right time—and now was the right time if ever there
were one.

My recent correspondence made me think that I was getting
close, as there had lately been some listings that were like those
my father described. Once I felt there were some good leads, I
would fly there and look them over. As you can imagine, the real
estate prices in La Paz are a lot more reasonable than in Brooklyn. For what it costs for a studio apartment in Brooklyn Heights,
you can buy a very nice house in La Paz.

But what would I—Morty Martinez—do in La Paz? I mean,
assuming I wasn't rich and didn't need to make money. And I
wasn't rich. I had saved almost five hundred grand on my own,
and the eight hundred from Vanderhoosen Drive put me comfortably in the black. I could buy a house and start a business in
Mexico. It could be almost anything. A restaurant, a small hotel,
a fishing boat. Anything but cleaning out houses.

Would Fanny be willing to leave Tangles and her career hair-
dressing to come with me to Mexico? Again, having only spent

one night with the girl, I was getting ahead of myself, but I could of course use help running a hotel, or I could set her up with her own hair place in La Paz. Perhaps she had money saved to open a place, but she probably had never considered La Paz.

Then again, part of my dream had been to set myself up and find a raven-haired Mexican beauty and start a family.

Either way, I was going to La Paz. Sooner rather than later.

The only thing possibly standing in the way would be Pete the Prick, if he took the money away.

Or so I thought.

So there I was at the library, checking the real estate sites, and of course my e-mail. I had a message from one of the La Paz real estate agencies. It was a listing with pictures. The pictures were of a stucco hacienda, the walls covered in cherry bougainvillea. There was one shot of the interior, with an opening to a court-yard. A courtyard with a fountain.

I held my breath, increasing the size of the photo. It was a three-tier fountain, but I could not get any more detail. The house was beautiful, the same design of which my father used to speak. I tapped out a reply to the message, asking for a close-up view of the fountain, and hit SEND. It would probably take a few days for them to get back to me, but in the years I had been searching, this was the first time I had seen any house with a courtyard with a fountain. This could be it.

I leaned back, more or less daydreaming, and briefly noted a tall, dark man, the one who had been standing in front of the house on Vanderhoosen Drive. The one with the turtleneck. He was at the computer across and down from me, and a librarian was showing him how to use it.

I was still thinking about the fountain in the picture, not about Danny Kessel.

TWELVE

RESEARCH SEEMED TO BE THE order of the day. The hairy cop who had come around to Mary's with the flyer was hot on Danny's tail. The two of them were looking for the same information: the location of Danny's sister.

Charlie took his heart medicine, telling himself that this would be the beginning of doing so every day just as his daughter had said he must. Just as he was swallowing, his phone rang, and he jumped. He hated that ring. It had become the sound of his financial peril. The sound of creditors pounding on his door. He put a hand to his chest and felt his heart thumping wildly.

He put on his reading glasses and peered at the small numbers on his cell phone. Yes, it was the nautical supplier again. Charlie needed to send them some money so they would send him the new rigging. Where would this money come from? Only one place, because he did not have any more. He expected the eviction notice to appear on his apartment's front door any day.

He dialed a number, the number of an old friend.

"Bobbie? It's Charlie Binder, how are you?"

"Charlie Binder!" The voice on the other end was gravelly, with the inflection of an older black man. "How long has it been?"

"How's Val and the kids?"

"I'm afraid I lost Val about five years ago. Breast cancer."

"Sweet Jesus, Bobbie, I am truly sorry to hear that. That cancer is a bitch. Lost Trix to lung cancer."

"And they say the men usually go before the women. I wish I had. Well, I did wish that, then."

"You got the kids, right, the family?"

"Yeah, yeah, I got Bartholomew, he's a dentist now in Long Island."

"A dentist? Hey, that's fantastic."

"Nice house, kids, you know . . ."

"And your daughter, I forget, Pam?"

"Pearl. She's a real estate broker down on the Jersey Shore. Divorced. He was a scumbag. Got one kid, kind of a handful, that boy."

"Sounds like you got a lot to live for. Keeping busy?"

"Things have changed so much, Charlie. Now I do everything on the computer, online, never need to go anywhere. Used to be I knew people at DMV, the Social Security office, state tax department. No more. I can get anything on anybody, and it is so much easier. Anybody could do it if someone were to set them up. But don't tell anybody! Heh heh heh."

"That's what everything is about these days, Bobbie. Computers, cell phones, gadgets, everybody plugged into some kinda machine. You seen these phones that screw into a guy's ear, got the blinking light? Talking on a cell phone now from the car. No more twisty cords."

"Heh heh heh—yeah. So what can I do for yah, Charlie?"

"I need a skip trace on a woman who used to live at 901 East 109th Street. Her name is Clara McNary. Married name. Maiden name was Kessel. Grew up in Canarsie, probably born there."

"Hang on." Charlie could hear the clickety-clack of a computer keyboard. "So should I ask what you're working on? You're retired, so I thought."

"Just a little project."

"Heh heh heh. Yeah, I hear yuh. This Kessel. She wouldn't be the sister of Danny Kessel?"

Charlie winced. "Your memory is as good as ever, Bobbie."

"Let me see what prison records have to say about next of kin. Is Danny out?"

"Figure he'll visit his sister."

"Heh heh heh." *Clickety-clack.* "You old rascal."

Charlie felt himself redden. "What?"

"Nothin', nothin'." *Clickety-clack.* "But do you know, this is not the first call I've gotten from some of the guys from the old days? Some of them actually tried to run down stolen money that was never recovered."

Charlie opened his mouth to say something but did not.

"Heh heh heh, don't worry, man. I'm not unreasonable. Just throw me a couple G's if you find him, how's that? I seem to recall there was five million missing. You find it, you can spare a few points for Bobbie."

"I always treated you right, Bobbie."

"Well, see you do this time or I'll ruin your credit rating and put you on contact lists that will bury you in junk mail and have your phone ringing nonstop. Heh heh heh, I'm kidding, I know you're good for it." *Clickety-clack.* "Awright, here we go. Clara Kessel McNary, Social Security number 686-56-2378, born July 8, 1977. Husband, Jonathon McNary, contractor. Married on Christmas of 2000." *Clickety-clack.* "They moved in 2005, to Spring Pond, New Jersey, where they have a mortgage of $546,437. He has a contracting business there, home improvement and such, looks to be doing pretty well." *Clickety-clack.* "Two kids, Johnny and Clara, enrolled at Spring Pond Elementary. You want her phone number and address?"

"Very funny."

"Heh heh heh. 71 Pleasant View Crescent, Spring Pond, New Jersey. 974-555-5565. Anything else I can do for you today, Charlie?"

THIRTEEN

DANNY GOT A SUBWAY STATION agent to explain to him how the fare cards worked and took a train to Fourteenth Street, then a PATH train to Hoboken, in New Jersey. It was there that he took a New Jersey Transit train to Spring Pond.

It was the beginning of rush hour, and the train was crowded with commuters. Many had white earphones, and Danny wondered why. Others spoke on their cell phones, and loudly, to their wives about what was for dinner. Danny wondered why. If their wives were making something they would not like, then what? Not like she would make something else. Before prison, most people read newspapers on trains, but now many had laptop computers. Kids worked their thumbs over video game gadgets. It all seemed even more like everyone was distant from each other, ignoring the world, shutting it out. It made Danny feel invisible. He was comforted that the conductors still punched tickets. At least that hadn't changed.

He had considered calling his sister Clara when he found her on the library computer, but he was afraid she would screen his call, and he needed to see her. He needed to find out what happened to their uncle, and he also hoped to have a place to stay for the night as he decided what to do next. He knew Jonathon would not be pleased to have an ex-con around but could hardly refuse him if he showed up on their doorstep. Or could he? Clara would not.

At the Spring Pond station, Danny went to the cabstand and had a driver take him through the winding streets and into a suburban maze of split-level and ranch homes.

When he got out of the car, he saw Clara immediately. She looked out the window as if she had been waiting for him. Odd, he thought.

She came through the screen door hesitantly, her belly large in a yellow maternity dress, dyed blond hair in a ponytail and flip-flops on her feet. Glancing both directions, she waited for him to approach. Her face was consumed with worry.

"I heard you were out, Danny. You should have called."

Danny looked both ways, wondering what she was so concerned about. The neighbors? Did the whole neighborhood somehow know there was an ex-con on the block? Would they come with torches and a rope?

"Is something wrong?"

"Jonathon isn't home yet. He won't be happy."

"I'm still your brother. And you're my kid sister. Who else can I come see when I'm out? You were the last one to stop writing."

"I'm sorry, Danny, it's just that . . ."

"It's OK—it actually made it easier not getting any mail, not seeing anyone. Can I come in or . . ."

Clara's shoulders slumped. "Of course." She led the way inside.

Danny immediately noticed the oddly painted wall, like whoever did the job was running out of paint. He didn't know it was a new fashion in interior design. He did not recognize any of the furniture, and he did not really expect to see any of Uncle Cuddy's stuff. This was all new. She led the way into the kitchen, where two little dark-headed kids sat. One was a boy about six, and the other was a girl about seven. Each held a spoon filled with SpaghettiOs midway to their mouths. They looked at each other, then at their mom, otherwise motionless.

"Johnny, Clara, this is Uncle Danny, Mommy's brother. He's been away a long time. Say hello to your uncle."

Almost inaudibly, the two tykes said in unison, "Hello."

"Pleased to meet you."

"Let's talk in the dining room. You kids eat your supper. Need more milk?"

They put their spoons of canned pasta in their mouths and chewed suspiciously but shook their heads. Their glasses were still half full.

The dining room had all the usual things, a sideboard, a china cabinet, a large wooden table, and some black lacquer chairs with high backs.

Brother and sister sat across from each other. She put a hand to her forehead.

"Jonathon is going to freak out when he gets home."

Danny spread his hands helplessly. "He's not going to cut me any slack? Look, I'm only here to see you for one night. It seemed like the thing to do when you get out. You see family. You are my family, aren't you?"

"There was somebody here."

Danny stiffened.

"What's that supposed to mean?"

"A man came by this afternoon, only a couple hours ago, and he was asking about you."

A long pause filled the room. Danny leaned forward.

"What did he say?"

Clara's hands began to wrestle one another. "Just that he heard you were out and he wanted to see you. That's all. That's how I knew you were out."

Danny's eyes drifted to the ceiling as he slowly leaned back in his chair.

"No name? What'd he look like?"

"He left a number." Clara pulled a slip of notebook paper from her bra and put it on the table in front of Danny. "He didn't leave a name, he just said it was important you call him. Short, with short reddish curly hair, and lots of hair on his arms. Older, maybe sixty something."

"Never seen him before? From the neighborhood, maybe?"

She shook her head.

"Sure?"

She nodded.

"Any tattoos?" That might mean someone from prison.

"Not that I could see."

"Well, I don't know what to tell you."

"How did he know to come here?"

Danny shrugged.

"Could he have been . . . someone from jail?"

"Nah. Don't know anybody like that from Sing Sing."

"At first I thought he was a cop, but . . ."

"A cop? Why?"

"Jeese, I dunno, he just seemed like it, you know. But a cop would have left a name. Look, Danny . . ."

"You tell Jonathon about this?"

Clara winced. "Yeah."

"Oh boy."

Someone entered the front screen door, and footsteps in the front hall made their way into the kitchen.

"Hey, kids—where's Mommy?" came a voice. A second later a tall, muscular bald man with a mustache was standing in the doorway, eyes narrowed.

Danny had forgotten how big Clara's husband was. "Hi, Jonathon." He was surprised when Jonathon actually shook his hand, but slowly.

"You can't stay, Danny, you know that."

Glancing at Clara, Danny responded, "Look, I don't know who that guy was that came here. I'm not in trouble or mixed up in anything. I only just got out, how could I be?"

"I don't know. What I do know is that I've got two youngsters in there and a pregnant wife in here. I'm responsible for them, you know? What kind of father and husband would I be if I let you stay, what with strange men with no names just dropping by asking questions? If trouble is following you, I can't have it here. I can't take the chance."

Danny thought about that a moment, then looked again at Clara. She was looking at the floor.

"You're right, Jonathon. I only found out about this guy when I got here. I'm sorry. I don't have any idea what it's about, but—"

"I can think of five million things it might be about."

Jonathon and Danny locked eyes.

"Hey, I—"

"Doesn't matter, Danny, what you say. Someone is still gonna think you know where it is."

Danny paced to the far end of the room, turned, and came back. "I just need ten minutes with Clara. Then if you could drive me back to the station, I'll go back to the city."

"I'm sorry, Danny. You are family, and I'm a family man. But I have priorities, you understand?"

Jonathon turned and went back into the kitchen. Danny could hear him pull out a chair and sit with his kids, asking them about their day, and them answering each question with one or two words.

Danny sat down again across from Clara. "How long has Uncle Cuddy been dead?"

"A month."

"When did they clean out the house?"

"Last week."

Last week. Fifteen years, and Danny missed the five million by a week.

"You know who cleaned it out?"

She merely shrugged and shook her head.

"Who got the people who cleaned it out? How'd it happen?"

"We had the real estate people arrange it."

"What real estate people?"

"The ones who are selling it. Something like High Class or . . ."

Or Upscale. Well, whoever had the five million hadn't had it long.

Clara smiled for the first time, a little tentatively. "Danny, remember the time we stole five dollars from Uncle Cuddy? Remember?"

Danny almost smiled himself. "I remember."

"And we took the five dollars down to the candy shop. We were going to buy . . ."

"Candy dots. We couldn't seem to eat enough of them."

Clara laughed softly. "Candy dots, on the long rolls of paper. And then those boys tried to take our five dollars. They were older. But you punched the one right in the nose and they all ran off, the one tripping and falling into that puddle that was always by the alley. We laughed ourselves sick. Remember?"

"Thank you for your time." Danny got up and went into the kitchen. "I won't bother you anymore."

Behind him he heard: "Danny, I'm sorry, but . . ." and she began to sob.

Jonathon looked up at Danny. "Done?"

"Done."

Scooting out his chair, Jonathon got to his feet and dug into his pocket. "Need money?"

"I could use a little, yeah."

His brother-in-law passed him a wad of twenties. "It's all I got on me."

They left the kids with their SpaghettiOs and went out to the driveway. A monstrous white SUV was parked there, and they got in.

On the way to the station, Danny reflected on his visit to the house on Vanderhoosen Drive. Even as Mary had said, the lock was stuck, and Danny more or less forced his way in, knocking out a piece of the doorjamb.

Utterly empty, except for the dust shadows on the wallpaper of where pictures used to be on the walls of long-dead relatives. You could not tell where the furniture had been, but Danny remembered where the couch once was—at a right angle to the front windows. There was a dust shadow opposite where you could trace where the huge old TV had been.

On his hands and knees, he slid an ice pick between the floorboards, working to loosen one of them. There was so much accumulated dirt and dust that he had to work at it a while until he lifted one edge. Danny stabbed the pick into the wood and lifted.

He remembered the night he and Joey paid off the Atlas armored car driver and put the remaining money under the floor. It was the night before the horrible day when the others were all shot up on the boardwalk, while Danny was trying to nurse Jimmy's oozing skin back at the safe house. Danny thought Joey meant to kill him the night they hid the money. In fact, he was sure Joey was at least considering it—then only Joey would know where the treasure was—but Danny never showed Joey his back as they slipped into Uncle Cuddy's house with the tools. Uncle Cuddy was in Florida at the time. Danny knew there was a space under the floor because he had helped his father fix the place after the boiler exploded, and remembered thinking at the time how much space there was between the floor and the ceiling of the finished basement, that you could put things there. But there almost was not enough room for those millions of dollars. That much money takes up a lot of space, and they really had to pack it in. Most of the night was required to get the floor back together. They even waxed it to make it look completely uniform, to fill in the cracks between the boards.

Fifteen years later, Danny stared into the same cavity in the floor.

His eyes now had a fine lace of wrinkles around them, and the crescent under each eye was now dark. A little gray had come into his hair at the temples, and there was a slight scar on his upper lip from a fight in the Sing Sing laundry—he'd been sliced by a razor blade.

His breath came hard, eyes blinking. He loosed a little moan of frustration, like that of a dog wanting to go outside.

The floor was empty.

"You OK?" Jonathon had stopped the SUV in front of the station.

"What?" Danny realized that he might have made that dog sound, that groaning whimper.

"Again, Danny, I'm sorry. But you understand."

Danny felt around the door looking for the handle. Could they at least have kept door handles in cars in the same place? "Thank you for the money, Jonathon. I'll pay you back."

"No, you won't. You won't be back."

They locked eyes.

"Maybe once I get settled . . ."

Jonathon was shaking his head. "Have you looked in a mirror?"

"A mirror?"

"I remember Danny Kessel as a good kid who was going to Yale. Who are you now? And what happens to those people?"

Danny absently felt the scar on his lip. "I think it all depends."

"There's a chance, but a small one. You know it, I know it. I've hired my share of ex-cons, and it almost never goes well for them. It's just the way it is. You'll have to turn it around, Danny. And the five million won't make that happen. It'll only get you killed."

The ice picks on Danny's forearms felt cold. He guessed under the circumstances stabbing him in the eye with one of them would only serve to prove Jonathon's point.

"You don't know that. Nobody knows that."

"God knows."

"God?" Danny suppressed a smirk. So Jonathon wanted to play the God card. "What does he know about the boy who was going to Yale? Where was he when it all went wrong? Where has he been since then?"

Jonathon tapped his chest. "God's either in here or he isn't.

You have to put him there. You used to go to mass on Sundays, you know."

Danny had to smile at that one. "Jonathon, you do fifteen years in Sing Sing and tell me where to find God between the cells and razor blades and shivs and needles and the gangs and the bugger boys . . . you live out here with all these white people and all these white SUVs filling your garages and your hearts with God and your heads with electronics. What do you know about God where I've been? Well, I'll tell you something: *He's not there*. Why? Because God doesn't live in hell. But somebody else does."

The train back to Hoboken had a different crowd, and, of course, it was after rush hour so there were fewer passengers. People going to night jobs. Security guards with stripes on their pants. A group of Guatemalan cleaning women headed to some office complex. Various people with white shoes, nurses and orderlies headed to hospitals and old folks' homes for the graveyard shift.

The sun was setting, and the low light flashed orange through the train window and on the giant Donna Karan sunglasses on Danny's face.

God should have been under those floorboards.

FOURTEEN

FATHER GOMEZ, FORGIVE ME FOR the previous observations about how Danny felt about God. But you see, I do not think Danny believed in God at all. I felt compelled to wonder how a model Catholic could become a ruthless monster with no regard for human life.

Anyway, when I got to my apartment, the gum wrapper was on the floor in the hallway. The wrapper I had put in the doorjamb. I saw this done in a movie once, as a way to see if someone had entered your apartment when you were away. Or as a way to know if someone might be in your apartment when you got home. So I entered carefully. The door was locked, but I could see paint scratched next to the doorknob, where someone may have used a pry bar or screwdriver to get in.

The door swung wide, but I stayed in the hall, listening. I put my head around the corner, my ears throbbing. Still nothing. So I stepped in.

Fortunately, the Balkan Boys had not wrecked anything. They were careful in their search. I could see that my bed looked a little more mussed than it should have, and the mismatched imprints on the rug told me they had moved the couch. Did they really think I would put the tight ones under the couch? I had to laugh. I could also see streaks on the kitchen floor where they had moved the refrigerator, and my sock drawer looked like a tossed salad. As if all that money would fit in a sock drawer.

You might think I would feel angry, or violated, but it was relief that I felt. Why? Because I had been able to predict their actions so well. This meant that I would probably be able to stay one step ahead of them. Also, it meant that they'd already come and gone and would not be back. Why would they return? Would they think I would move the money back to my apartment?

For a moment I thought that might be a clever idea. I concluded that it would be too cute. Too cute ideas have a way of backfiring.

I am sure they wondered why all my belongings were on the floor. My impression is that the Balkan Boys are not that bright, just muscle. If Pete were with them, though, he would no doubt understand that I had needed to flatten the money. He has found tight ones and knows what a pain in the ass it is to unroll the money that has been tightly wound for decades, through the wet humid heat of summer and the broiling dry radiator heat of winter.

It would have been best had I not left those on the floor. But what was I to do? Forgo Fanny, not wave the red flag when the bull entered the ring? Besides, they already knew I had the money, or at least the absence of it would not dissuade the Prick from thinking I had it.

Now, what would their next move be? If anything, they might shadow me, try to follow the leprechaun to his pot of gold. So all I would do is not go to the money for a few weeks. I was sure they did not have an interest in shadowing me for months, 24/7, much less the time to do so.

I almost began to straighten up my apartment when I remembered that Fanny was looking forward to doing that together, the nutty girl. Sweet Fanny. Women's minds work on so many levels at once.

Fanny had a late hair appointment and would be over at eight. I had two hours to prepare. How to spend it?

As I have said, my place is nothing special, but this did not mean there were not things I could do to prepare my lair for her visit. So I dropped by the market and bargain store for a few purchases.

First, one must fix the bathroom, because men simply see this as a place for hygiene. Women do not see it this way. This is a place where they spend more time than we do, and much of that time is taken with making themselves beautiful, so I suspect that a bathroom has much to do with their self-image. This is why I make an effort to make sure the bathroom is clean, and of course to attend to essential details. For example:

The toilet paper must dispense over the top of the roll. This is the way women prefer it, I do not know why, just another small female mystery. I purchased some of the triple-thick variety as well, not the cheapest I could find.

Kleenex—men see no difference between facial tissue and butt tissue. This view is not universal. I sometimes even blow my nose in paper towels. I purchased a big colorful box of the kind with moisturizers in each tissue.

The bowl and all hardware must be clean—but it is not enough to make it clean; there must be evidence that it is clean, so I purchased one of those chemical hockey pucks for the tank, and the water turned a beautiful aquamarine, transforming my toilet into a little blue oasis. If there were a small beach, the Ty-D-Bol Man could lay out a towel and feel as if he were in a tropical paradise.

I do not know how much Fanny had already inspected my medicine cabinet, but it was best to purge it of stray ointments and pills. Even men like to keep certain aspects of their hygiene a mystery, if for no other reason than to keep the illusion that we are never frail or sickly or in any way physically unattractive.

I had purchased a small wicker wastebasket with plastic flowers on it to replace the white plastic one that had Q-tips stuck to the bottom.

The final touch was a fuzzy toilet seat cover, matching black rug, and new shower curtain. How does one clean a shower curtain, after all? I have tried, and it is like trying to wash a dog. It does not seem to want to be cleaned, and when you are done, the whole bathroom is covered in water.

Two other items needed attention. Refreshments, and making myself irresistible, more so than I am naturally, anyway.

Food is always tricky. I knew she liked lobster and champagne, but we did that the night before.

I knew she liked Yago, so I picked up two four-packs and put them in the freezer for a quick chill. The red fruity sticky wine makes my mouth itch, so I bought some vodka for me, the expensive kind with a plastic blue jewel glued to the bottle, very classy. I would mix this with pineapple juice, so I bought a can of the concentrate. I hoped to get her to drink the vodka, of course. I find that these days most women will, and it was essential that she not just sip Yago. Sober women are like throw pillows. Useless. You can put them on the bed, they look attractive, but you cannot sleep with them. So I found my blender and cracked some ice trays. I would make blender drinks. In my bag of purchases were some new wine goblets, ones without chips on the rim.

Early in a relationship, women do not like to be seen gorging themselves, so I do not try to do anything too fancy like chili con carne or a turkey or anything. Also of course, the food sends a message. Sandwiches would tell her I did not respect her. Oysters would suggest I was anxious to rush her into bed. Which I was, of course, but even as they do not like us to know what they're thinking, it is never wise to let them know exactly what we are thinking. It had to be something small to eat, bite-sized, so even if they eat a lot, it does not look that way, and, of course, you do not want anything that has any possibility of making them barf. Nothing ruins the prospect of sex like barfing, man or woman. Well, maybe diarrhea, or a heavy period, but you see what I am saying.

I decided on crackers, cheese, and grapes. The crackers, of course, could not be from the cracker aisle. As tasty as they are, a Ritz is not sexy. You have to go to the fancy cracker section, which for some reason is never with the other crackers but on a high shelf, and the boxes are white and look like wedding invitations. I am many things but not a cheese master. There are rules for date cheese, though. It cannot be hard as you do not want them to have to hack away at a block of cheese like they were sculptors working a block of marble, and it must not make the breath bad in any way. Well, a little garlic is OK if you both eat it, cancel each other out. I rely on the French when it comes to cheese, so I bought a couple of the little white packages of soft herbal cheese. The white packages almost matched those of the crackers, which made me think they should sell them matched so men are not left to try to figure these things out on their own.

Grapes! I cannot emphasize enough their importance when entertaining. Say what you want, but grapes—white or red—are dead sexy. Something about their smoothness, the way people put them on their tongue. I need not elaborate. Who was it that asked her man to peel her a grape? And Cleopatra, on her barge—they fed her grapes almost constantly, and they tell me she was a hottie of the ancient world. So I think we all understand about grapes.

I made a nice plate of the grapes next to the cheeses and would splay the crackers later. No sense letting them go stale.

I changed the sheets to my best ones, the ones I never use myself, the ones with a tropical bamboo pattern. Then I showered and shaved and plucked my ears and trimmed the nose hairs. Perhaps this is too much detail, but you get the idea. I was preening.

OK, so she was coming over to clean shelves, yes? So how was I to dress for this shelf-cleaning date? Casual, to be sure, but a T-shirt, like a sandwich or pizza, sends the wrong message. A clean white shirt and button-fly jeans would do the trick. The white showed off my dark complexion. And the button fly is like grapes. I do not think we need any further explanation on that.

You see, women are such sensual creatures, so sensitive, every little thing can influence their mood, good or bad. As I have demonstrated, they work on many levels at once. To keep them happy and focused, you have to keep all their senses pleasantly occupied. Taste, sight, texture . . . grapes, button fly, lack of ointments, new flowery wastebasket . . . I needed sound. Some gentle Latin jazz would be perfect. Something like salsa or merengue music is like oysters—it tips your mitt, makes them wary. No, the best music for this is bossa nova or rumba. These songs have the subtle bongo beat of fucking, but sort of hidden. Yet unmistakable if you're thinking about fucking at all.

Holy Mother of God! I almost forgot smell. Very important. It has been my experience that they can smell things men can't. Like dogs, they can pick up many subtleties in the air. You have one pair of stinky socks in your hamper, one chicken bone in the garbage, one insignificant fart all the way across the room, and the woman is turning her nose one way and the other, asking: *Do you smell that?*

Scented candles. They are pleasing to look at and mask the smell of any stinky sock that may have secreted itself under the bed. One in the bathroom is wise.

I clapped my hands. All was in readiness.

My cell phone rang. I recognized the number and smiled.

"Querida!"

"Can I take a rain check?"

"But . . . what about the . . . the shelves? I cannot leave all my possessions on the floor."

"Just one more day? I had a really long day. I just wanna go home and soak in a hot tub."

Soaking in a hot tub. More than once I have cursed the man who invented bathtubs. Men must constantly compete with a mass of hot water and Calgon bath beads.

Women are delightfully unpredictable, yes? Sometimes.

I collapsed onto the couch, a balloon deflated.

"Whatever your heart desires, *corazón*." I was wondering if I could freeze the grapes.

"Promise you won't put the things back?"

"I promise."

"What will you do tonight?"

"I was thinking of washing the shower curtain."

"What?"

"Just kidding, *querida*. I guess I will go down to Oscar's and catch up with what's going on in the business."

"Morty?"

"Yes, *encantadora*."

"I'll make it up to you."

"Yes?"

"I have a cute little thong and high heels."

I suddenly found myself standing, the balloon fully inflated.

"Tomorrow, yes?"

"*Yes.*"

FIFTEEN

QUEENS IS WHAT I LIKE to think of as New York City's third borough, after Manhattan and Brooklyn. Just as Swedes and Norwegians both live on vast white glaciers, each borough thinks their patch of snow is better than the one across the fjord. That said, I must tell you that all the boroughs defer to Manhattan as the boss. To do otherwise would make you look like an idiot. You will not find the Empire State Building on Flatbush Avenue. You will not find the Stock Exchange in Flushing. You will not find Times Square in Hunts Point. You will not find Central Park across the Verrazano Bridge.

The pecking order of the others is of course a matter of major dispute. Well, except when it comes to Staten Island. I think it is safe to assume that the Bronx, Queens, and Brooklyn all acknowledge that Staten Island is at the bottom of the totem pole, starting with its southern, isolated geography. Brooklyn, Queens, and the Bronx suspect it is only a matter of time before Staten Island secedes from the city and settles into its proper legacy: part of New Jersey. Perhaps they could rename it East Bayonne.

So the three each think they are better than the others, though I think the Bronx has a pretty tough case to make. Yes, they have their precious zoo, but let us face facts: The South Bronx is a pretty formidable stumbling block on their walk of fame. I would stroll naked down Brooklyn's Utica Avenue in Crown Heights before I'd stop for gas on Melrose Avenue in the Bronx.

I think Brooklyn and Queens agree on this point, so that leaves just the two of us to argue who is second to Manhattan. Obviously, I believe my native Brooklyn to be far superior to Queens. As with Staten Island, Brooklynites secretly believe Queens will one day secede to Long Island. Or should. For the most part, they are indistinguishable. Bedroom communities, strip malls, and so on. No character, no what they call moxie.

Queens's sole claim to superiority—as far as I can see—is that each of its neighborhoods has a postal address as a town like anywhere else in Long Island. There is Rosedale, a neighborhood in Queens, which has a postal address of Rosedale, New York, plus zip. In Brooklyn, the neighborhoods are not part of the address; we just live in Brooklyn, New York. This is why people in Queens take an attitude with us. Can you imagine?

This is also why I can be sure Charlie Binder, as he sat in his car across from Oscar's Grille, was disdainful of my neighborhood. He was from "Rosedale, New York," as was his partner Stevie when they worked this neighborhood on the NYPD years ago. Stevie used to call my neighborhood "Brooklyn's Armpit" because geographically it sits under the arm formed by the Rockaways. Then again, it is my impression that police generally have some level of disdain for the neighborhood they work in. How could they not? People don't call the cops to come over for Aunt Bee's apple pie, to crank the ice cream machine or strum a guitar on the porch. They call the cops to their home because their husband has bashed them over the head with a bottle and locked them in the bathroom with a pit bull. Day after day cops are subjected to the worst a neighborhood has to offer.

Charlie didn't know it, but he had been one step ahead of Danny all day, mainly because he had a car and Danny was walking or taking public transportation. He got to Mary's and Clara's before Danny. In truth, if Charlie had started a little later in the day he would have run right into his man.

So why had Charlie come to this neighborhood, anyway? What made him think to find Danny here?

Certainly, it is reasonable to expect that when a man gets out of prison he will return to his home, and Danny's registered next of kin was his sister. Which is why he drove to 901 East 109th Street first off. Again, had Charlie stopped for a bialy and coffee, he might have saved the life of the asshole who lived there.

But there was another reason Charlie was fixated on my neighborhood. As you may have guessed, he and his partner Stevie were detectives who worked on the armored car holdup. They were the ones who never found the money. And it was Stevie who was mortally injured in the shoot-out on Coney Island's boardwalk.

You might imagine Charlie held a grudge. He did not. Danny did not blow a fist-sized hole in Stevie's abdomen. Joey, the one who helped hide the money, shot Stevie. As Joey lay there bleeding and moaning on the beach, Charlie walked up and shot him in the head. Sure, there were other cops there. To them this was justified. You shoot a cop and justice is often swifter than usual.

Surprisingly, Stevie's death had little to do with the search for Danny. Charlie just wanted the fucking money. Not to solve any case, either. Charlie was retired. He more or less considered this

his nest egg, his ship pulling into port, which would hopefully go a long way toward pulling his sailboat out of dry dock. The boat was more expensive than supporting a Park Avenue mistress.

In order to locate the stolen money, Charlie and Stevie had tried tracking the gang's movements since they made the boost. Yes, the cops knew the bunch of them went directly to their shabby hideout at the end of Flatlands Avenue, but a police search revealed that the money was not at the hideout. The crooks must have stashed it.

Danny was questioned thoroughly after his capture, and though he denied knowing anything about where the money had gone, the police were certain he knew. How were they certain? Look, cops not only see a neighborhood at its worst, they also listen to people lie all day. First thing out of a perp's mouth is "Wasn't me." When of course it was him. After years and years of this, the better cops become attuned to what is and isn't a lie purely through observation, and these better cops they make detectives.

So they knew he was lying. Had Danny personally been one of those who hid the money?

They tracked the gang's movements as best they could from the day of the robbery, and it turned out that the only one who could be tracked to anywhere other than Coney Island or locally in Flatlands was Danny. He had taken cash out of his bank's ATM not far from Oscar's—the gang knew better than to spend any of the money they had stolen so soon—and they knew his sister and uncle lived nearby. He could have been visiting them, or he could have come to familiar ground to hide the money.

The inside man, the armored car driver, was questioned, of course, but the police never made the connection between where he lived and the gang lived, much less Uncle Cuddy. I can only guess they were so intent on cracking Danny that they never thought they needed another suspect, and since the gang tried to burn the truck, they probably could not imagine that it was an inside job.

Charlie was convinced Danny knew where the five million was and that the stash was somewhere nearby. Maybe Danny buried it in the cemetery, maybe in the park, maybe in his sister's or uncle's backyard. Charlie had already established that the sister had moved and the uncle recently passed away. When he went to the sister's old address, the door was open, the torn screen door locked, and there was no answer. He would try back there again the next day. Once Danny knew the uncle was dead, and if the money were somewhere in the yard or on the grounds or stashed in the attic, he would go to the real estate agency on the sign out front to gain access.

Five million in twenties: Charlie knew that took up a lot of space. You would need to dig a large hole to bury that in, and chances were that after all this time there might be a depression where this hole was. He walked the entire park searching the ground for clues. He walked the edges of the cemetery, where there were no graves. Nothing.

The more he thought about it, the more Charlie felt they would not have dug a hole—too much work, and worries about people seeing the disturbed ground.

He backtracked to the uncle's place later in the day and tried the door—it was open, and the doorjamb was broken. Someone had forced their way in. Danny? He strolled each floor, tapping on walls, and climbed through the hatch into the attic and crept into the dank basement. Nothing.

Of course, the place had been cleaned out recently. Was it possible the movers or cleaners found it? Outside chance. If they had, everybody would know about it.

So Charlie spent the balance of the day canvassing the commercial strip, focusing on cheap restaurants and bars and hotels. The bump and thump over by the highway seemed like the kind of flop where Danny would stay, but the girl at the desk said she had not seen him. On his way home, Charlie planned to stop back there and check with the night clerk—maybe he'd seen Danny.

It is pretty common knowledge that an ex-con will almost always go to see family, or go back to a familiar neighborhood, as soon as they get out. What they should do is go on vacation somewhere, but most have little money. Danny's sister and the uncle were the only identifiable links in his old stomping ground.

Charlie climbed out of his black SUV, bleeped the lock, and headed for the crummy bar across the street.

CHAPTER

SIXTEEN

MARY WAS WORKING LATE, LOST in the morass of her own lousy bookkeeping. That is the only explanation for why she was there so late.

The only explanation for why she was there when Danny tapped on the glass door.

I am sure she could not recognize him at that distance and probably yelled for him to go away. He kept knocking, and she came over and saw it was Tom Roberts, the man who looked at the house on Vanderhoosen. She probably thought he must be interested in the house.

Mary unlocked the door and let him in.

I could play gypsy on this one, Father, but Mary was my friend. This one I will leave to your imagination, not mine.

SEVENTEEN

I ENTERED THE DARK CONFINES of Oscar's and did not beat about the bush. After cordially nodding to those at the bar, I went and sat down across from Pete the Prick at his table. His seat was in the corner, with his back to the wall. The Balkan Boys were nowhere to be seen.

You know of Pete's character, but not of his looks. He was shorter than me, with a sharp nose and sharper hazel eyes, and a dark waxy complexion that was scarred from acne. You could see a series of white scars on his scalp, as he keeps his dark hair cut to within an inch of his scalp. One presumes these scars come from fights, perhaps someone smashing a beer bottle on his head, I do not know. I will say this for Pete: He had very nice teeth, and he showed them often, though rarely in what one would call a smile. This was a tightly wound man, always clenched. You could see the muscles in his jaw flexing, his hands in fists, his brow squeezing his eye sockets. When I looked closely at him, I really did feel sorry for him, as he is obviously not a happy man. My guess would be that nothing is ever enough for Pete, and that he feels constantly threatened and must do what he can to feel in control or on top.

"Whadda you want, spic?"

When he speaks, I do not feel sorry for him at all.

"Can I buy you a drink?"

"I'll drink your money. All of it if I could."

"Oscar? Whatever Pete is having, and my usual, please." I turned back to Pete, smiling lightly but not gloating. My intent was not to egg him on. My intent was to try to put his ambitions toward my eight hundred grand to bed. "You look well."

"Who was the slut you banged last night?"

You thought they called him Pete the Prick for nothing? This is a difficult man. I find it best not to answer any of his inflammatory questions, as they only lead to more inflammatory questions.

"How is business? I hear you are doing well."

"What is this, gloating?"

I shook my head wearily. "No, Pete. I'm just trying to get along. We both work in this business, we are both feelers. There is plenty of work. We compete, but we both make a living. So why be enemies?"

He attempted a laugh. "What do you take me for, spic? Some kinda asshole?"

Of course, I was tempted to answer that question, but did not. The drinks arrived—his was a scotch and grapefruit juice. Horrible drink, horrible man. I sipped my ginger and cognac.

"These rumors of my finding a large sum of money has made people feel cheated, resentful. I would simply like to dispel the rumors if I can."

"Well, you can't, spic, get it? We know you found a mother lode. *We know.*" He scooted his chair out and stomped out the door, his drink untouched.

With a show of resignation I stood and met the eyes of Slim Jim, Buddy, Buddy Dyke, Mim, and Oscar. "Well, I tried."

Oscar's boulderlike head cracked open at the mouth. "Wasting your time, Morty."

"Has anybody seen Frog and Hugo?" I asked.

"Don't think Frog'll be in," Mim looked up from her tabloids. "Heard his mother is sick or somethin'."

I cocked an eyebrow. I knew his parents had been dead for some time, but I shrugged this information off. His reasons were his own. I took a stool between Buddy Dyke and Slim Jim. "So how was everybody's day?"

"Has Pete come lookin' for the money?" Buddy Dyke asked, flexing.

"Watch out for them Balkan Boys," Buddy added.

"You carry?" Slim Jim made a pistol shape with his hand.

"This rumor has got to stop," I groaned. "Is there nothing else to talk about?"

It was at that moment a stranger walked into the bar. All eyes scanned him and then returned to me. We all understood. This was a cop of some kind. Something in the way he kept his right thumb on his belt, near where the holster would have been.

"Drink, bud?" Oscar tossed a coaster on the bar, and the stranger approached it.

"Beer." The stranger was in shorts, windbreaker, and deck shoes. He was covered in ginger hair in what might have been described as a pelt were it not for the fact that he shaved his face. In one hand was a cardboard valise.

Ah, this must be the man who visited Mary.

Sure enough, no sooner did he have his beer than he slid a

piece of paper from his valise and held it up for us to see. "Hate to trouble youse all, but seen this guy?"

This was the very same flyer Mary had on her desk.

Buddy and his daughter took the flyer from him and inspected it closely.

"Nah," they finally said in unison. "Why? You looking for him?"

The furry stranger placed a fifty on the bar. "Let me buy a round for the house, you know, for taking your time. I appreciate any help."

The flyer made its way down the bar. I only glanced at it and shrugged.

Slim Jim held it at arm's length, turning it one way and the other. "Looks familiar, but . . ."

"Gimme," Mim demanded. One glance. "Sure, this is that kid Danny Kessler. I mean, Kessel."

Oscar took a look. "She's right. It's Danny. He out?"

"Who is this Danny Kessel?" I inquired.

"One of the gang that held up an armored car ten, fifteen, maybe twenty years ago," Mim said. "Caught him. Went to jail. Others all killed in a shootout."

"Why you lookin' for him here?" Oscar asked the stranger.

"His old neighborhood. Figgered he might come back to the stomping ground."

"Never did find all that money," Mim said, grinning. "Did they?"

"Jeese." Slim Jim scratched his belly thoughtfully. "You think they hid it around here? Maybe buried it in the park?"

The stranger did not answer. "If any of you see him, I'll pay you a hundred dollars to call me. One phone call for one hundred dollars. That's light work." He held up a one-hundred-dollar bill.

"We'll keep an eye out." Oscar polished a glass enthusiastically.

The stranger put a small stack of business cards on the bar. "Thanks. Number is on the card. 'Preciate your time."

With that, the stranger vanished back out the door. I saw him climb into a black SUV across the street.

The stack of cards went around, and I examined mine, front and back. "There is only a phone number, no name."

"Bounty hunter," Oscar said with authority. "This guy is trying to recover that money, all right."

"Hundred—that's not so much." Buddy frowned.

"Like he said, it's a C-note for less than a minute's work." Slim Jim looked at the ceiling, making mental calculations. "That's . . ."

"Six thousand dollars an hour," I added. "What some lawyers make, they say."

"Jeese." Slim Jim scratched his belly again, now with both hands. "Lawyers make a lot of money."

Mim began wheezing, and we were immediately concerned. It was anybody's guess when she might just keel off her stool, her heart and organs finally dissolved in Canadian Club. She was grinning, though, and we relaxed when we realized she was laughing.

"What's so funny, Mim?" Buddy Dyke cracked her knuckles nervously. "Never seen youse laugh before."

"Danny lived on the other side of the basin. But his Uncle Cuddy lived right around here." Mim was looking at me. I was as yet confused by her crusty merriment.

"Around here? Jeese." Slim Jim tottered to his feet, as if he were going to go look for the money any minute. "Where?"

Mim's laughter broke into a bark, her rheumy wet eyes twinkling at me. "See if you can guess, Morty."

It was suddenly feeling very warm in the bar, and I finished my drink in a gulp. "Why do you ask me, Mim?"

"He lived . . ." Mim surveyed the others, then came back to me: "On Vanderhoosen."

It took a second or two—or was it hours?—for me to realize what she was suggesting.

"So?" I said, my voice cracking.

"Ooo!" Slim Jim thumped the bar. "Didn't you clean out a house on Vanderhoosen Street, Morty? Wasn't that . . ."

My compatriots were all fingering the little white cards with the phone number on them.

"Look, this money, it is a rumor . . ." My protest was feeble.

Oscar leaned both forearms on the bar and brought his granite head close to mine. "Morty, you found the money from the Atlas armored car heist."

"And that cop was lookin' for it." Buddy jerked his thumb at the empty doorway.

Mim was laughing so hard she loosed the queen of all farts, a sound roughly equivalent to a foghorn sounding from within a vat of pudding.

"And so is Danny Kessel," she roared.

EIGHTEEN

WHAT GOES THROUGH A MAN'S mind when he realizes all at once that there are three hard cases out to get him?

Panic.

First, as we know, I had Pete the Prick breathing down my neck.

Then there was the furry cop. I use the word "cop" loosely indeed. If he were real police, he would have badged us. Nothing a detective or undercover cop likes more than flashing his badge and watching people's eyes bug out. He was some independent operator. A dick, perhaps, or bounty hunter.

Then there was the ex-con, Danny. I knew nothing of this man, except that he had been a part of an armored car holdup. Well, I certainly did not imagine he accomplished that with a feather duster, which meant he was likely armed and dangerous.

Then there were my peeps at Oscar's. I did not care for the way they were looking at those white cards with the furry cop's phone number. As soon as I had left, I had little doubt that they were all clawing their cell phones to see who could call first. And for a measly Ben, a C-note. Bastards.

What goes through a man's mind when, out of nowhere, everyone seems to be against him? For me, the flight instinct was the first thing to enter my mind.

I left Oscar's as casually as possible, laughing off Mim's theories and the speculative mood of the rest of them, and walked calmly to my car. Once behind the wheel, it was a challenge to contain my panic. It is difficult for a man to admit that he is almost overcome with fear. I did not sob, but tears fell from my eyes.

I am not an idiot. It was unlikely that Mr. Trux managed to save eight hundred thousand dollars. Do the math, Father Gomez—you would have to save almost thirty dollars a day for eighty years to sock that much away, and without dividends or interest. So I suspected this quantity of cash must come from someplace not entirely legal. Even so, I still had it, and it was secure. The problem was the word was out about what I'd found. It wouldn't be long before the cop and this Danny person found out about it.

Specifically, what did I have to fear from them?

The cop would lean on me, tell me I'd better cough it up or he'd make trouble for me. Who knows? He might get physical.

This Danny person was probably capable of anything. Anybody who spends a considerable time in prison has lost all subtlety. After menacing me, he would probably move to Plan B pretty quickly, which would involve physical coercion. Torture. Then he might kill me once I told him.

When a man panics, he is reduced to one of his most primal states, and perhaps the most primal of all instincts is that of flight. Yes, even more so than the act of mating. After all, what man, caught in bed with another man's woman, does not immediately put wings to his feet? He does not stay and keep mating.

My mind raced with the images.

Of me at the storage locker, stuffing the backseat of the Camaro with the Scottish suitcase.

Of me on the highway, headed for the Throgs Neck. No, wait, south on the Belt Parkway, toward the Verrazano Bridge, Staten Island. From there I could either head toward Florida on I-95 or toward California, and La Paz, on I-78.

Of me by the dashboard light, big green highway signs passing over me, the barrage of white stripes slipping past, the red taillights ahead, pulling me onward.

Of the sun rising, of gas stations, of fast food, of sleeping in rest stops. I would go and go and go and go until I was so far away I could not be found. I could access the rest of my money in the bank from wherever I ended up.

Ah.

But where were those Balkan Boys? I scanned the surrounding cars—they could be in any of them. To drive to the storage lockers would probably be to hand the money to Pete the Prick. You have to understand, he's an extremely competitive person and will do anything to win. Going home would be dangerous. Who knew who would be waiting for me there? I couldn't go to Fanny's—I did not know exactly where she lived, and I did not even know her last name. Well, maybe she told me and I forgot between the champagne and the cold duck. Besides, any woman can tell you that men edit what women say, tuning out what sounds to us to be unimportant. Last night her name wasn't very important.

I decided to indulge my first instinct, at least partially. I needed distance, and room to think without looking over my shoulder. If I took to the highway, I should be able to spot the Balkan Boys tailing me, maybe give the idiots the slip in a rest area on the turnpike, and then find a motel for the night.

So I began, down the commercial avenue of two-story brick buildings, shuttered shops and stoplights, toward the parkway and the highway.

As I did, I saw police cars ahead, their flashing rollers lighting up the house fronts like the disco dance floor at Octavio.

Cop cars were in front of Upscale Realty, just around the corner from the avenue.

I slowed as I passed, trying to see what the trouble was. I hoped Mary was all right.

"Officer?"

A uniform cop pacing next to his car waved me away. "Keep moving."

I saw where another cop was stringing yellow plastic tape across the sidewalk, telling a small crowd to move back. Pulling ahead, I parked at a hydrant on the avenue and jogged toward the store.

"Officer, what has happened? Is Mary all right?"

This was the officer who had been stringing crime scene tape, and he was equally as testy as the first cop and kept scratching his mustache and adjusting his hat.

"Who are you?"

"I am Mary's friend."

"What's your name?"

I hesitated. See? Give a cop two seconds and he will start the interrogation. "It is me, Bob, I am her friend."

There were more sirens coming down the avenue. That wasn't good. The more cops, the more serious something like this was. The itchy cop was chewing hard on his gum, his hands moving from mustache to hat, clearly agitated.

"Sir, I'll need you to wait to talk to the detectives."

My veins were iced with dread, mostly about Mary's fate but also the prospect of being scrutinized by the police.

"They want to talk to me? But why?"

"You were her friend, you said, right?"

Were.

"Mary is dead?"

He squinted at me. "How did you know that?"

"You said 'were,' indicating she is now in the past, yes?"

"Did I?"

"My God . . . how did she die?" You know someone is really a friend when their troubles can suddenly replace your own. What had she said to me, the last thing, about bad things happening to good people? Eerie.

A flock of other cop cars—some unmarked—and an ambulance stuffed themselves into the side street off the avenue. Any hope I had that the itchy officer was mistaken about Mary was fading. You don't get this many cops showing up to a heart failure or slip in the bathtub. Besides, I knew there was no bathtub at Upscale Realty. Then again, maybe there was a tub under all that mess.

The itchy officer was being called over to where the new arrivals were assembled. You could tell the detectives right away. One was thick and Hispanic, the other slouchy and probably with an Irish name. The officer pointed a commanding finger at me.

"Wait right there." He ducked under the tape and trotted over to his superiors and the EMS people. A reporter was in the mix, a man named Dexter Lewis. I went to high school with him. He was always recognizable at a distance by his Panama hat as much as by his clubfoot. Dexter lurched around like Juan Valdez with one giant honking black hobnail platform shoe and one small black ballerina slipper. He was teased and tormented relentlessly back then by the other kids. I was always nice enough to him, and when we ran into each other on the street these days we said hello and exchanged pleasantries. He worked for the local paper, the *Brooklyn Gazette,* and was often the first on a neighborhood crime scene.

I had told the itchy cop my name was Bob. It seemed essential to slink away. If Dexter looked my direction, though, he would recognize me, and when I had vanished, and the cops got upset, he might ID me.

Wasn't it just hours ago I was worrying about grapes? Wasn't I considering French cheeses and fancy crackers and blender drinks and shelf cleaning? And do not imagine that I had forgotten about the thong and high heels.

Slowly, like a ghost, I drifted back from all the light and hubbub, seeking the corner of the building and a clear shot at my Camaro on the avenue. It was maybe fifty feet to the corner, and I kept my eyes trained on the fuzz and Dexter. Gawkers straggled around me toward the crime scene. I continued to back slowly toward the corner, toward the avenue, away from the police tape. Now if the authorities and a certain reporter would only keep their attention away from me.

I was next to the building, my hand dragging along the bricks, feeling for the corner.

My fingers danced along the brick, touching the cracks, the mortar, anticipating the sharp edge that would be the corner. I dared not take my eyes from the police and the Panama hat.

At last.

I spun around the building corner. Directly into Speedy, my foreman, knocking the tiny brown man to the ground.

"Speedy!" I knew it was him immediately by the little straw

cowboy hat he wore, the brim rolled tightly on the sides. I moved to the other side of him, away from the police, and helped him to stand.

Speedy scrambled to his feet, hat in hand, cursing in Spanish. "Morty, what the hell is wrong with you? Jesus Christ, you about ran me over."

"Come on." I grabbed him by the elbow and led him to the hulk of my rusty white Camaro at the hydrant.

He shook free of my grip.

"*Dios mio!* What the hell is going on? Where are we going?"

"Mary is dead, killed." It was then that I could smell the sweet peachy Thunderbird on his thick black mustache. He was a little drunk, and he was always irascible when drunk. "We have to get out of here."

"We? Why do I have to get out of here? I want to go look."

I put my hands way down there on his shoulders, trying to remain calm, trying to be fatherly. "Speedy, have I ever lied to you?"

"Not that I know of."

"I am telling you that it is very important that you get in the car, we move away from here and the police in particular, and that we have a little talk. The cops will not let you see anything anyway, and in fact, they might want to take you down to the station and ask you questions all night long."

"Your car is better. Mine isn't running too good. Questions? Me? The police?" This notion seemed to make him teeter slightly, as if he were losing his balance or about to pass out. I took the opportunity to open the passenger door and guide him into the seat. I trotted around the car, got in, and moved us away from the hydrant and the police.

"Morty, are we in trouble with the police?" Speedy chewed on his mustache nervously. I could see he was wearing what he always wore: plaid shirt, jeans, work boots, and of course his little cowboy hat. He couldn't have looked more like a migrant worker if he tried. In fact, I think he did try. It was his way of gaining the trust of the laborers. But you would think when off duty he would wear something else. A tracksuit, maybe, and loafers.

"Not yet."

"Not *yet*? We will be? But I have not done anything?"

I checked my rearview mirror. There were a couple cars behind me, and so I made a turn into an alley to see if any followed me. One did, what looked like an SUV of some kind. The headlights were higher than a sedan.

"Speedy, remember all those tight ones?"

I saw the white of his eyes expand. "Yes, of course."

"You have any idea how much money was there?"

"I try not to think of it. It is not mine."

"Well, it was a shitload, and I think there are people who want it." I checked my mirror again as the alley came to an end and I made a left at the cemetery. The SUV had drifted back, but I saw its headlights swing slowly into line behind me. "You got some of it, and if people want it back, they will take mine and yours."

"Who are these people that want to take our money, Morty?"

"Let's just say the person who stole it, and someone who probably wants to steal it from him."

"*Dios mio.* So what do we do?"

"The first thing we have to do is shake the Balkan Boys."

"Balkan Boys?" He seemed alarmed. As he should have.

"Pete the Prick is trying to steal the tight ones from me and has the Balkan Boys shadowing me. They are following us now—don't turn around!"

Of course he did turn around, briefly.

"We need to go someplace for the night where they can't get us, where maybe we can sneak out the back after a while. Know any place?"

"*Dios mio*. The Balkan Boys are after us. And the police. Are there others? It sounded like there were others, the ones who own the money."

"Speedy, we own the money. Nobody else. A long time ago, it was legitimately owned by someone else, then it was stolen. Think, Speedy, where can we go?" I glanced at the headlights in the rearview. "We cannot go to my place, or yours . . . a barrio bar or something? After-hours place?"

Speedy sank his face into his hands, as if weeping, but I know this was the posture of thought for my friend. He seemed to need the darkness of his hands for the process of contemplation to be successful. It did not take long before he raised his face and showed me his big white teeth. It was a smile, of course, but a particular wolfish kind of smile men recognize.

"Chica bar!"

NINETEEN

AS SPEEDY AND I DROVE to the chica bar, the police examined the scene of the crime at Upscale Realty.

So did Dexter. As a star reporter, he was well connected and sort of had special privileges other reporters sometimes did not. That is to say, he had influence with local politicians and elected officials, which I guess are the same thing if you think about it. Anyway, the cops trusted him not to use information and circumstances against them and had always championed their causes in his editorials. He did this almost purely out of a desire for the kind of access he was enjoying at Upscale Realty. He was allowed to put on the plastic shoe covers and roam the crime scene while the forensics people put things in Baggies and took photographs.

There was a lot to look at because the place was a mess, and the forensics people were rolling their eyes and shaking their heads at the task before them. It was like looking for a pin in a pile of grass clippings.

Dexter prided himself on being highly observant of things that were out of the ordinary, that were out of place. He stood in front of the desk where Mary had been killed. Her body had been photographed and removed, but there was blood on the desk and much clutter. Dexter's eyes came to rest on the flyer on Mary's desk, the one of Danny that Charlie had dropped off.

How had this flyer come to be here among her house listings, lien searches, and applications? The paper it was copied onto was still very white, unlike copy paper that has been exposed to light for a few weeks, and it was near the top of the pile of blood-spattered papers on her desk. So he knew it was recent.

Dexter did not want to draw attention to the flyer. If the police found it and thought that this was important evidence, well . . . they were the experts, not him. At the same time, he felt it was important, so he leaned down for a quick look at what little of the flyer he could see. Yes, it was a mug shot. It did not look like there was a name on the flyer.

So how would a real estate broker come to possess this flyer? Unlikely she made it herself unless she moonlighted as a private detective. More likely that someone would have given it to her. Would someone have just given it to her, just given it to a single real estate broker? It was clear to Dexter that whoever made this flyer was looking for this person and had given it to Mary as part of the search. This person would be canvassing the neighborhood, and thus there were probably other people out there with this same poster. So even as Dexter could not touch anything at the crime scene, much less take this flyer, he determined to ask around to see if anybody else had found it.

Dexter glanced down again at the flyer. Perhaps this was nothing. Then again, perhaps this was the face of the killer staring right back at all these police. Would they think to notice it? A picture of the killer was not the sort of thing they usually expected to find at a crime scene, so Dexter figured it might take them a while.

Detective Ruez was suddenly standing next to him in front of the desk. He was a barrel-chested Hispanic man in his forties with a cleft chin and nervous but dull eyes.

"Notice the blood spatter?" Ruez pointed with his cleft chin. "She was sitting down. Which is why he got her in the eye, not the gut or chest."

"Wow, I didn't notice that." Dexter adjusted his Panama hat and smiled admiringly at Ruez's cunning detective work. Ruez was probably right. Of course, her body was next to the toppled chair, so Dexter did not consider this a novel observation.

The other detective, who had a very faint mustache, shambled up next to Dexter's other flank. He was one of those adult males who would never quite shed his boyish looks, and though he wore a tie and jacket, he tended to squirm as if the clothes made him uncomfortable. His name was Pool, and he nodded his head thoughtfully. "Must have been someone she knew. Some of the neighbors we interviewed said she locked the doors after five but often worked late. So she must have let him in. No sign of forced entry."

"*Him*?" Dexter asked naively.

Ruez and Pool shared a dull look and said in unison: "It's always a he when it's a she."

"Yes, I have noticed that, too. You are right. Most likely a he." Dexter was outwardly admiring their insights while inwardly wondering when they would see the mug shot for the blood spatter. You know, like the forest for the woods.

It was moments like these that made Dexter feel like a genius.

Wasn't it Einstein who invented the atom bomb?

TWENTY

SPEEDY AND I DROVE TO Queens, the clumsy Balkan Boys in tow, to a Latino area that I would not normally go to but was no doubt familiar to most of the day workers. That is because it is where most of them lived in shabby rental homes, six to a room, like in a bunkhouse on a ranch. Their lodgings were illegal, of course, and every once in a while the city cracked down on them as they do on many small crimes—mainly for show.

You may wonder what day laborers do when they are not crowding street corners in their steel-tipped work boots. They make very little money, and most of what profits they make are sent to their families in Mexico or Central or South America. Of course, they must eat, but most of that is rice and beans, almost exclusively. You could not spend a lot of money on rice and beans if you tried. So once you have the food and shelter part taken care of, what do you have left?

As they say, men do not live by rice and beans alone.

We drove into an area that was houses on one side and auto shops and wrecking yards on the other.

"Here." Speedy pointed to a driveway with a chain across it.

"Here?" It looked like the entrance to a scrap yard of some kind, but then beyond the streetlamp glow I could make out a row of cars.

"Beep the horn. Just one small beep."

I did so.

A dark man in a tight white T-shirt appeared from the lot ahead. He was a large man, the kind that flexes his muscles in front of mirrors, and he stepped over the chain and swaggered toward us.

"It's me, Speedy."

"Speedy who?"

"Come on, Pitu, you know me."

The large man took a flashlight from his belt and shined it through Speedy's window, blinding us.

The light went out, and by the time my eyes could see more than green blobs I saw the large man in the tight white T-shirt standing to one side of the drive holding the chain.

So I drove in and parked next to the other crappy cars. They were even more rusted than mine.

We climbed out.

"Speedy, what is this place?"

"Come on, Morty, I will show you."

He started off to a far corner of the lot, where I could see Pitu's white T-shirt. As we got closer, I could see he was standing next to a door leading into what looked like an abandoned manufacturing plant of some kind.

"I like to tip Pitu—give him ten bucks, Morty."

I fished out a ten-spot and handed it to Pitu at the door. He took it without a smile or thank you and opened the door.

Bomba music and light lay beyond the door. I shielded my eyes and saw tables filled with little thick brown men like Speedy.

Except they had their hair carefully slicked back and wore equally slick, brightly colored shirts and tight white or black pants. They far outnumbered the thick little brown women scattered amongst them in frilly dresses. Some of these women sat in the men's laps, some just sat next to them holding their hands, and some others sat with men playing cards.

At six foot, I was a giant amongst these people. Pitu the bouncer was my height but stronger and could easily have picked up two of these laborers and slung them around like chicken for the pot. I am serious: These people were not over five feet tall, and many were closer to four feet.

"Chica bar, man." Speedy showed me those teeth again. "Cerveza?"

I followed Speedy. This club was arranged inside an old one-story brick plant loaded with rusty machines like lathes, conveyors, hole punches. These machines were more or less pushed to the far side of the room, behind a short bar. In the center were tables on a dusty concrete floor. Some fading streamers hung from the ceiling, and speakers provided the music. It was not fancy, but it was inexpensive.

This is where the day laborers came to drink and gamble—and be entertained by women, but it wasn't what you think. I had heard of these places. The "chicas" are not prostitutes, strictly speaking, but hostesses, like geishas. They simply flirt with the men and give them some womanly comfort. They dress like wholesome virgins from back home.

I seriously doubted the day laborers could afford actual sex from anything but the filthiest streetwalker.

Speedy led the way to the bar. It was tended by a big woman with arms as large as her legs. That is to say, she might have measured only up to my chest in height, but her proportions were impressive. I had no doubt that she'd mopped the floor with a few rowdy laborers now and again. She was in a frilly dress also but did not look too friendly. Her eyes painted me top to bottom with suspicion while her mouth rattled off something disapproving in Spanish to Speedy.

Speedy laughed, waving off whatever she had said. "Cerveza, Mamma."

I put my hand on the bar, which was down around my waist. There were bottles behind the bar, none with labels. Mismatched tumblers with clear liquid were put in front of us, and next to that Mamma placed a paper cup of what looked like beer.

We tapped glasses and put away the clear liquid. The liquor was not powerful. I would say it was watered, whatever it was. The flavor wasn't bad, but it also was not good. Something like candy corn and lawn cuttings. The beer was thin, too. Probably dregs, unfinished kegs from real bars.

"Can we talk here, Speedy? Anybody speak English?" It was then that by the light of the bar I noticed what looked like lipstick on his neck. "Hey, where were you tonight, you rascal?" I wiped my finger on his neck and showed him the pink.

He blushed. "A girl. Should that surprise you, Morty? We can talk here, they don't understand much American. So how are we going to get out of this? I don't want to give back that eighteen grand. I can use it, you know?"

Two of the little brown chicas came up to the bar next to me to pick up some drinks for their table. Their brown eyes were disproportionately large as they looked up at me. The one whispered something to the other, and they erupted in giggles. I turned back to Speedy.

"Here is the situation. There is an ex-con, his name is Danny, and he stole the money but is back looking for it. Obviously, he hid it under the couch in the Trux place, and we found his tight ones. There is some sort of detective looking for the ex-con, probably to take the money from him. There is Pete the Prick, who has the Balkan Boys following me, trying to steal the money from me because he knows I would not go to the police. Now Mary has been killed, and the police wanted me to stay at the crime scene to talk to me, but I left and ran into you."

"Who killed Mary? And why?"

"This is a question I cannot answer. Perhaps it has something to do with Danny, or the furry cop."

"Furry cop?"

"The private detective has very thick body hair. You can see it on his arms and legs, sticking out the back of his shirt . . . like that. I think of him as the furry cop and will call him that until I learn his name. If I learn his name. I would rather not."

"Oh."

"My first idea was, of course, to take the money and leave."

"Leave *Brooklyn*?"

"Yes, leave Brooklyn."

"And go where, Morty?"

See? I told you how people in Brooklyn have the peculiar notion that this is the best of all possible places to live. They do not know of places like La Paz.

"It would not be wise to even tell you where I was going because I might still go, but I cannot."

"I am confused, Morty. Why not take the money and run?"

"Because I put the money someplace safe, and I cannot go to it without risking the Balkan Boys following and taking it."

Another round of drinks appeared down around my belt buckle. We drank the candy corn and grass clippings liquor in silence.

Speedy burped. "What if we rounded up some day laborers to protect you? Then you could go get the money."

I pulled thoughtfully on my lower lip. "I had not thought of that. Still seems risky. What if these munchkins decided to take it from me once we got to the hiding place? Are they to be trusted?"

"Mumpkin? What is this?"

"Not important. Could they be trusted?"

"I tell them, they do. They respect me. And we don't have to say what we're going to get."

"Come on, Speedy. They all know I scored."

He shook his head. "You don't understand them the way I do. They are very . . . traditional. Not in their nature to steal, to think of stealing."

"I believe you believe that. But when it comes to this much money . . ."

"How much was it, in all?"

"Just as I will not tell you where I would go, I will not tell you how much. It is better you do not know these things. It could be dangerous. What if they grab you and torture you? Better that you know nothing. Which brings me to another concern. Even if I leave, it will only be a matter of time before they come looking for you to try to make you tell them where I am, where I hid the money."

Speedy downed his beer and once more put his face in his hands. When he showed me his face again, it was serious but hopeful. "We could go together. Two is better than one. You drive, then I drive . . . we go, not stop. But please, someplace warm, yes?"

Looking deep into his eyes I considered this. But I also wondered how long it would take Speedy to think of some way of driving off with all the money. There I would be in an IHOP parking lot somewhere in Arkansas, hurling curses at the gods for my ill fate.

"You would leave Brooklyn?"

"How can I stay like this?"

"Let us keep that as one of our plans. It is best to have alternatives. I am hoping that there is some way to work this so we do not have to spend the rest of our lives looking over our shoulders, wondering when Danny or the furry cop will show up."

"I see what you are saying, Morty. This is very difficult. We are in real trouble."

The two chicas returned. One next to me, one next to Speedy. We were getting the big-eye treatment.

"Morty, let me dance with this chica. My head hurts. I will be back. She is so sweet, I would hate to insult her by turning her away."

Off he went, and I was glad for it. I needed time to think, and those eyes next to me were not helping. So I turned, smiled, and attempted to send her away.

"*Gracias, chica, por favor . . .*"

She took me by the hand, pulled me toward a chair, and then with all her might pulled me down into it. In truth, I gave in. She seemed so determined, I was afraid she might cry or something if I said no. And let us face facts—it is very hard to say no to large brown female eyes.

I did not know what she was going to do next, and tensed. Little thick brown people were dancing all around me, the women's skirts slashing my chair, the music thumping, laughter.

Ah, what a sweet child. Brown Eyes began to work my shoulder muscles, probably much as she had worked corn flour into tortillas in her village down in Wherever. This was exactly what I needed. I was tense, as you can only imagine, the muscles in my neck and shoulders wound up like your grandfather's grandfather clock. I suppose as an experienced chica hostess, maybe she could spot a man in need of a massage.

It was so relaxing, Father, I cannot tell you. This chica—I realized that she was a miniature version of the woman I would want in La Paz (assuming of course that the Fanny thing did not work out). And this made me realize how distant La Paz was now.

To tell you the truth, my eyes started with tears, and it was all I could do to summon the strength not to sob right there in the chica bar.

How had I got into this horrible mess?

And how on earth would I get out of it?

I would gladly donate a portion of the money to a good cause if only fate would show me the way out.

The key was Danny. To make him think I did not have the money. Perhaps I could make him think Mary had it? That does not seem like something I should do to a friend, but she was dead now, so what did it matter? If I could only make him look somewhere else.

Like teaming with Speedy, this was one idea. Not a very good one, especially if it was Danny who had killed Mary, because if he had I had no idea what she told him about me. If only the police would find him, arrest him.

Ah.

But then they would find out he was looking for the money, and the police would then be looking for the money, looking for me.

Now the chica started on my temples—the muscles there were wound tighter than a cuckoo's cuckoo clock, and my brain felt like it was slowly detaching from my skull and floating to the ceiling.

My eyes were half closed as I gazed across the noisy room, watching the little thick brown people dance. The men were smiling and clapping, the chicas holding their skirts and swinging this way and that. This was not *Saturday Night Fever*—the dance was clearly something traditional, from their homeland. Their big brown eyes were alight with festivity and the thought of home. Poor bastards, stuck here in Brooklyn to make a buck. I always thought they looked so miserable in the winters here, too, so out of their element and slightly dismayed by the season's torment. I supposed many of the ones I was watching had worked for me at some time, but I will be brutally honest with you. I have a very hard time telling one laborer from the other, they look so similar to me. I need Speedy not only to translate but also to tell one from the other. Frankly, if it were not for Speedy's straw fruit-picker's hat, I might not recognize him immediately, either. I do not mean to sound superior or anything when I call them little thick brown people. Can I help what they look like? I do not think you would want me to lie and say they were tall thin white people when they were not. You and I both know Norwegians do not come here to do day labor. Perhaps in California, I do not know.

My chin was on my chest, my eyes lowered toward the floor; the chica began to knead the base of my skull. My brain seemed to drift somewhere near the manufacturing plant's filthy ceiling. What bliss. Now I was watching all those little dancing feet. It seemed to me, the way they were dancing, a chica would put her foot someplace, pull it away, and then he would put his foot in the same place, as if to cancel out her step.

Like the laborers and their chicas, I was in a dance with four people out to steal my money. Could I make steps that would cancel out theirs? This was another idea worth further thought.

Sometimes things get hectic with my business. When they do, I return to the basics of my business philosophy, which is quite simple. Running a business is ninety percent priorities. I have a house to clean, and they want this for Thursday. If I order the Dumpster first, it is useless if I have nobody to fill it. So I arrange the labor first, I call Speedy. You see?

Now my massaging chica reached forward as far as her little arms would go, raking my chest muscles, her breasts smashed into the back of my head. I am not sure which felt better. Or if I had ever had the back of my head massaged with a woman's breasts before. I recommend it highly.

Priorities. I could do nothing with those idiots in their SUV outside. Speedy had a good idea when he suggested mobilizing some of the laborers—and here they were, already assembled.

As if sensing my resolve, the chica suddenly ceased her work and tweaked my cheeks, giggling like the munchkin she was. My brain plopped back into my skull, and I gave my head a shake to make sure everything was attached and in working order.

"*Muchas gracias, chica.*" I handed her a twenty, and her eyes went wider than I thought possible.

"*Más?*" She was clearly eager to work me over for another twenty, but I smiled and said thanks but no.

I turned to find Speedy at my elbow, his face sweaty from dancing.

"I am better now, boss."

"I, too, feel better. And I now know what we must do first."

"I saw you with that chica, boss. Her nipples—they were up around your ears."

"Very relaxing, having tits on your ears. I was surprised."

"Can't get a whore to do that, either. Not the way a chica can."

"Speedy, round up some of the boys."

"Yes?"

"Yes."

TWENTY-ONE

FROM OUR VANTAGE ATOP THE manufacturing plant, the red SUV was clearly visible. It was down the block, parked across the street and on the other side of a streetlamp's pool of yellow light. A string of about ten laborers crunched ahead of me on the gravel roof in Brooklyn's orange night glow. Sneaking across the roof in their brightly colored shirts and tight white pants, they were not too unlike escapees from a Jamaican steel drum band, only smaller, and not Jamaicans. Perhaps you have not seen a Jamaican steel drum band, but I think you see what I am saying. They did not look like East Brooklyn commandos dressed brightly as they were.

It had not been difficult to recruit the laborers. In fact, it was difficult to pare it down to just ten. They are a mischievous lot, and to them this seemed like great fun.

Mamma, however, got involved and wanted to know what we were up to. Pitu appeared, arms folded.

Speedy explained that there were two men in a red SUV who were watching the place. We noticed them when we came in. They were not police or Mafia but a couple of local boys who wanted to shake Mamma down for protection. Speedy said these two were not connected to the mob, just a couple of jokers.

Mamma said she already paid protection and would make a call.

The laborers complained that she would ruin their fun. Mamma was a tough woman, no doubt, but when it came to the men, she really did care, really did want them to have a good time. So she looked at Pitu.

He turned his head this way and that, thinking, or working his neck muscles, I am not sure which. Pitu asked if they had guns, which would mean he would need to use the sawed-off, and pointed out that if there were gunshots, the police might come, and then there would be a lot of explaining to do.

Speedy assured him these two punks had no guns. Perhaps baseball bats or brass knuckles.

Pitu chuckled. He was not afraid of baseball bats or brass knuckles. The sound of their heads being crushed in his hands would not draw the police.

So as they say, the game was on the foot, and up the ladder we went to the roof. Approaching the red SUV from the ground was impossible. With the way the laborers were dressed we would have been spotted in a second.

Speedy was in the lead, I was at the end. He led them along this rooftop to the next one, jumping down about five feet, past roof vents that looked like giant rusty mushrooms. Soon we were behind the SUV, and at the far edge of the single-story manufacturing plant. Beyond was a vacant lot, mounds of stray rubble piled randomly. One was up against the side of the building. One by one the thick little brown men, our brightly clad commandos, jumped to the top of the rubble pile and then turned to the chain-link fence along the road.

When we were all assembled in the shadow of the vacant lot, we surveyed our target.

An arm dangled lazily out the red SUV passenger window, a cigarette burning between the fingers. Some sort of twangy, warbly music wafted through the humid night air from the vehicle, like something you might hear playing in a Russian coffee shop in Brighton Beach.

The quarry was still unaware.

It would have been too noisy for all of us to climb the fence. Instead, one of the men found a length of angle iron from a scrap pile and used it to pry the fence fasteners at the post. A squad of men peeled the fence back.

We would have to be quick. So quick that the Balkan Boys would not have time to exit the vehicle. Our festive commandos did a little pantomime of what they would do, communicating in silence, all squatting and then raising their arms as they stood.

Speedy held up his five fingers and counted down.

Four . . .

Three . . .

Two . . .

Crouched, the men ran toward the vehicle and collected behind the SUV where they could not be seen in the rearview mirrors. Fortunately, the streetlight was in front of the vehicle, so they were mostly in shadow.

I remained back in the vacant lot—I was too tall and would have risked being seen.

Speedy held up his five fingers again and counted down.

Four . . .

Three . . .

Two . . .

All at once they crowded the SUV's passenger side, squatted, put their hands under the quarter panels, and heaved.

They may be small, these thick little brown men, but they are powerful for their size.

Up went the SUV—the hand hanging out the window vanished, the cigarette landing on the ground.

The car flipped and crashed over onto the driver's side. You could hear the safety glass pop and shatter, and the Balkan Boys begin to shout angrily.

Back came the colorful laborers, laughing and chattering. I stood atop the pile of debris and boosted them one by one back up onto the roof, Speedy last.

Four of them had hands down for me to grasp, and we locked grips. I used my feet on the brick to get traction, and as I did so, I saw the four of them strain, and heard them curse, from the burden of my weight.

Just as they grabbed me by the elbows, I felt a hand latch on to my shoe from below. I also felt the cold terror of falling back to the ground, of having the Balkan Boys standing over me with baseball bats, of being beaten within an inch of my life.

"*Arriba!*" Speedy shouted.

I wiggled my foot, trying to shake free, but I was wearing calf-high boots. I could feel someone trying to grab my other foot, too, so I lifted it.

"Speedy, lift! Lift!" I shouted.

"*Arriba!*" he growled. I think more of the laborers were now pulling on the ones who had me. So you had me being pulled by a bunch of munchkins on the roof while at least one Balkan had me on the ground, and I could feel myself getting stretched, my joints cracking, my tendons thrumming.

I was hissing with pain and anxiety when a shape appeared to one side above me. I could not see what it was, but it was about three feet around, circular, and a few of the laborers threw it in my direction.

I ducked my head, heard a metallic bang, and was suddenly released from below. I catapulted up onto the roof.

A cheer sounded among the men, with no shortage of laughter.

Wobbling to my feet, I looked at Speedy in the night's orange glow. He was clapping me on my shoulder and pointing down.

Those thick little brown men had yanked off one of the rusty mushroom cap vents and thrown it at my attackers. The Balkan Boys were now rolling around on the ground in their overalls, cursing in a Slavic tongue.

That is when Pitu and Mamma turned the corner, into the vacant lot.

They had baseball bats.

I told you Mamma looked like a tough customer.

I watched for a moment, long enough to see Pitu and Mamma go to work and to hear what sounded like a bone breaking. Perhaps an arm.

"Thank the men for me, Speedy."

He rattled something off to them, and they all cheered, drowning out the shouts and cracks of bats from below.

"But Speedy, this is our time to get going. So let us make tracks. Yes?"

"*Yes.*"

TWENTY-TWO

CHARLIE BINDER WAS WAITING IN a canyon of four-story brick apartment buildings for me to come home. He was in his black SUV outside my apartment building. Thinking.

How do I know? Because Speedy and I drove up to the intersection three doors behind him, that is how. And he was sitting in the SUV I'd seen him get into outside Oscar's. And I think it is reasonable to assume Charlie, like most people who wait, was awake and thinking about something.

Like about the call he got from somebody not ten minutes after I left Oscar's. Charlie would have been just about to look in again on 901 East 109th Street, where the lightly torn screen door was locked, the inner door open, and nobody answered.

The place where Clara Kessel used to live, and where he was hoping the current owner had seen Danny.

Of course, the rude man at 901 East 109th Street *had* seen Danny, which was his misfortune. The rude man was just out of sight of the front door, around the corner in the hallway, his body in a fetal position and stiff with rigor mortis. He wasn't a very nice person, as we know, and so it wasn't like a lot of people were dropping by and calling. So Rude Man was dead, Danny had killed him, and nobody knew about it.

Yet.

The call Charlie received from Oscar's kept him from investigating and finding Rude Man dead in a fetal position in the hallway of 901 East 109th Street. Charlie drove by all the police activity off the boulevard, where Mary had been stabbed with an ice pick, not knowing about that, either. Had he learned of that, he might not have been waiting at my place.

How much had the person who called from Oscar's told him? Had they told Charlie that I found the money or simply that Danny might be found looking for me? I did not know.

"Man," Speedy began with a heavy sigh from the passenger seat, "everywhere you go there's someone looking for Morty, waiting in an SUV."

"If I am going to lie to the furry cop, I need to know what he knows," I said, squinting at the black SUV. The clock on my Camaro's stereo read 12:30. They would be kicking Mim out of Oscar's about then. She stays past closing, right up to where they turn out the lights and pry the old owl from her perch.

"So we're not going to go get the money, Morty? Make a run for it?"

"True, the Balkan Boys are out of commission, for now. We could go get the money. We could start driving. But while we have a little breathing room, I would like to try to see if I can turn the furry cop—"

"Furry cop. He sounds like a wolfman."

"—and Danny Kessel away from us. Like I said, Speedy, we'd still be looking over our shoulders if we went now." Also, to be honest, I was not all that sure I wanted to tie my future to Speedy.

I did not really know how far I could trust him with eight hundred thousand dollars in cash.

"Morty, I gotta get home. My dog, she has probably shit all over the place by now."

I thought a moment. "It is unlikely they will be looking for you yet. They only know about me for now."

So I dropped him off at the house where he rents a room.

The light in his room was on, and a shadow went across the shade. I had a moment's panic. Had someone already targeted him? Was Danny in his room with pliers, ready to make him talk? I watched the window a minute longer, and the shadow passed again. I laughed softly to myself for my worry. It was the shadow of a woman's form. Of course, the lipstick on his neck. She was waiting up. He would probably get scolded for staying out so late.

I drove to Oscar's.

Sure enough, there was Mim and her beehive wig tottering down the boulevard with her cane. If she was sober, she did not use the cane, but after toppling over a few times on the way home, she had started arriving at Oscar's with the third leg.

I drove up behind her, pulled over to a sleeping meter, and got out.

"Mim," I called. I could hear her huffing and puffing as she struggled to stay upright after twelve hours of continuous Canadian and colas. How some people take that kind of punishment and survive never ceases to amaze me. Then you have all kinds of people who think their bodies are delicate, that if they are deprived of their wheat germ, honey, and green tea their bodies will go to pieces. You have to wonder whether the human body is a lot tougher than many of us think.

To get Mim's attention, I had to stride over to where she was passing a shuttered bagel shop and put a hand on her shoulder. I think the surprise almost killed her right on the spot.

"Christ, Morty, you scared the ever living shit outta me!" Mim was choking on her fright.

"I am sorry, Mim. Please, over here, lean against a car. You do not look good."

She staggered over to a car and pushed her bony frame up against it. I think this was one of the few times I had ever seen her off of that stool at the far corner of the bar.

I did not spend a lot of time waiting for her to recover. She might croak before I got any answers.

"So who made the call?"

"Morty, look—"

"Mim, I don't care that somebody *made* the call. The cop would have found out one way or the other anyway. I would want a friend of mine to score a hundred bucks." I tried to keep the sarcasm out of my voice when I said "friend." "What I need to know is how much one of you told him."

"We talked it over after you left and drew straws." She gasped, still trying to recover. The orange streetlight made her pale, creased face look like a rubber mask. "Slim Jim won. He called the cop, the cop came back to Oscar's, gave Slim the C-note."

"Yes, but what did he tell the cop?"

"That you cleaned the uncle's house, and the word on the street was you found money in the house, and so we figured Danny Kessel might come looking for you. Can I go home? I'm abouttah puke myself."

"Is that all?" Was that not enough? I could have wrung all their necks for this.

"The cop asked how much money."

"And?"

"We said we didn't know but that it was a lot. Morty, did you find the five million?"

"Five million?"

"Yeah, that's how much they stole from the Fargo truck."

"Five million?"

"Five million, that's what I said. How many fucking times I gotta say it? Excuse me . . ." Mim leaned over and shot a stream of Canadian and cola puke at the car's tire. I jumped back to keep from getting splattered.

Five million? So where was the other four million two?

"Mim, I will tell you honestly, I did not find five million, not even near that amount. I do not have these people's money. I do not have the money from that truck heist."

Reeling upright with a groan, she drew her sleeve across her mouth. "They gonna think you did."

"What do you think I should do?" You must be wondering why I would ask an old puking tottering mask-faced drunk a question such as this. Mim had been around a long time, that is why. While I am not a complete idiot, and had genuine hope that I could work this out myself, I was open to suggestions from just about anybody. When you are in a jam, a third party sometimes has a useful perspective, even with puke on their sleeve.

"You hafta tell 'em you ain't got their five million. Or prove someone else does. Shit, Morty, I gotta get home before I fall over."

So I took her arm and walked her around the corner to her building. She only puked once more, and I was thankful she lived on the first floor so I did not have to try to drag her puke-spraying body up several flights of stairs.

Back at my Camaro, I thought about what she said. Now,

perhaps my money was just part of the five million, and maybe it was not. A variety of possibilities presented themselves. First of all, it was not certain that the five million was ever hidden in the house I cleaned. This was the best possible alternative because Danny would not have any reason to come looking for me.

Ah.

Mary was killed for some reason, though. Perhaps this was a coincidence. Then again, perhaps Danny killed her to get keys to the house, or to make her tell him who cleaned the house.

Second, if the five million had been hidden in the house, and I did not find it, could it still be there, and Danny just hadn't gotten it yet?

This was a good alternative also. Then he would go get it and he and the Wolfman could go off and leave me out of this.

Third, if Danny had looked for the stolen money and not found it where he left it, then it meant somebody else got it. Who? How was I to know? It could be almost anybody. One of Danny's relatives, maybe, or the old man Mr. Trux, or one of his kids, or a plumber or a contractor . . . the five million could be long gone.

This was a bad alternative because convincing Danny and the Wolfman that I did not have their treasure would not be easy. I would have to find who did take it and put them on a trail leading away from me. My task would be a difficult one.

What I needed to do was discover whether the situation was one, two, or three. Unfortunately, the Wolfman probably had none of the answers as yet. Odds on, only Danny knew whether he had found the money or not, and where it was hidden. Unfortunately, it was not a simple matter of asking him. I did not know where he was. Finding him—or him finding me—might put me in great peril. But if I waited until Wolfman found Danny and asked him, and if the finger ended up pointed at me, I would be locked into alternative number three.

My brain hurt. I was trapped, and yet I had to head them off.

Once again, I thought of how I would gladly donate a portion of the money to a good cause if only fate would show me the way out.

There was someone standing at the driver's window.

"Morty."

I will be brutally honest: I screamed like a little girl and honked the horn by accident.

"Ooo, Morty, don't do that. You scared me."

It was Frog at my window, his aftershave stinging my nose.

"My God, Frog," I groaned. "You scared the shit out of me. Why did you sneak up on me like that?" I rested my head on the steering wheel.

"Sneak? I just walked up. Man, did you hear about Mary?"

"Yes, Frog, I heard. Horrible." My head was still on the steering wheel.

"Who would kill Mary? Why?"

"I . . . I don't know. What are you doing around here at this hour? They said your mother was sick or something." I managed to pry my head off the wheel and lean back, my heart lunging in my chest.

"What? No, no, she's dead, remember."

"Yes, of course I do. But that is what they said down at Oscar's."

"I had some errands. Who do you think would kill her? Someone we know, maybe?"

"I . . . I don't know."

"I heard there was a guy passing around flyers with another guy's picture on them. A con of some sort. You don't think that maybe—"

"Well, Frog, everybody else knows, so you might as well. That picture was of Danny Kessel."

"Danny Kessel . . . you mean that guy back when, the guy who stole the five million and the cops never got it back?"

"Danny's uncle lived on Vanderhoosen. I cleaned out his house. Near the one you cleaned."

I heard Frog hold his breath.

"On *Vanderhoosen*?"

"On Vanderhoosen."

"Ooo, *Christ*."

"I did not find five million dollars in that house, Frog. Please say you believe that."

"Yeah, yeah, sure . . . so what you're saying is that he's looking for the guy who cleaned the house?"

"It is possible. Very possible. And he went to Mary to find out who it was."

"Ooo, *Christ*. You don't think she told who it was, do you?"

"It is possible he got the information from her one way or the other."

"Morty, what're you gonna do? Go to the cops?"

"And hand over the money I *did* find? That is *my* money."

"Yeah, don't go to the cops. Don't go to the cops. Can I help?"

"I don't know, Frog."

"You have my number—keep me informed of what's going on, OK? *Christ*."

"Good night, Frog, I will call you."

"Take it easy, man, OK? And don't go to the cops."

"Yes."

I heard his footsteps retreat rapidly.

So what could I do that did not involve meeting with Wolfman or Danny?

As I had done with Mim, I supposed I could try to fill in a few more holes in what I knew to try to get a clearer picture of what alternative faced me. If I knew how Mary was killed, or what the cops knew, perhaps that would tell me if Danny was hunting me, and I would know I was in the worst possible spot.

Ah.

I could not just walk into the police station and ask them the particulars of the case.

But I could walk into the *Brooklyn Gazette* and ask Dexter, the clubfooted reporter.

TWENTY-THREE

IT WAS AFTER ONE IN the morning. Why would I think to find Dexter at the paper at that hour?

True, I did not know him well, but I read the *Gazette,* and Dexter had had a number of big stories, scooped the Manhattan tabloids a time or two on a big mob trial, had an exposé on Latino gangs that went national, and had won some journalism awards—something the *Gazette* was proud to note at every opportunity. Hands down, he was their star reporter. In barrooms across the borough, beery patrons wondered aloud if Dexter had outgrown the *Gazette,* and why he had not moved off to bigger and better things at the Manhattan papers. Some wondered if the *Gazette* and Dexter were becoming one and the same. It was said he had a bed under his desk and could be found in his office pounding out his stories late into the night. It was said he slept little.

Through the heavy glass doors of the sleepy glass office building was a rent-a-cop and security station.

"Is Dexter in? I am a friend."

The guard looked like he could barely stay awake as he poked and prodded his phone.

"Hello, can you tell me if Mr. Lewis is in?" he said into the receiver. He had the roller-coaster accent of Jamaica. "Hold on." He put the phone to his chest and looked to me. "Who are you, now?"

I told him; he told them. He put the phone down, turned a sign-in book to me, and handed me a building pass. "Turd floor, mon."

Exiting the small elevator on the third floor was like falling into a cold lake of air-conditioning and fluorescent light. The reception desk was empty. Beyond that was the hum of ventilation and the flicker of computer screens. Cubicles stretched to the far side of the fluorescent lake and glass-wall offices on the far shore. The cubicles were empty. No people were in sight.

"Ooo. Morty?"

Far to my right, at an office in the corner, was a head sticking out of an office. It was mostly a bald head, with hair around the sides.

"Dexter, hello." I was a little taken aback. I had not seen him without his Panama hat and remembered him with a thick head of hair. Perhaps his hat was both his trademark and his camouflage.

"Come!" He waved at me, smiling, and his shiny head retreated back where it came from.

I found my way over to his doorway and was greeted by a grin and hearty handshake. "Morty, this is a huge surprise."

Dexter was in a white shirt open at the neck, brown suspenders, tan modified chinos, and black mismatched blocky shoes. His small, dark, cluttered office was stacked with papers, and the shelves crowded with awards large and small. There was also a photo of his parents, and of him at the mob trial. That there was no photo of bride and brood was not much of a surprise. A man must often choose between family and his ambitions.

His Panama hat was on a coatrack in the corner.

"Here . . ." Dexter cleared a stack of papers from a chair next to the door. "Sit, Morty."

I sat, and he lurched around to the other side of his desk and collapsed in his chair. There was a window behind him, looking east, and in the distance I could see the lights of Coney Island, the Parachute Drop tower clearly visible. His office's fluorescent lights were not on, only an old lamp by his desk that looked like a flying saucer. It lighted his desk and little else.

I have to say, as pleased as I was to find Dexter in his office at this late hour, I became a little worried by how overjoyed he seemed to be to see a man who was just an acquaintance, and probably a reminder of some pretty rough times in high school.

"I'm glad to find you in, Dexter. It has been a long time."

He didn't answer this, just nodded his head and smiled. "You know, Morty, I haven't forgotten that you were one of the few people back when, back in the day, who didn't bust my chops about the foot. You were jake, and I appreciate that to this day." He leaned forward on his desk, shoving a laptop computer to one side. "And yet I know we are not friends. There's no reason, just that we only know each other from then. Am I right?"

"Yes, of course. You seem very happy."

Dexter seemed to be hardly able to contain his pleasure. "Ooo. Happiness!" He held a finger aloft. "Somebody once said, 'Happiness is satisfaction disguised as joy.'"

"I suppose so. You are wondering why I am here."

His grin blossomed into a smile that spread across his stubble, his eyes shiny, his head shaking slightly. "I know why you are here."

"You do?"

"Somebody comes to see me late at night I get all happy. Why? Because I know I'll get a satisfied feeling, you know? Why? Because the only reason anybody comes to see me at an hour like this is to tell me something I might not know, and I get satisfied knowing things other people don't."

"And this makes you happy. I understand."

He leaned back in his chair, out of the light, tapping his fingertips together. His eyes were twinkling with lamplight. "And I get a great deal of satisfaction trying to figure things out, putting one thing together with another until I understand secrets. You were at the Upscale Realty murder scene. I saw you there."

I guess my eyes widened, because he reacted by chuckling.

"Don't worry, Morty. I know you didn't do it."

"Did someone say I did?" I found myself standing.

"Relax, Morty, relax. Here . . ." He leaned down, and I heard the puff and soft thump of what must have been a college refrigerator door open and close. He set two Miller beers on his desk, opened both, and handed me one. "I also know the cops wanted to talk to you—what was it you said your name was? Bob? But you lit out. Don't worry. I didn't tell them who you were. I did go by your place looking for you later. Word has it you and Mary Duggin were good friends."

"Yes. I saw her earlier today." I sank back into my seat. "You are right. I probably can tell you a few things—possibly related to her death—that you do not know. But I must make myself clear, Dexter. I not only came to give a little information but to get it."

He reached out and thumped the desk, a jaunty display of applause. "Morty, you and I might be friends yet. Glad to hear you say that. I don't like idiots, and I would have been disappointed if you were an idiot."

Now I had to decide what to trade him for what I wanted to know, without dragging me into it. I decided to get what I could out of him first. That would help me decide how to massage the information. I didn't need Dexter chasing my money and the story of how I got it for the *Brooklyn Gazette*.

He waved a hand at me, for me to start.

"I want to know what happened to Mary."

"Stabbed. Here." He pointed to his eye.

I shivered. Poor Mary. I really did like her. She had a good soul.

"Do they know who did it?"

"No."

"Any leads?"

"You mean the police?"

"Yes, do they have any suspects?"

"Not yet."

"Any idea of . . . the nature of the crime? Was it a robbery?"

"Petty cash missing, looks like. He used the key from around her neck to open the strongbox."

I shivered again. My check was probably still in there, with the business name and phone number and the subject: "House Cleaning/Vanderhoosen."

"Of course," he continued, "they don't know what else may have been in there that the perp was looking for. Do you know, Morty?"

"I'm not done. So are they convinced it was just a robbery?"

"They're not sure."

I wasn't getting what I needed.

"But you wanna know what I think?" I heard that giant black shoe bump the underside of the desk. "I think this guy did it."

He held up the flyer. The flyer the Wolfman had been passing around the bar. "His name is Danny Kessel. He got out of prison yesterday. Stole . . . but you know this, don't you?"

Reporters were as good as the police at reading people.

"I know that flyer. A cop of some kind was passing it around Oscar's."

"Yeah, I know. And I know you were there."

"Where did you get that flyer?"

"Mary's desk. It was sitting right there. The cops let me hang around the crime scene. But this isn't that one. Once I saw it, I realized somebody was looking for a con. This is a prison photo. How would she have it unless somebody was canvassing the neighborhood?"

"You know who the cop was that was handing it around?" I asked.

He tossed the flyer on the desk. "Not yet. I was hoping you could tell me."

"I do not know. But I know he drives a black SUV."

"Morty? Tell me something I don't know for a change. I'm not an idiot, either."

We looked into each other's eyes for what must have been thirty seconds.

"I see," he finally said, breaking eye contact and leaning back once more in his chair. "So. If you won't tell me, it means that the information you have about this might implicate you or someone you care about. Hmm?"

I looked at the ceiling.

"Now what could a feeler have to do with all this?" He, too, looked to the ceiling, as if reading my thoughts up there. "Well, that is something of itself. You know, if you're somehow mixed up in this, Morty, I might be able to help. If you help me. Otherwise, I have to go out on the street and spend all kinds of time asking questions about you, where you hang out, who you hang out with . . ."

Fanny. He would find out about her, and the tight ones, and figure it all out in a short time, I was sure.

I leaned forward, elbows on my knees, making a show of my anguish.

"OK, Dexter, I will tell you. But you must believe me that I am an innocent party in this who has been drawn into harm's way. I think maybe Danny Kessel thinks I recovered his money. I cleaned the house owned by his uncle. I found a little money. But not five million, I swear before God."

His eyes: squinting. His lips: pursed. I was being examined very closely.

"Look, we feelers often find money. Ask Frog."

"Frog?"

"Yes, Franco, he hangs out at Oscar's. He does apartments, mostly."

"Mostly . . ."

"He does the occasional house. Did one next door to the Trux place."

"Trux place . . ."

"The place I cleaned, Danny's uncle."

"Hmm."

"So I found some money. And as I often do, I shared some of it with the day laborers. They went out drinking, and word got out that I had found a lot of money. It is unfortunate that my discovery comes at this time, when Danny—"

"Not five million?"

"Not even close. It was more than I have ever found. But if it was five million . . ."

"You wouldn't be here now. You'd be long gone."

I clapped my hands. "As you say."

"But nobody knows for sure that Danny hid the money in the house, right? You haven't run into him yet, that right?"

"I have only run into Wolfman, at Oscar's. But he is parked outside my apartment right now."

"Wolfman?"

"Yes. The cop with the flyers. Very hairy man. I think he shaves his nose."

Dexter chuckled about that. "And he's staking you out?"

"Yes. The idiots down at Oscar's sold me out for a hundred bucks. Mim—"

"Mim?"

"An old-timer, sits at the far end of the bar. She recognized the photo, knew it was Danny, knew that Danny's uncle lived there on Vanderhoosen Drive . . ."

"And 'cause there were the rumors of the money . . . got it." Dexter began to rock in his chair. He was liking my story. Probably because it was the truth. "And you won't go to the police because . . ."

"Hey, I got that money fair and square. The next of kin signed a release of all the house contents to me. All a hundred percent legal. The cops will take that money away as evidence or something. I got plans."

"Plans?"

"There is a place I want to buy. A place far from here, start a new life."

"You lived here all your life. You don't like Brooklyn?"

"You would not understand. It has to do with my family. I want to buy my family's house back in . . . well, out of the country."

Dexter was now playing with a pencil, tossing it in the air and catching it.

"Morty, this is one fucked-up story. Thank you. I owe you one."

"All I ask is that you try to help get me out of this. I am not the bad guy."

He caught the pencil and pointed it at me. "Just the lucky guy."

"*Almost* lucky." I stood and began pacing. "Shit, man, I got nowhere to go. I cannot even go home. Wolfman is waiting for me."

Dexter struggled out of his seat and staggered over to his coatrack. "Let's go."

"Go?" I watched as he slid on his Panama hat. It was like watching a soldier put on his helmet.

"We have a date with the Wolfman."

TWENTY-FOUR

ARE YOU SURE THIS IS the best idea?" I was sitting in Dexter's Mustang convertible, one of the new ones, in black. The top was down, yet somehow Dexter's Panama didn't ever seem in danger of flying off as we drove over. Perhaps he flexed his head muscles to keep it on, I do not know.

"First rule of journalism: Go to the source. Besides, how would you get home otherwise?"

I shrugged and climbed out of his car. Better him than me—nobody better to put one over on a cop than a reporter. Besides, I was beat. It was almost two thirty. I could hear the siren song of my pillow.

His car growled around the corner onto my street, and I stayed by the corner watching.

The Mustang's taillights flared as it pulled to a stop next to the Wolfman's SUV.

I watched. Dexter lurched out from the driver's door and leaned in the open passenger window of the SUV.

That was my cue.

My building is two in from the boulevard. There is nothing but sidewalk, signs, and a couple small dying trees. The brick buildings are at the back of the sidewalk. No bushes or anything like that to block the view from the SUV. Only parked cars along the entire length of curb down to my building.

So I ran at a crouch behind the parked cars, dodging the street hardware as I went. At the spaces between cars, I shot an eye out to my left, toward the SUV, the Mustang, and Dexter. Each time there was a flash of streetlight and a glimpse of the cars across the street. It was like a slow-moving motion picture, frame by frame, interspaced with a view ahead along the sidewalk, sign posts, streetlamp, and skinny trees.

In front of my building I stopped and got an eyeful of the Mustang and Dexter standing at the SUV. Gently, I fished my building keys out of my pocket so as not to make any jingly sounds. I found the front door key—but also saw the key to the locker.

The locker with the eight hundred grand in it. This was all worth it, right? I did a flash review of the evening.

Buying grapes and flowery trash can. Fanny's voice on the phone about the bath. At Oscar's, realizing I was in deep, deep shit. The itchy cop and crime scene at Mary's. Running down Speedy on the boulevard. The sweet massage from the chica. Mamma and Pitu beating the crap out of the Balkan Boys. Mim spewing. Frog frightening. Dexter Lewis pointing his pencil at me and saying, "Just the lucky guy."

There I was crouching behind a car, like a criminal, in front of my own apartment, caressing a silver key to eight hundred grand and savoring my dream of my La Paz birthright.

I gave my head a shake. *Daydream once you're inside, idiot!*

Confirming that Dexter was still blocking Wolfman's sight-lines, I scuttled like a crab up to the apartment vestibule, slid the key in the lock, and gently swung the door open.

Halfway open, it stopped.

I shoved, and it seemed to shove back.

My breath stuck to the back of my tongue like a mollusk—I dared not move. There was someone in the vestibule.

No, you idiot—look, it's the wooden door wedge.

From the street, I heard Dexter laugh about something—and at first I thought it was at me, but he couldn't even see me from where he was talking to Wolfman.

I pulled the door open a little, reached around, and moved the stupid wedge the landlord keeps there for propping the door open. Next I knew I was safely in the light of the vestibule, mailboxes on the wall above me.

Which reminded me: I had completely forgotten about the white envelope from the genealogical people. The one containing my ancestry. I could picture tossing it on the backseat of the Camaro, the white envelope wedged in the corner when I shoved the Scottish suitcase into the backseat.

I slid the next key into the next door and pushed it open into the hallway, keeping an eye out the window to see if Dexter was still standing there. Yes, they were still out there. And I was undetected.

Still crouching, I pushed the door closed and turned.

"What the hell is this?"

You have heard the term "jumping out of one's own skin"? My muscles and skeleton dashed up the stairs leaving only my skin, brain, and eyeballs in the front hall.

It was the monster frog, of course—my landlord. The monster frog's belly stuck out of his green-and-white-striped pajamas like a hairy bloated cantaloupe, a cellophane-wrapped stogie in his top pocket, a Mets baseball cap on his head, green flip-flops on his feet.

God only knows what he was doing up at that hour, standing in the hallway, watching as the door slowly creaked open and I backed into the building.

I had collapsed into a sitting position against the wall, clutching my brain to make sure it did not leave only my eyeballs down here with the monster frog and the inevitable inquisition that I would now have to deal with after this ferociously long and complicated day.

"Did I scare yah?" He now stood over me, hands on his hips.

I could not imagine why he would ask such a thing when the answer seemed clear.

"Good God, man, what are you doing standing around in the hallway at this hour?" I had a hard time keeping the peevishness from my voice.

"My goddamn hallway. I'll stand here all night long if I wanna. There's people standing in the street talking, I was gonna go tell them to get the fuck away from here. Now I find you creepin'. Morty creepin' in my hallway."

Brooklyn: a borough of over two and a half million souls. Every year we have a couple hundred murders, double that number of rapes, double *that* number of assaults, and thousands and thousands of thefts. If any one of these were to happen in front of my building, I have no doubt my landlord would close his shades and plug his ears. But two men talking in muted tones at three in the morning? It is *this* that upset him enough to get out of bed, exit the building in his green-striped pajamas, and tell them to go away.

Then again, this is the man who feels up all the garbage bags for contraband—that is, recyclables. A year ago I tossed a small recyclable milk carton in the garbage, and I still hadn't heard the last of it.

My skeleton and musculature slumped reluctantly back into my skin with my brain and eyeballs. I worked my jaw to make sure it might be able to form words.

"It is perfectly simple," I began, not having a clue what I would say next—and knowing that nothing was simple anymore.

"You know those two out there?" he grumbled.

"I do not even know who you are talking about. I did not notice anybody."

"Well, they're out there, and they're talking. In front of my building."

Monsters lead small lives.

"I assure you that I . . . you see, it is my girlfriend." When in doubt, blame it on your girlfriend or wife—other men are only too willing to accept this variety of excuse.

"Ooo. The one from . . . from . . ." He waved his thumb toward the west, unable to bring himself to say "New Jersey."

"Yes. That is the one."

"That figgers."

"I was out with someone else, and I think she may be suspicious, so I wanted to be careful coming home. You are a man of the world, you know how it is."

More like a man of the four-story brick building in East Brooklyn. I doubt he had left the neighborhood for twenty years. This didn't keep him from tugging up on his pajama bottoms as if his cock were hanging down to his gnarled yellow toenails.

He sniffed and looked somewhere off into the middle distance, probably picturing his last conquest, sometime when Nixon was in China. I shuddered. I could only imagine what that lucky girl looked like, much less what they looked like together. I tell you, I gagged.

"You OK? Youse ain't gonna barf in my hallway, are yah?"

"No, I am fine, really." I got unsteadily to my feet, my stomach somehow being the last part of me to rise up from the floor. "Well, it was nice talking to you. Good night."

"I tell you, Morty." He was saying this to my back as I tromped up the stairs. "You got an interesting life."

Interesting? The irony of that made me chuckle. "Good night."

"And Morty . . ."

I paused.

"Yes?"

"No more milk cartons in the garbage. We'll get a ticket."

CHAPTER

TWENTY-FIVE

AS I REACHED MY FRONT door, I looked toward the floor for the gum wrapper.

Ah.

I neglected to put the gum wrapper in the doorjamb eighteen hours or so ago when I left with Fanny. Why? Because I knew the Balkan Boys had already been there. Back in that blissful, carefree world eighteen hours ago, I did not know Danny Kessel was hunting me.

I unlocked the door and stepped in.

I heard something move.

Who was it that turned into a pillar of salt? Medusa? That was me.

For about two seconds, until I heard the movement again, over by the couch.

A weapon. I needed a weapon, and fast.

A flash-fast mental inventory of my apartment zoomed in on the image of my baseball bat. I do not play baseball. I would venture to guess that most Brooklynites do not. But even as it may be customary in South Jersey to keep pigs inside your house or in California to keep your convertible Bentley in the garage, in

Brooklyn most people keep a baseball bat somewhere handy. You know, just in case there is trouble. It is not like Brooklyn is particularly dangerous, do not get me wrong, but we are a cautious people, many of us having lived through times that were more dangerous. This weapon is customarily kept somewhere near the front door, where presumably a frontal assault on your apartment would occur.

Mine was in the coat closet. Near the front door, yes, but not next to the front door. I had moved it when straightening up my place for Fanny. To get it would require moving toward the person in my dark apartment and opening the closet and feeling around in there to find my bat. Far too many movements involved, and I would surely expose myself to being clobbered by the uninvited guest.

The kitchen. If I ran to my left, I would put distance between me and my intruder and have both knives and mop handy to defend myself. I began my dash for the kitchen even before I finished thinking about whether this was the best option.

I made two long strides before my feet shot out from under me and I was landing on my back, the air whoofing from my body.

Idiot. I had forgotten about all the junk that was still thrown around the floor. I slipped on a book or something.

Well, I thought to myself, *this is it, the intruder will be on top of me in a moment, knife to my throat, or bashing my skull in with a brickbat.*

I didn't have much time to dwell on my fate, because there was a woman screaming. In my apartment. Somewhere over by the couch. All I could see was small splotches of light from the windows in stray patterns across the dark cave of my apartment. It was like some kind of eye test or something the doctor gives you.

Of course, I figured whoever this woman was in my apartment was being attacked by the intruder, so I scrambled to my feet and charged in that direction.

My forward motion was stopped somewhere over by the coffee table. By the lamp—but I did not remember a lamp in the middle of the living room, and it hit me sideways. The intruder had swung my floor lamp at me. The blow landed on the side of my chest and spun me rather than stopping my forward progress. I knew my shins were approaching the coffee table, and I knew that would really hurt, so I vaulted for the couch.

I landed on someone there, the woman. I know this because what I landed on screamed even louder than before. More like a shriek.

The impact of me hitting the couch thrust the back of it against the windowsill, and the spring-loaded shade shot up into the roll with a sharp slap. Street light filled the apartment, spilling across the couch, the coffee table, the floor lamp on its side in the middle of the living room.

There, beside me—well, technically sort of under me—was Fanny, her eyes as wide as pizza tins, her tiny fists held up over her head as though she thought this might protect her somehow.

"Where did he go?" I shouted.

"Morty!"

Thinking she saw the intruder behind me, I spun around.

Nobody.

I looked back at Fanny.

"Where is he?"

"Morty, you scared the ever-livin' shit outta me!"

My brain chemicals swirled from panic and confusion to reason. I pointed a finger at Fanny.

"You are the only one here? Yes?"

"*Yes.*" She folded her arms. A sulk was setting in.

"Ah."

"Morty, why—"

"What are you doing here, Fanny? How did you get in?"

"I felt guilty about making you keep all your things on the floor. So after my bath . . . you know, you should lock your front door, Morty. Anybody could walk in here. Intruders could walk in here."

I slumped back into a puddle at the end of the sofa. "Well, it was locked when I just got here."

"That's because I locked it to keep out intruders."

"Yes, my sweet, but you see, when I heard you move I thought you were an intruder, so I made a dash for the kitchen but tripped on all my belongings on the floor—"

"Of course you did, because you leave your front door unlocked so they can get in. If you locked your door you wouldn't—"

"Yes, I hear you Fanny, but to be brutally honest, I do lock my door."

"Well, it wasn't locked when I got here."

I felt the growing bruise on my side where the floor lamp had hit me, and there was a dull warm spot on my back where I had fallen onto the floor. "So it is my fault that I tripped over my possessions on the floor. It is my fault that—in my own home—I got hit in the chest with the floor lamp, is this what you're telling me?"

"Yes."

"Ah."

There was an uncomfortable silence—as there often is after a man's logic has been made into a pretzel by a woman's.

Fanny was angrily staring at the ceiling. She was in shorts, with a tight tank top. In the low light I could not make out colors. Her dark hair spilled fetchingly over her shoulders. Her nicely curved legs were drawn up and swiveled to one side, so that I could make out the delicious curve of her bottom.

I reached over and began to stroke her thigh.

"What are you doing?"

There is of course no explaining to a woman that when it comes to sex, the male mind will render almost any diverting altercation trivial.

I leaned down and kissed her kneecap.

"*Querida,* this is all just an unhappy mix-up. If you think about it, it is funny, yes?"

"No."

"I come home, and I trip over my books and things in the dark thinking you are an intruder, and here you are, thinking I am an intruder. It is ironic. Irony is not something to fight about."

I moved closer to her, a ripple of pain shooting up my ribs, and began to stroke both thighs. Her arms were still folded, her gaze at the wall, her mouth sucking on her teeth in anger.

"Fanny, even with the mix-up, I am very pleased to see you. I have had a really rough day. You would not believe it."

"And just what are you doing coming in at this time of night?" Her eyes slashed at me briefly before returning to the wall. "Did you know you have grapes in your freezer?"

"Yes. Would you like some?"

"No."

My resolve to bed her wavered slightly. As I had just said, and as you know, Father, I had had a very trying day. To cap it all off, I now had to tangle with a petulant woman. I was not sure I had the strength.

"Everybody has gone crazy. They think I have a large sum of cash, and they are following me. It took a while to shake them, to get back here safely. You cannot believe what I have been through." I briefly wondered what Dexter was discussing with the Wolfman, and whether they were still down there bothering the monster toad.

Fanny's eyes were trained on me. "Large sum of cash? You mean money?"

I have never found women to live up to the avaricious nature that is sometimes ascribed to them. Still, the mention of this money seemed to have turned Fanny's mood.

"Yes, my sweet. When I clean houses, I sometimes find cash, which is legally mine. I found some the other day, but rumors about how much exploded, and everybody thinks I have truckloads of cash hidden somewhere."

She put her hand on mine. "Finding money must be exciting."

"It is in my blood. I am descended from conquistadors; finding treasure, it is what my people have been doing for centuries."

"What's a conquistador?"

"A conquistador is a Spanish explorer and fortune seeker. All my books, like the ones I tripped over, tell stories of how they came to the New World and brought home to Spain gold and riches. Some of the time, anyway."

"That would maybe explain the way you talk. Do . . . what do conquistadors do with money when they find it?" She drew her nails lightly down my forearm. This is something that gives me an almost automatic erection. I cannot tell you why. You would have to ask Pizarro, my penis, and as yet he has not spoken aloud.

I moved up next to Fanny, and she slid down, her big brown eyes looking up into mine. The anger was gone.

"Well . . . we put it in a safe place."

"Here?" She reached a hand up to stroke my neck.

I shook my head slightly, smiling at her. "Here is not safe for money."

Her eyes turned playful. "I don't think your place is safe for me, either. There's an intruder, and I think he's about to attack me."

She was right.

TWENTY-SIX

SO WHERE WAS DANNY WHILE all this was going on?
Back at the bump and thump. Had Charlie Binder followed his
original plan to show the motel night clerk the mug shot, instead
of sitting in his car in front of my building, annoying a monster
toad in white-and-green-striped pajamas . . . well, things might
have turned out differently. Or if he had chosen to go a second
time to the torn screen door at 901 East 109th Street and found
Rude Man's corpse.

But I was the hot wire linked to what he thought was his
money. Thanks to my cohorts at Oscar's.

What did Dexter say to Charlie there on the street in front of
my apartment?

"Nice evening." Dexter smiled. At that moment I was hiding
up at the corner ready to sneak into my building. Ready to be
scared shitless by my nosy landlord and then be scared shitless
by Fanny the intruder.

"Yeah," Charlie replied flatly, eyeing the man in the white
Panama hat.

"I bet you're looking for Morty, am I right?"

Charlie did not reply. He was thinking about the pistol he kept under the driver's seat.

"The reason I ask is because, well, I don't think he'll be coming home anytime soon." Dexter followed this statement with a helpful smile.

"How's that?" Charlie felt it was probably best not to divulge anything he didn't need to.

"You're not the only person looking for him. People wanna know about that money they say he found. I'm not sure he really did, but . . ."

"People?"

"Yeah, all kindsa people. Not sure which kind you may be, not my business."

"Who are you?'

"Dexter Lewis. I work for the *Brooklyn Gazette*. Reporter."

Charlie tensed. This was not good. As every cop from Canarsie to Carlsbad knew, an unexpected reporter is always a bad thing.

"I'm following this myself," Dexter continued, holding up the entire conversation. "Oh, don't worry, I'm not after the money, just the story."

"Maybe you'd better not follow this one." Charlie tried to smile. "I know people at the precinct here. This is none of your business, *capisce*?"

That made Dexter laugh. "Hey, I do, too, what a coincidence." He held up a hand and began to count them off on his finger. "There's Captain Tom Farfel—I was at a cocktail party at his house last week, I'm surprised I didn't see you there. You know Tom finally got that in-ground pool? Chief Detective Grimes was there, an old fishing buddy, we go every year for fluke in Barnegat Bay. We musta spent an hour talking about stripers.

And the Brooklyn DA was there, too—Phil Greene. Yeah. The *Gazette* supported him in the last election, stand-up guy. I wrote the endorsement myself."

Charlie squirmed in his seat, the pelt of hair on his back becoming like a wet sponge from sweat.

"Anyway, if you wanna find Morty, I'd forget about hanging around here. You missed the boat. There musta been five cars out here waiting last night, and Martinez never showed. They say he's gone to ground somewheres. Mighta even left the state. Anyways, wait if you want, I just thought I'd give you a tip. And now that there's a murder connected with this . . ." Dexter read Charlie's face. "Oh, you didn't know? Looks like someone offed Mary Duggin over at the real estate office, the one that reps the house where Morty found the money. You know the place? Sure, if you're here, you musta been there. So I'd watch it if I were you, because the boys at the local P are looking for suspects. I think maybe you better get in touch with your pals and let them know you were there and that it wasn't you who killed her. You know, just to be on the safe side. That's what I would do. You know them as well as I do, I'm sure they'll understand you were just there . . . what were you doing there?"

Charlie started his SUV. "I get it." And he drove off down the block.

Dexter jotted down the license.

It was times like these that Dexter believed his own hype. He wasn't just a good reporter, he was almost a superhuman reporter. He knew people so well, what made them tick—and what made people tick was fear, uncertainty, and self-preservation.

That's how he got me to spill the beans, after all. I did what was obviously in my best interest. Or so it seemed at the time.

"Ooo. What's going on out here?" A man in green-and-white-striped pajamas was standing on the sidewalk, hands on his hips. "You got any idea what time it is? People in this neighborhood is tryin' t'sleep."

Struggling with his clubfoot, Dexter made his way over to this man. I could have watched this part myself had I not been engaged in a bullfight at that moment.

"Hiya. Nice night. Sorry if we woke you. It was inconsiderate."

"Damn right it was."

"Like I said, sorry. I'm Dexter Lewis."

"I ain't shakin' your hand. I dunno you."

"I just said who I was." Dexter said this as if he were both amused and a little mystified. "And if you shake my hand and tell me who you are, then we will know each other. Am I right? You live here, at this address?"

"Me?"

"You came out of this building, didn't you? You know, I can find out who you are through your address, but I find a handshake much more friendly. Right?"

The man in the white-and-green-striped pajamas opened his mouth a few times to say something but hurried back inside instead.

Adjusting his hat, Dexter turned to his car, a lopsided smile on his face.

Fear. Uncertainty. Self-preservation.

Works every time.

Or almost.

TWENTY-SEVEN

A HAZY, UNCARING SUN ROSE over the Atlantic, the giant reflective eye of a predator watching Brooklyn as if it were a cowering rabbit. I stood at my bedroom window in just my underwear. A checkerboard of flat and pitched rooftops stumbled away to the east, melting into the orange haze of dawn. Even at that early hour you knew it would be the first truly oppressive day of summer. One of those days when you ask yourself whether a shirt is necessary. In just shorts and sandals, throw a towel over your shoulder and head out for the day. You put the towel on the car seat, then take it with you through the day so you do not leave sweat everywhere. A cotton barrier between you and seat backs all over town. Same as a shirt, yes? But cooler. This is fine for me, of course, because I have a good chest, with muscles and not too much hair. I think I have attractive nipples for a man. This would also be fine for someone like Fanny, who has great tits.

Then the mind turns to the patrons at Oscar's, who have—shall we say—more pedestrian body types. I would not want to walk in there and see that crowd without their shirts. Pale, matted, and flabby as corpses. A shirtless day at Oscar's would be like a zombie happy hour. Not so happy.

I suppose you would remind me, Father, that we are all God's creatures.

Anyway. I was looking out my window at that predator eye in the sky staring down on East Brooklyn and its alleys. I said it was uncaring because I was worried about what this day would bring. Whoever was up there, the mind behind that eye, I don't think this God or what have you even knew of my problems. But I wondered if the eye could see what was to come, whether there was a way out, whether I would find it. Whether the eye could see me driving into La Paz, Fanny in the passenger seat with some silly sandals on her feet she bought in a junk shop, the eight hundred grand in the Camaro's trunk, and Danny Kessel somehow dead, shot down trying to escape the police.

And a predator's eye? This day was lying in wait for me, like a cat at a mouse hole.

I glanced back from the window at Fanny. As before, the sheet was wrapped around her like a giant white three-hundred-count cotton tentacle, one of her thighs and both legs fetchingly exposed below. The graceful sweat-kissed arch of her back leading to the smooth white shoulders. The wild mane of dark hair spilled across the pillow. The regal nose smashed into the mattress. The spark of drool coming from her luscious, distorted lips.

The very picture of heaven.

I have found it interesting that heaven and hell sometimes seem to crowd each other.

Priorities. That was the only way to know my next move.

I left the bedroom and carefully looked out of the front window to the street. Wolfman was gone, and the other cars on the block all seemed innocent enough.

My keys were on the small table before me. The locker key's

glint seemed to be winking at me. I doubted the Balkan Boys were watching me now, as they were probably still at the hospital. Wolfman was off my butt. Speedy was probably tucked in bed with the girl on the window shade. The world was looking the other way. I could grab the cash and run. Sounds easy to do, just leaving Brooklyn, where I grew up and where I know all the places and people—but it wasn't. As much as I longed for my ancestral home in La Paz, to connect with my heritage and my people, to start a new life, this is something that you prefer to ease into. If I grabbed the cash and hit the road, leaving most of my meager belongings, I would not be leaving so much as running. There is a big difference. And in some ways, I thought that I might yet outsmart that predator in the sky. Several good things happened the day before, as crazy as it all was. Then there was that fountain in that courtyard four thousand miles away. Did it have the Martinez coat of arms on it? Was it possible I had actually located—and could buy—my ancestral home? I could hardly wait to get to the library to check my e-mail.

I realized that the only one who might be watching me now was Danny. True, he was the rottenest banana in the bunch, but at least the field of pursuers seemed to have thinned a little.

But what of the five million? Even if Danny caught up with me, I did not have it to give to him. I seriously doubted he would accept eight hundred grand. If only I could find out who did have it, or had the rest.

My thoughts turned to Dexter, my clubfooted friend at the *Brooklyn Gazette*. I had to wonder what he and Wolfman spoke of on the street last night, and I knew it could be important to how I should proceed. I wanted to know if Wolfman was off my trail so that I did not get blindsided.

I went to my wallet for the card he gave me when he dropped me off.

"Morty," Dexter said as he handed me the card, "keep in touch. I'll help if I can. But you have to know—I'm after a story. It's what I do. Understand?"

I understood. I was grateful at least Dexter was after a story and not me—that is, if it is possible to separate the two. I trusted him only so far.

Dexter, on the other hand, trusted himself too much.

TWENTY-EIGHT

DANNY WAS IN HIS MOTEL room, half asleep, watching the friendly people on the morning shows. The petty cash he stole from Mary was on the dresser. On the bed next to him was his cell phone and a check. My check. The one to Mary for the house cleaning, with my phone number on it. Even he knew it was too early to call me, but he was waiting to do exactly that.

There was a knock on the door, and he waited for it to happen a second time to make sure he had not dreamt it.

He stood, drew a sheet over the phone and check on the bed, and placed a pillow atop the money on the dresser. Danny smoothed his hair and carefully put on his jacket. Especially the right sleeve.

The sleeve with the remaining ice pick in it.

TWENTY-NINE

DEXTER'S NIGHT HAD BEEN A busy one. Aside from scaring off Wolfman from in front of my building, he managed to do some research back at his office, stop by to wake Frog and interrogate him, and visit the house on Vanderhoosen Drive. Dexter could have gone home at that point, gotten some sleep, but there was one more thing he wanted to do. It was a long shot, but worth a try. Just as the sun was coming up, as I was looking out the window across the Brooklyn rooftops, he was pulling into the parking lot of the Luna Motel—the bump and thump.

He had spent many hours parked out in front of the bump and thump. Watching and waiting. Especially as a younger reporter. Before he had dirt on everybody who was anybody in Brooklyn, he would do this to get compromising information on people. Local businessmen, small-time politicians, what have you. These were little fish swimming in and out of the bump and thump, cheating on their wives, on their girlfriends, and some-times both. Dexter had no interest in ruining their lives, but little fish know things about larger fish, who know things about big fish, and there are scams going on all over the place, cushy deals, kickbacks—wherever business and politics cross paths, corruption is sure to follow.

To uncover what was up and break a new story, all Dexter really had to do was extort information from the little fish and work his way up to the big fish. In part, this was how he built his career with the *Gazette*. So while other people his age were out drinking and chasing girls, Dexter in his twenties was more or less watching other people fuck.

How had Dexter known to target the bump and thump? It was the only place to rent a room for a night in the neighborhood, and he knew Danny's relatives no longer lived around there. Other than the Brooklyn Bridge, my hometown is not much of a tourist destination, especially out east. East Brooklyn does not really have any reputable motels, only the other kind. When your relatives come to visit Brooklyn they stay on your couch. The idea of Uncle Pete and Aunt Fran staying in one of these motels would not even enter your mind.

Of course, checking the Luna was not a sure thing, but it was a percentage play, and Dexter knew he had to work Mary's murder as fast as possible to stay ahead of the police. To his advantage, it took the cops a half day or so to stop filling in forms and filing reports and to start getting down to the business of actually looking for the perpetrator. Plus the cops had families. Many slept at night. Dexter did not.

As I was considering the sun's predator eye, Dexter left me a message on my cell phone, which was still on night mode: off. Then he left his car for the motel lobby. Apparently he didn't see the sun, not the way I did, or maybe he would have stayed in his Mustang. It is hard to say why he left the car, why he did not continue to wait outside to see if Danny would appear. I guess we all get impatient. And as we have seen, Dexter was not shy about approaching strangers.

He determined from the desk clerk that a man fitting Danny's description was staying in room 404. He had to knock three times before the door was answered.

I can only imagine what Danny thought when he opened the door and found a clubfoot in a Panama hat standing outside his door.

"Are you Danny Kessel?"

"Who are you?"

"Probably your only friend."

Danny did not like this one bit. He had no friends. Not in a long time. So immediately this man was lying to him. Was this the guy who went to Clara's house, looking for him? Clara would have mentioned the hat and clubfoot for sure.

"Really?"

"Can I come in? Really shouldn't discuss this in the hall."

"Please." Danny took a step back.

"Thank you." Dexter lurched into the room, over to the window. Danny closed the door behind him; he knew this could not be a cop. Detectives do not wear hats, and if they did, it wouldn't be a white hat. Also, he was pretty sure the NYPD wouldn't hire a clubfooted person.

"I know about the money, Danny. And so do other people. You'll never get it like this."

"Like what?" Other people . . . was it one of them that visited Clara?

"You're barking up the wrong tree."

"Please explain."

Dexter's eyes drifted to the pillow on the dresser, then to the sheet in an odd position on the bed. Danny followed his gaze and tensed.

"The money is gone, am I right? It's not where you hid it fifteen years ago at your uncle's, is it?"

Danny did not answer, only moved his right shoulder nervously.

"And now," Dexter grinned, "you think you know who may have found it."

Looking at the floor, hands dug into his pockets, Danny moved away from the door, closer to Dexter. "Please, go on."

"You're looking for this person with the idea of making him give it back. You spent fifteen years waiting to get your hands on the money. You earned it, right?"

"Where did you come up with all this?"

"This is what I do. Find things out. Tell stories. You have an interesting story, Danny. I think it deserves a happy ending. I can help you write that ending. But not if you go for the money. You killed Mary Duggin to get the name of the house cleaner you think has that five million. There was a flyer with your mug shot on her desk, and a private eye asking questions about you all over the neighborhood. How long do you think before the police find you?"

"Could you please tell me exactly what you're suggesting?"

Dexter folded his hands and touched them to his lips the way a minister does when delivering the final thought in a sermon. He was smooth, all right.

"Two ways this can end, Danny." Dexter held up a finger. "One: The cops find you, and if you break for it they'll shoot you down. They have a long memory—they know how Joey killed that detective years ago. They'd like nothing better than to shoot you."

Dexter held up two fingers. "Two: You come with me, we go

down to the precinct, and you turn yourself in. Let's face it, Danny: You were out, what, less than twenty-four hours and you murdered someone? You don't belong out here. You know that, don't you?"

Danny knew Dexter was right about that last part. His brother-in-law Jonathon had said pretty much the same thing. He did not belong out on the street. "You're not a cop?"

"I'm a reporter, with the *Brooklyn Gazette.*" Dexter put out his hand, chin raised, head tilted in a kindly and forthright manner. "Dexter Lewis."

Danny knew he did not belong on the street, but he knew he did not belong back at Sing Sing, either. He had no friends, no family. His only connection to the world, to his past and his future, was the millions that had been in the floor. It was the only thing he had to lose.

Stepping closer to Dexter, Danny swung his right hand forward casually as if to shake hands.

Instead, he pushed an ice pick into Dexter's chest.

The penetration of the cartilage and muscle sounded like someone snapping a celery stick.

Dexter did not know what happened at first. "Ooo, hey, whoa . . ."

Then he took his hand away from where Danny pushed his chest and saw the blood.

Eyes wide.

Grin now grimace.

"*Jesus Christ!*" Dexter staggered back, fumbling for his cell phone.

"Sorry." Danny batted the cell phone from Dexter's bloody hand and kicked the clubfoot out from under him. Dexter fell on the bed trying to yell but only gurgled with panic.

With the bedside phone, Danny proceeded to smash Dexter's face. The whole phone, base and all, the receiver and cord jumping all over the place. The forensics people could not be certain how many times he hit Dexter's face, but the phone was in about a dozen bloody pieces when Danny finally stopped.

What was left of Dexter slid off the bed to the floor; on the white sheets was the silhouette of his head in scarlet blood. It was like some art project from grade school where you trace your hand to make a Thanksgiving turkey.

Down at the front desk, the night clerk's shift was ending, and he glanced at the phone switchboard. The red diode for 404 was blinking—receiver off the hook. Common enough. Probably someone knocked it off the base during some sex thrashing.

They say pride arrives before the fall. For Dexter, I think it was the handshake.

THIRTY

IT WAS ABOUT THAT TIME that I was turning on my cell phone and waiting for the ridiculous thing to find a signal. I never could understand how the phone could start every day telling me there is no signal when it is four floors up and in direct line with the cell tower. It tells me this for five minutes until it seems to suddenly decide to go look for a signal and finds one. I will be brutally honest—I don't know how the things work to begin with, but this is like plugging a lamp into a wall socket and having to wait for the bulb to find the electricity.

So I set the idiotic phone on the coffee table and picked up the floor lamp, the one Fanny had slugged me with, which was still on the floor. It was one of those cheap black standing lamps with a saucer-shaped disc that shines the light on the ceiling. The saucer was dented and came off in my hand when I tried to secure it back in place. I put it next to the door to take down to the trash on my way out. I could see what I had tripped on. I went over and picked up the book I had stepped on. The cover had torn off, but I recognized it as the biography of Cortés. Now there was a guy who got into a lot of trouble, and often managed to get out of it somehow. I tossed the book on the shelf and surveyed the rest of the stuff. I hoped Fanny would let me put this stuff away soon. I was getting tired of looking at it, much less tripping over it.

Hmm, Fanny. I wondered if I should wake her and have sex or whether she would be too grumpy. It was not even six o'clock, and I have never known a woman who really enjoyed having her sleep interrupted for any reason. Still, it was worth a try. If the day went very badly, or if I was somehow killed, at least I would die knowing I had had sex that morning and the day was not a total loss. This is the way men think. Perhaps with the exception of priests, I do not know.

So I was on my way to the bedroom when my phone suddenly realized that there was a megawatt cell tower five blocks away. It cheeped. That meant a message. I stopped and looked at my caller ID. Dexter's number. I was about to dial and see what the message was when the phone cheeped again, but longer. There was an incoming call. I did not recognize the number.

I do not know about you, Father, but for me, there is virtually no good that can come from an unexpected early morning phone call. One's mind always turns toward death—someone has died. However, when my phone rings at odd hours and displays a number I do not know, it is almost always Russians. Drunk Russians who leave slurred messages in Russian that I cannot understand. Somehow, they misdial my number, and in their drunken state they fail to listen to my message, because if they did they would know I was not the person they were calling and would not leave long messages in slurred Russian. I could only imagine what they went on about.

So I let the call go into voice mail and dialed up my messages.

"It's Dexter. I had a very interesting conversation with your friend Frog. Meet me at the house on Vanderhoosen at noon."

So I tried calling Dexter to find out what Frog had told him, but there was no answer.

It was at this time, of course, that Danny was listening to my message greeting.

"Hello, this is Morty of Martinez House Cleaning. Please leave a message after the beep and I will return your call as soon as humanly possible."

He was just trying to decide whether to leave a message on my phone when there was a loud blurping sound in the corner. It startled him, but he quickly realized it was Dexter's blood-stained phone in the corner, on the floor.

He did not like the ring and so went over to make it stop. When he picked it up, he looked at the number. It was the one he had dialed on his phone. It was the number of the house cleaner he had been calling.

What did this mean? Dexter and the house cleaner were talking to each other . . . did this house cleaner know Dexter was on his way to the bump and thump?

He glanced over at Dexter's pulpy red face, or what was left of it. The *Gazette*'s star reporter was still crumpled next to the bed, twitching. Danny resolved to move him into the bathtub, out of sight. It was disgusting.

Danny wanted to answer the phone, but the brand was different from his own. He did not know that it folded and needed to be opened to answer the call. So he pushed a button on the side and it stopped ringing. My call went into Dexter's message box.

I left a message asking Dexter to call me and then checked to see what the drunken Russians had to say.

Very curious. Nobody spoke, but I heard a phone ringing, and it got louder, and then someone whispered, "Sorry." That was it.

Of course, Danny's phone was leaving a message in my box when Dexter's phone rang, and the message I was listening to was a recording of Danny picking up Dexter's phone and not being able to make it work.

I did not know this at the time, though, and thought that the message was very odd. Stranger than drunk Russians, even. I looked at the number again. I was sure I did not recognize it. I was half expecting a call from Pete the Prick to give me hell about his boys getting a little batting practice last night, but I double-checked, and it was not his number. My phone did not recognize it as anybody in my contact list. It could also have been the police tracking me down to ask questions about Mary's murder. That was a call I did not want to answer, but would have to eventually or they would come find me.

Had I listened to the sound of someone calling me when another phone went off in the room, and the person got distracted, forgetting to leave me a message? Well, whoever it was, if it was important, they would call back.

That is when my phone lit up again, this time with Dexter's number. So I answered.

Danny was trying to dial Dexter's message box, to retrieve my message to Dexter, but had inadvertently dialed my number instead.

"Dexter?"

There was a pause on the other end, and I heard nothing. Danny thought he was listening to a message, not a live person.

"Hello?" Still I heard nothing, so I hung up. I figured that Dexter must have lost the signal. Or my idiotic phone did. I looked at my signal indicator and had full bars. He would call back. I set the phone down and went into the bedroom to molest Fanny.

Meanwhile, Danny stared at Dexter's complicated phone,

which told him the call was over. Not much of a message. Or had he maybe called my number by accident? He was unsure. These phones were frustrating him. If there was one thing about the outside world that made him feel more alien than anything else, it was these phones. So he put them both on the dresser next to the pillow on top of Mary's petty cash, grabbed Dexter's mismatched feet, dragged him to the bathroom, and rolled him into the tub.

Danny surveyed the motel room. There was no hiding what had happened there. The bed, the floor, the streak of blood across the carpet and into the bathroom . . . he would have to rent the room until he had the millions and could get out of town. If he could just figure out how the phones worked, he could track down this house cleaner.

He filled his pockets with his belongings and both cell phones, put the DO NOT DISTURB placard on the outside door handle, and went down to the desk. It was time for a change of clothes and a car. If he did not have the money in two days, he would just leave town—there were too many bodies, and the police would eventually find him if he kept bouncing around the neighborhood in the same clothes day after day.

Almost out the door, he glanced in the mirror. There was a splotch of blood on his forehead. He spit on the corner of the bedspread, wiped it off, and went downstairs to the front desk.

"Checking out?" The night clerk was just getting ready to leave, had his college textbooks in his backpack, but the day girl was late—again. It was the same clerk Danny had seen his first night out.

"I need the room for two more nights, please—here." Danny slapped two hundred-dollar bills on the counter. "Keep the change."

"Hey, thanks." People often tipped him thinking it bought extra discretion. What it really bought was textbooks, not to mention beer.

As the night clerk watched Danny leave by the motel's back exit, he glanced down at the light for the phone in 404. It was still blinking. And that other guy, the one with the giant black shoe, had come in and gone up there. Maybe he snuck out.

THIRTY-ONE

CHARLIE BINDER HAD NOT GIVEN up. In fact, he had spent the night following the reporter.

That's why he was in the parking lot at the Luna Motel early that same morning, waiting for Dexter to come out.

He got tired of waiting.

He approached the night clerk, who was just stuffing forty bucks into his wallet.

"Can I help you, sir?" The clerk glanced at the wall clock—where the hell was Cheryl?

A twenty landed on the counter. "Guy with the white Panama. Which room?"

The clerk was raking it in, all last minute. Cheryl's tough luck. "Four oh four."

He watched the ginger-haired man in sailing togs disappear around the corner, and then glanced at that red diode for the 404 phone again. Cheryl could have trouble in 404. Two men? Fine. Three? Trouble. A lot of going in and out? Drugs.

Upstairs, Charlie reached the door and unholstered his .38 but held it inside the pocket of his windbreaker. He knocked. Then again, listening. Nothing.

A cleaning cart lady was at the end of the hall, and he paid her twenty to swipe her pass key on 404. She scurried away.

Gently, he pushed the door open, then spent about thirty seconds scanning the room.

"Holy Mother . . ." He spotted the blood, the shattered phone, and the drag line to the bathroom. There was the sound of movement, from the bathroom. Charlie crept into the room, his gun now drawn. Carefully, he circled across the carpet, stepping over the drag line. The bathroom door was only open a crack. He stood to one side. Another sound, like a gasp. With his foot he pushed the door, but it would not open all the way. He stopped and listened for a full minute. No sound. He pushed again on the door with his toe. Wouldn't budge. He poked his head around the corner into the dark bathroom while his other hand grasped the light switch.

He flicked it on.

It was only moments later that the night clerk was in the parking lot, unlocking his Chevy Impala, when he saw the guy in sailing togs walk rapidly out the front of the building, climb into a black SUV, and roar off down the road.

Something was up—this he was sure of. The drug thing? It did not bother him. What he did not like was a bunch of men and one woman. That usually turned ugly. One night the cops had to come and rescue some poor girl in 310. She had been in there for days, chained to the bed. The bastards had put a lot of things up inside her. Sick.

Cheryl had finally showed up. This was her problem.

The clerk was about a half mile up the boulevard in his Chevy Impala when he pulled a U-turn.

"HMM-4556, HMM-4556, HMM-4556 . . ." The clerk was repeating Charlie's license number.

Fifteen minutes later, the Luna Motel security guard and the night clerk showed up at room 404. They banged on the door, then they keyed it.

The door swung open and they were dialing 911 a second later.

Dexter was in the middle of the room, on his side.

THIRTY-TWO

I WAS BLISSFULLY UNAWARE OF all this. I was coupled with Fanny. We lay spent on the bed, me on my back, she draped across me.

"Morty?"

"Yes, *querida*?"

"Did you really find a bunch of money?"

When it comes to women, a man has a number of alarms that sound when certain topics come up. The most obvious is their weight, the "do I look fat in this dress" question. A man only has to answer that wrong once to learn that certain topics are too dangerous to address. There are numerous others, of course.

One of them is money. I once mentioned to a girlfriend that I had come into a couple thousand dollars, and she was of the immediate notion that I should spend it all on her. I had only myself to blame with Fanny because I had offered the information when I came stumbling in last night. I needed to explain to her how difficult my day had been, and there is no explaining the story without the money part.

But there are not only dangerous questions but dangerous circumstances. This was a doubly dangerous circumstance: the post-lovemaking question. A woman senses a man's defenses are lowered at this point. It is the perfect time for her to ask, for example, "How much do you love me?" Or: "Are we ever going to get married?"

So I was doubly cautious: She was both asking a dangerous question and asking it under dangerous circumstances.

I have found the best way to answer a question you do not want to answer is to redefine words, rephrase the question.

"Find? My pet, I do not find money. I make it. The house I cleaned? I did not charge. Why? Because I thought I would find money in the house. Why? Because I have a sense about these things. Sometimes I am wrong, and lose money on a house cleaning. Sometimes I am right, and make money. It evens out. This is my business."

Fanny played with my nipple, deep in thought. That is, Fanny was deep in thought. My nipple was just pensive.

"Where did you put it?"

"In a safe place."

"A bank?"

"You cannot walk into a bank with"—I caught myself—"that much money and deposit it. They will ask questions, the police come, and it is likely you will never see that money again. They will think it is drug money, illegal money."

"So what's a safe place for money if not a bank?"

"Some people think under the sofa is safe."

"Who?"

"Some of the houses I clean. I find money hidden under the couch. Often in peanut tins. They call these—"

"That's too obvious." She punched my nipple playfully. "So where did you put it?"

I answered the question as carefully as I did quickly. Just

knowing that it was in a storage locker would not give her any critical information about the exact whereabouts of the eight hundred grand.

"I have a storage locker."

"That's a good place."

"Yes, I think so."

It was then that my phone rang. Under the circumstances— with a naked girl in my bed—I would not normally answer the phone, but better to answer the phone than any more questions about the money from Fanny.

"Morty?"

"Frog?"

"What the hell is with that freak ringing my bell at four in the morning?"

"Hmm?"

"The guy with the foot, in the hat . . . the white hat. He came here and woke me at four this morning, asking me questions. Morty, I appreciate you have a problem, but don't drag me into this thing."

"Frog, I did not send Dexter to you. I just mentioned your name in passing as another feeler. Had I known—"

"Well, what did you tell him about me?"

"I am not sure I remember. Again, I only mentioned you in passing." What I did remember was Dexter's message:

It's Dexter. I had a very interesting conversation with your friend Frog. Meet me at the house on Vanderhoosen at noon.

"Frog, I apologize, I had no idea he would even contact you, much less wake you. What did he ask you about?"

"Ooo. Gotta go, Morty—call you back."

He hung up.

So I guessed I would find out at noon from Dexter.

THIRTY-THREE

DANNY NEEDED NEW CLOTHES. HIS were beginning to smell, and he needed a new look to stay under the cops' radar.

He knew where a mall used to be, and after a long walk he found it was still there. Things had changed, no more Chess King, but he remembered the Gap. It was there that he sought out his new wardrobe: a brown plaid long-sleeved shirt, chinos, white Converse All Star low-tops, socks, white briefs, a reversible belt, and a lightweight brown zippered jacket. After his purchase, he went to the mall bathroom to change and dispose of his old clothes.

At Sears he found two more ice picks and boot laces. As was his practice in prison, he always discarded a shiv once he used it. That was a big factor in not getting caught in prison. Even if you were present when someone got killed it did not necessarily implicate you. In prison, you are almost never alone with just one other person, so killings always happen with people nearby. Prisoners who witnessed a killing would never divulge this to the authorities. Those that did usually ended up dead no matter how the guards tried to protect them.

Even as Danny was back in the mall bathroom rigging up the two ice picks in his sleeves, he told himself that he would have to cut back on the stabbings. A witness who was not a prisoner would be sure to tell the authorities.

Killing Rude Man was unnecessary. He knew it was reactionary on his part, like a reflex left over from prison.

He did not want to kill Mary, but she refused to tell him who cleaned the house and picked up the phone to call the police when Danny got angry. It was just as well, though, because the contents of her strongbox were useful. First, the check for the cleaner, Martinez, with his phone number. Second, there was a thousand dollars in mixed bills, which was in the same envelope with the check. The cash was useful on its own, but it was interesting that all of it was old bills—more than fifteen years old. Was this part of the five million? Since it was in the same envelope with the check, it could have been from the cleaner.

Dexter was asking for it, and had it coming. Did he really think that much of himself, that he could talk Danny into turning himself in?

Danny knew if he continued to ice pick people, the chances of getting caught sooner rather than later would increase. He was renting room 404 two more days, and he reasoned that as long as nobody went in he had at least that much time before the reporter's body was found and he should get out of town. Forty-eight hours to find the cleaner—me—or whoever took the money, and get the five million. He hoped that I had his money. When I moved the couch to clean, Danny figured, one of the floorboards popped up and I discovered it. Otherwise, it got complicated, and he might not find the five million at all.

Danny walked from the mall and found a small park where

he could study his and Dexter's phones to try to make sense of what happened earlier when he tried to use them.

He had my phone number—but not a way to find me. Until he managed to check Dexter's messages, and heard the one I had left.

"Dexter, Morty returning your call. I'll see you at the Vanderhoosen house at noon."

THIRTY-FOUR

IT WAS THE UPS DELIVERYMAN who detected something was wrong at 901 East 109th Street. He knocked on the screen door with one hand, his other hand holding the plain brown package containing pornography. He heard something inside, he did not know what, and put his hands and face up against the screen to see inside.

"Hello?"

He heard the sound again, a squealing or squeaking sound. The deliveryman grew up in a rough section of the Bronx, and the sound was familiar. Rats fighting? Then he saw a rat scuttle across the hallway.

"Hello?" The screen door was locked. He detected the faint smell of decay, and he looked at the houses to either side. An older woman in a flower-print housedress next door was watering her flowerpots on her stoop.

"Excuse me . . ."

She squinted at the deliveryman.

"Do you know the man who lives here? Have you seen him recently?"

She smiled. "He's an asshole. The less I see of him the better. Enjoy your day." She went inside.

The deliveryman was undecided about what he should do. Rats don't necessarily mean anything is wrong. The guy could have a rat problem and left his screen door open when he went out of the house to get the paper. No wonder he had a rat problem: You could smell the garbage was spoiling.

He posted one of those annoying yellow delivery stickers to the screen door and walked slowly down to his brown van. Calling 911 seemed overkill. He would have to come back the next day with the package. If the situation were the same, then he would call the police.

Twenty minutes later he was at a light on the boulevard two blocks away when a cop car pulled up next to him.

"Excuse me, officer?"

Ten minutes later two police officers forced open the screen door at 901 East 109th Street and found a pile of rats feasting on Rude Man's chest cavity. One officer barfed on the spot; the other made it outside before he puked.

THIRTY-FIVE

THE FORENSIC PEOPLE AT THE Luna Motel, room 404, were as overwhelmed as they were at Upscale Realty. When they turned out the lights and turned on the black lights, there were thousands of semen stains covering virtually all the surfaces of the room. All were tagged, and then they turned on the lights and began tediously sampling and documenting each one.

Detectives Ruez and Pool were there, wearing their shoe covers and staring thoughtfully down at the blood drag across the carpet into the bathroom.

"Dexter's not going to make it." Ruez shook his head.

"Bad shape." Pool made a clicking sound in his teeth, an expression of regret.

"This'll be murder for sure." Ruez sighed.

"Think a girl was involved? You know, thump and bump . . ."

"Angry husband or boyfriend comes in, smashed his face in with the phone?"

"Whoever it was didn't pull punches." Pool looked at the shattered phone, which had been poured into an evidence bag and was sitting by the door. "Funny that Dexter was at the Upscale murder scene just last night, and now here dead."

"Funny?"

"You know." Pool looked at his partner. "Not ha-ha funny. A coincidence."

"Or not."

"Think Dexter was following something on the Upscale murder, got close to the murderer?"

"Low percentage. It's a thump and bump. Had to do with sex." Ruez smiled faintly. "Did we find Dexter's cell phone yet?"

Pool said no with a frown.

"Not in his car?"

Pool said no with another frown. "We called the paper, they're checking his office."

Ruez sighed. "Let's go look at the security tapes. But we need that phone."

Pool headed for the door. "Possible the killer took it?"

"Why would the husband take it?"

"Maybe his number was on it. Voice mail, you know, like that."

"Hmm. Let's have the paper give us the cell provider, download the incoming and outgoing calls, messages."

They started down the hotel corridor for the manager's office, the plastic on their shoes going *screnched screnched screnched*.

"Ooo." Pool winced. "Hear about Rat Man?"

"Guy they found eaten by rats?"

"Whew!" Pool waved a hand in front of his wrinkled nose as if there were a stench. "Glad we didn't get called in on that."

If Ruez and Pool had taken the phone research a step further, they would have had the provider triangulate the signal and locate Danny and stop all this carnage and destruction right then and there.

But they did not.

Idiots.

THIRTY-SIX

FANNY AND I LEFT THE apartment about nine. She was running late. I was carrying the busted lamp down to the trash.

"*Cara mia,* you must tiptoe down the last flight of stairs," I whispered.

"Morty, I have to get to work, come on."

"My sweet, we do not want the landlord to come from his lair."

"His what?"

"His lair. Like a monster from a cave under the stairs."

"Morty, can't you talk like everybody else? It's not always cute."

I threw up my hands as she tromped down the last flight of stairs. I could picture the monster toad in his gloomy grotto, his leviathan ogre wife parked in the corner surrounded by abused Entenmann's boxes and torn Cheetos bags. He hears feet coming down the steps, and the monster toad wonders: Who is this? Can I make this person miserable? And so he pries his bulk from the sofa and goes to the door.

Like clockwork. As soon as Fanny hit the ground floor, my landlord emerged.

"Who are you?"

Fanny shrieked, startled, and the monster toad looked up at me.

"Whatsimmatter with her?"

"You scared me," Fanny scolded.

"Morty, you know we live down here. Tell her not to stomp on the stairs."

"Yes, of course. Sorry."

"I wasn't stomping," Fanny protested. "I don't stomp."

"Morty, is this the girl from . . . *Jersey*? The one from last night when you came creeping in?"

You see what I mean? He emerged to make my life miserable. Though to be brutally honest, I do not think he had any idea that what he was saying was making me miserable.

Monsters are horrible by nature.

Fanny was staring holes through me as I tiptoed the last few steps to the landing.

"You're not from New Jersey, are you?" I asked Fanny.

"What *girl* from Jersey?" When a woman puts her hands on her hips while talking to you, there is often going to be trouble. "You were creeping?"

"Oh, then this is the other girl," my landlord added. He was talking to me like Fanny was not even there. I just blinked at him, looked at Fanny, and laughed. Hey, when things like this happen, you can either laugh or cry. Take your pick.

"This is Fanny." I said this like an introduction . . . and tried to ignore the growing suspicion and awkwardness.

My landlord just glanced at her as if she were a photograph.

"Well, make sure Fanny doesn't stomp down the stairs, OK?"

"Sure." I smiled at him reassuringly and guided Fanny out the front door.

As soon as we reached the stoop she ground to a halt. "What *girl* from Jersey?"

I groaned. "Fanny, he is insane. That is why I wanted you to walk softly down the stairs, so he would not come out of his apartment."

"Why didn't you say so?"

"But I did, my sweet."

"No, you said something about your landlord being a liar."

"*Lair.* I meant his apartment."

"You could have just said so. What about this *girl* from Jersey?"

"There is no *girl* from New Jersey."

"Then why—"

"I told him that. It was to make him stop bothering me. I had the . . . money bag in my hand and he came out and—"

"What, like a shopping bag? What the hell are you talking about, Morty?"

"Look, *querida*, please, we can discuss this as I drive you to work, yes?"

"*Yes.*"

So I managed to shovel my way out of the pile of shit my landlord dumped on me—and I did it by telling her the truth. It was too fantastic not to be true. Though I felt like an idiot telling her I transported the money in a cheesy plaid suitcase, and said it was in a duffel bag to simplify the story. Although I think she was beginning to think I was an idiot anyway for telling my landlord that I was taking my shirts to New Jersey. What could I say: It seemed like the thing to do at the time, yes? Anyway, Fanny was still vaguely suspicious and cool when I dropped her off at Tangles.

I had a couple hours before I had to meet Dexter at the

Vanderhoosen house. Where to? The library—I wanted to check my e-mail, see if the real estate people had sent me the photograph of the Martinez three-tiered fountain.

I parked at a meter on the parkway, shoved some quarters in, and headed for the library entrance.

I checked my e-mail: no message from the people with the fountain. I looked over the pictures again. It sure looked like the place. I could almost transport myself there, feel the salty warm breeze, taste the air tinged with the smoke of burning palm litter, hear the birds and the hum of hummingbirds flitting through the bougainvillea, see the stark shadows tracking along the stucco where lizards sunned. It was like I had been there in a former life. Perhaps I had.

I checked out some other listings and the La Paz site, mainly just daydreaming. I checked the time and realized I had better log off and go meet Dexter.

Exiting the library, I had the image of the fountain in my mind. Steps away from the library entrance, I received a tremendous shove from behind—I tripped and fell, rolling to my side on the cement sidewalk.

My attacker? Pete the Prick, standing over me with a two-by-four at the ready.

"I want that money! I know you fixed that bid with Mary! The tight ones are rightfully mine!"

I told you, Father, about how he had nice teeth, but that he rarely used them to smile. He was not smiling, but the teeth were literally snapping at the air with every syllable, spittle flying.

My arms were held out to protect myself. If he started in with the two-by-four, I would take a serious licking.

Think, Morty, think.

I obeyed Martinez's First Rule of Combat: Don't.

"Pete, you are right! The money? The tight ones? They *are* yours. But if you hit me, if you hurt me, I will not be able to take you to the ten thousand, right?"

I could tell: He really wanted to hurt me, and in a bad, bad way.

"Balkan Boys are busted up, why shouldn't *you* be?" He was frothing mad, to be sure.

Here is this insane man brandishing a two-by-four threatening to seriously harm me on a public street. Citizens are passing by, giving us a wide berth. There is even a security guard in the library watching from behind the glass doors. Is anybody calling the cops? I know New York has a reputation for being a cold place, but despite my predicament, this is not true. If you ask directions, New Yorkers will stop and give them to you in great detail, with other natives dropping in on the conversation to give their version of the directions. But when it comes to physical altercations, not many of us will intercede. Cowardice? Not as such. I think it has more to do with survival of the fittest. If you are weak, it is your fault. That is not to say that a New Yorker would not protect a child from an adult, or a woman from a man, but not a woman from a woman, and not a man from a man. The good news is that after you are beat up, lying there bleeding, a New Yorker will call the EMS and do a nominal job of making sure you do not die. A small consolation, I know, but a consolation nonetheless.

"I am different from the Balkan Boys because I have something you want, Pete!"

"Ten thou? Is that all?"

See how clever I was? When you bring up money, like sex, it will distract most people.

"I swear, Pete, that is what I got. Those little lying brown bastards exaggerated! You must have had that happen! Yes?"

His eyes began to wobble in their sockets as his rage succumbed to a morsel of thought. I figured I had better keep working on him.

"I'll give you the ten thousand and then we can have peace, yes?"

"No, no, no peace, ever." His rage boiled anew. "You give me the money and I still hate your guts, spic."

"Pete! I cannot give it to you from down here, can I? You have to let me up so I can get it, yes?"

He took a swing at me with the bat, and I pulled my hands away just before he smashed my hands into skin bags of shattered bone. Well, I knew this was going to be a predatory day, did I not?

"I could smash you into a pulp, throw you in the car, and twist your cock with vise grips until you told me where to drive to find it, how's that?"

"Pete! Pete! Listen to me!" He had really given this some thought, yes? "If you did that, what would keep me from going to the police afterward? I mean, unless you aimed to kill me, and if you did, you would surely get caught with all these witnesses and sent to jail for the rest of your life and never see the money. Yes? Yes?"

His eyes got all wobbly again as his brain tried to process what I was saying.

"Get up." He still had his weapon ready, so I was cautious.

My eyes stayed on him as I slowly rose to my feet, hands out,

palms down in a calming gesture like one might use on an escaped gorilla. *Easy, big fellah.*

"Your car or mine?" I asked, if nothing else to try to keep his
mind off hitting me.

His eyes wobbled and then he said: "Your spic-mobile, what
else? Try anything cute and I'll ram this board into your cock so
hard your eyes will fall out."

I never before would have suspected Pete was capable of such
colorful descriptions. This was his second reference to maiming
Pizarro, and I had to wonder if Pete the Prick got that name for a
reason other than his personality.

As I walked ahead of Pete toward my car, I was busy thinking.
I could not really take him to the money or he would see that
there was a lot more than ten thousand and want it all. I was not
about to give him all the money, though I might have parted
with ten grand to get this asshole off my back. A small price to
pay when you look at the larger picture.

No, I could not take him to the storage locker. I glanced at my
watch. I was supposed to meet Dexter.

Can you see where this was going?

Who better than Dexter to defuse this situation? I could say
the money was still in the house and, with Dexter there, get a
little room so I could run for it or something if necessary.

At that moment, though, Dexter Lewis was in intensive care
at East Brooklyn Hospital. The ice pick narrowly missed his
heart, puncturing his left lung, and he was able to climb from
the tub after he heard Danny leave. That is when he heard someone else come into the room—Charlie. Though he heard this
person gasp upon seeing him on the floor, Charlie left without
helping him. Dexter was blinded by having the phone pounded

into his face but managed to crawl out of the bathroom. That is when he was discovered by the Luna Motel staff and was rushed to the hospital.

So Dexter would not be meeting me at the house on Vander-hoosen Drive.

Danny would.

THIRTY-SEVEN

DECKED OUT IN HIS NEW outfit, ball cap pulled low over his Donna Karan sunglasses, Danny had decided to wait inside his uncle's house on Vanderhoosen Drive. Inasmuch as Dexter had said that there were people looking for him, Danny figured that it would be better to be seen as little as possible. Especially loitering around his uncle's house. The doorjamb was already broken, so he had no trouble getting in.

So when I drove my rusty white Camaro up to the curb, and beheld the shabby two-story brick house, I expected to see Dexter waiting for me out front. I did not even see Danny. My heart sank. This would make escape more difficult. A lot more difficult. And if I gave Pete any clue that I was bullshitting, he would likely make good on his promise to mangle Pizarro.

I might have to enact Martinez's Second Rule of Combat: Go for the balls and run.

"Here?" Pete shouted.

"Yes. I found the money here but moved it to a different location in the house."

"Why would you do something so fucking stupid as that?"

"Because it is the last place anybody would think to look. The place where I found it."

"You're a fucking spic idiot. Come on, get out."

So we got out and walked up to the stoop, Pete keeping his distance and making the Martinez Second Rule of Combat difficult to enact. I knew the key to the front door was in a magnetic container under the mailbox—but Pete didn't know that.

"We have one problem," I sighed. "I do not have the key. I gave it back to Mary. And we cannot get it from her now."

"Bust it in, faggot." He prodded me in the back with the two-by-four. Even if I gave him the money, even if it were there, he would go to town on me with that two-by-four, I was certain.

"I will try. But people may see and call the police if we break in the front door. Perhaps we should break in the back door, a door with glass panes that would be easy to break. Yes?" This may seem like I had a plan, but I did not. Just stalling, looking for an opportunity to escape.

"*Yes,* asshole."

So we went through the side yard, which was a narrow driveway of maybe ten or twelve feet between houses. I could not help but notice someone move in front of the window in the house next door, which was odd, because that house also was empty. It was the one Frog had cleaned a few weeks back. Could Dexter have gone to the wrong house? And gone inside?

We reached the rear entrance to the kitchen, and I opened the flimsy wooden screen door. "Could you hold this screen door open while I try to force my way in?"

Pete merely snorted, took a step closer, and held the screen door.

Let me tell you, it is very difficult to enact my Second Rule of

Combat on someone standing behind me. Turning quickly would give him enough time to react.

The door was locked. I slipped off one of my tennis shoes and smashed a glass pane in the door. Carefully, I removed any remaining shards that might cut me, reached in, and unlocked the door. Pete watched me closely, so much so that I did not think that trying to slip a shard of glass into my pocket—perhaps useful as a knife—was wise unless I wanted to be castrated with a two-by-four. I turned the knob and the door swung open.

Exactly as I had left it. Cupboards all bare, greasy stains on the wall surrounding where the stove had been, striped rectangle of dust on the wall where the refrigerator had been.

"Where is it?" Pete jabbed me with the two-by-four.

"Upstairs. The attic." It was either that or the basement, and I would rather flee running down stairs than up. At least if I fell in my haste I would not fall back toward Pete. I say this all calmly enough now, but I will be brutally honest: I was shitting bricks, my back soaked with sweat, my heart doing jumping jacks in my chest. At the same time, I was coiled like a spring, ready to do what I had to save my skin. I was sure Cortés felt like this when the Aztecs were after him at Tlaxcala.

I led the way up the steps, and that two-by-four jabbed me a couple times along the way. A little reminder of what was in store for me.

I went to the hall closet and pointed at the ceiling.

"A hatch?" Pete looked up with disgust at the square wood panel that led to the attic.

"Yes, a hatch. Do you want to . . ."

"What am I? An *idiot*? You go up. And if you don't come down with ten thousand bucks, doctors will be pulling splinters from your balls. Got it?"

A reply to the third threat on Pizarro seemed unnecessary.

"I need something to stand on to get up there, and all the furnishings are gone."

"You're stalling, spic. The money isn't up there, is it?" He started waving the two-by-four, winding up for the beating.

"Well, if you beat the shit out of me with that before I go up into the attic, how will you ever know? For Christ's sake, Pete, would I lead you up here and corner myself in the closet or the attic if the money was not here? Try thinking with your head for a change." Perhaps it was bold of me to push back like that, but it worked. Pete stepped back. He was still fuming, but he was also looking around for something I could stand on to reach the hatch.

Directly across from the closet was the bathroom, and on the wall of the bathroom was a wooden cupboard. Pete set his two-by-four on the sink and began to grapple with this cabinet, to try to pull it off the wall.

Unfortunately, the door to the bathroom opened in. Otherwise, I would have slammed the door shut and bolted down the stairs and not stopped running until I was in La Paz standing before the three-tiered Martinez fountain.

The cupboard jarred free from the wall, white dust pluming out from where the wall anchors had burst from the plaster. Pete turned it toward me.

"Here, asshole, use this," he said from behind the cabinet.

It was then or never.

I could not kick him in the balls without having the cabinet fall on my knee. Then we would both be injured. Instead I did a high kick into the cabinet itself just as hard as I could.

He stumbled back, his shins hit the edge of the tub, and he fell into the shower, the cabinet thudding down on top of him. I heard what sounded like his head hitting the shower wall, and a strangled yelp—that must really have hurt. Even if he was still conscious, I figured that little mishap should delay his pursuit long enough for me to make it to the Camaro and zoom off.

I did the switchback staircase to the first floor in two jumps, turned toward the kitchen, and came to a screeching halt.

There, just inside the door through which I had entered, was a man in woman's sunglasses, a brown Gap ball cap, and department store duds. I did not recognize him as the man I saw standing in front of the house, or the man at the library computers, or the man in the mug shot. My immediate thought was that this was one of Pete's henchmen, one I had never seen before. But how would he have come to this place?

All I could think to do was say, "Excuse me." I turned and went for the front door.

"Martinez?"

I was already at the front door, yanking it open, when there was a hand on my shoulder, spinning me around.

"I'm talking to you!"

Not a wise move on this stranger's part, because as we know I was in Martinez Combat Mode.

He spun me around and my knee came up fast and hard.

A man sort of hates to do this to another man, but at the same time we know exactly how devastatingly effective this maneuver is, don't we, Father?

My knee found its mark. The stranger's body jackknifed.

"Oof!" he grunted, his jaw muscles visibly locked in bashed gonad anguish.

There was a clunk on the floor next to him. It was a meat hammer. It seemed to have fallen from him when he contorted. A meat hammer?

The stranger was jerking his right shoulder strangely, but I did not take time to continue my study of him. I burst through the front screen door, scrambled into the Camaro, and sped off down the street.

Danny, of course, had been trying to move his right arm to grab his ice pick, but the contortions resulting from the explosive agony in his groin prevented him from this act. He staggered back against the wall, gasping, wincing, hearing me fire up the Camaro.

All herky jerky, he managed to straighten up, tears streaming down his red face.

Then he heard another sound. From upstairs. There was a crash and an unintelligible shout.

Someone was stumbling down the stairs, roaring like a wild and rampaging ape.

Pete the Prick turned the corner into the living room, the two-by-four in his hand. He saw in his peripheral vision someone standing against the wall. He did not know who. At this point, he was so enraged that he swung the weapon in an attempt to injure whoever it was.

Can you see where *this* is going, Father?

Danny had gotten hold of his ice pick by now.

It went badly for Pete the Prick. But I cannot say I miss him.

THIRTY-EIGHT

THE POLICE STILL DID NOT have a clue about what was going on.

They had found Mary stabbed, and it looked like a robbery because the cash box had been looted.

They had found Rude Man half eaten by rats. They had yet to figure out that he had been stabbed. From what they could tell there was no sign of foul play, so an autopsy was not scheduled until the next day.

They had found Dexter with his face caved in by a phone and stabbed in the chest. He had undergone emergency surgery for the chest wound and to try to save one of his eyes. Even though he seemed stable in intensive care, he had not regained consciousness—and the doctors were not sure if he would.

To the police, these three unfortunate incidents had nothing connecting them.

So the cops were searching for a tall, dark man in a turtleneck and large sunglasses, the one on the fuzzy motel security tapes, the one who had registered as Tom Roberts. They were not looking for someone in a Gap cap, large sunglasses, plaid brown shirt, chinos, and white Converse All Star low-tops. The chances of them picking up Danny were slim indeed.

The only thing tying any of this together was the small wounds, but they were not even in the same place on the bodies. Mary got it in the eye, Dexter in the chest.

The people like me and Frog and the barflies at Oscar's who might have had a clue were not getting involved with the cops, and the cops had no real reason to seek us out for questioning.

They did have one thing to go on. The guy who rented room 404 at the Luna Motel. They got a full description: tall, dark complexioned, turtleneck, sport coat, scar on lip, women's sunglasses.

And our friend Wolfman Charlie? He was still looking for the damn five million. That is why the bastard simply walked away from Dexter as he lay there in a smear of blood on the motel bathroom floor. Charlie headed home to Queens for some sleep, his gun a little more handy than before.

Ah.

But remember? The motel clerk memorized Charlie's license plate. And the motel cameras got a picture of him and his black SUV.

Which was why he got a phone call that woke him up.

"Charlie. It's AJ. Howareyah? How's the boat?"

Charlie blinked at his alarm clock, and at the afternoon sun in the window, unsure of what time of day it was.

"Coming along. Almost finished. What's up, AJ?"

"I should ask you. Detectives in East Brooklyn are hot for you, got you on tape at the scene of the beating of a reporter. Whatsupwidat?"

Charlie's heart felt like it tripped and fell, and for a moment the room swam about him.

"Tape? I don't understand."

"Luna Motel. Says you was in the room where some reporter there got the shit beat out of him. He may not live. They need to talk to you, Charlie, you unnerstand? They're callin' here askin' questions. I said I'd give you a call. Courtesy, seeing as how you're a cop."

"I don't understand, AJ . . ." Charlie sat on the edge of the bed, batting away sleep's cobwebs.

"They have your make of vehicle, your license, a witness, and the motel security tape. They say you was there, Charlie. Were you?"

"Yes, I was at the Luna Motel. I was trying to track down Danny Kessel, you know."

"I know. Why else would you be in the Armpit of Brooklyn? Go on."

"I started to follow the reporter, because I knew he was looking for Danny. Thought he would lead me to him. So he goes to the motel, and I follow him up to a room. I knock, no answer, so I leave."

"Uh huhn. Well, you gotta come down."

"Come down?"

"You know the drill, Charlie. You gotta tell the detectives what you know."

Charlie groaned.

"When?"

"Now, Charlie, now."

THIRTY-NINE

AT THIS STAGE OF THE cat and mouse, I had had enough. Pete was not about to let me alone, but for the moment, I knew he was out of my way. This was a window of opportunity I might not get again.

A window of opportunity to get the money and make a run for it. There could be no hesitation once I had the Scottish suitcase in hand—I had to hit the highway and not look back, leaving my crappy furniture to the monster toad. No way could I go back there now.

Let us not forget, Father Gomez—I still had Danny to worry about, and at that point I had no idea I had just crushed his nuts. I had no reason to think that was Danny in the Trux place on Vanderhoosen Drive. To be brutally honest, it was the Donna Karan sunglasses that threw me. You do not expect a hardened murdering cutthroat degenerate con like Danny to be wearing giant Donna Karan sunglasses, do you, Father? I am certain your answer would be no.

So I drove directly from Vanderhoosen Drive to the storage place off the boulevard, a renovated factory with idle brick smokestacks. I kept an eye on my rearview mirror just in case I was being followed and steered around the block a few times to be sure. I pulled in past the guard, parked, went in, and walked up three flights to my mini storage locker.

I pulled out my keys.

No locker key.

I stared openmouthed at the keys in my hand, but that did not make the key appear.

How was this possible? My keys are on a steel split ring, and none of the other keys were missing. Did I take the key off?

Of course not, you idiot. You have looked at that key a number of times, seen it winking and blinking and all that while you fantasized about a fountain four thousand miles away.

Last I saw it was that morning. Now it was gone. The keys had not left me at any time. Well, when I was undressed, of course, last night, I did not bring them to bed with me and . . . the shower!

I tell you, Father, I almost fainted. But moments later I was back in the parking lot lifting the battery from the Camaro, looking for the paperwork.

Gone. That bitch had really done some searching, yes? So much for Speedy's father's hiding place.

I climbed into the Camaro and revved her up. I think I set a new land speed record between U-Stor-It and Tangles. Check next year's Guinness Book.

All those seemingly innocent questions about the money. Her wanting to help with my shelves so she could search my apartment. Instead of her date with Calgon, she came into my place to search while she knew I was at Oscar's. Then that sneaky bitch Fanny stole the key to the storage locker while I bathed. Searched my car enough to find the paperwork, too.

My phone rang. I did not recognize the number but answered just the same.

"Morty," a small voice squeaked over the line. "It's Hugo."

No kidding.

"Look, Hugo, I am kind of busy—"

"You seen Frog? He's missing."

"What do you mean *missing*?"

"Car is gone from his apartment complex, and when I was cashing my check down at the bank, the teller said she was sorry to see Frog go. I asked what she meant, and she said he was in earlier transferring his money to another bank."

"So?"

"A bank in Switzerland. Morty, I think Frog skipped town."

I scratched my head, my face contorted with confusion. I know because I saw my face in the visor mirror.

"Switzerland?" I knew that the last time I spoke with him that morning he was kind of jumpy about Dexter. Where was Dexter, anyway?

"Hugo, call me if he shows up. I am chasing something else down at the moment—talk to you later."

What the hell was going on? No, I am not asking you, Father, because I now know. But at the time I did not.

CHAPTER

FORTY

CHARLIE BINDER SHOWED UP AT the East Brooklyn precinct as I was closing in on Tangles. He did not know how he was going to play it because he was not sure how it was going to be. Would they treat him like a fellow cop? Or like a suspect? He knew the interrogation techniques.

There were two detectives in the interrogation room; one was white and one was Hispanic, both young. Charlie knew that was not good. It was not good because they were young and would not be as forgiving as someone of Charlie's generation. It meant he was going to be treated like a suspect. Back in the day, it would have never gone down like this. You could get a pass on things like this if you were a fellow cop.

"Hi, Charlie, thanks for coming down," the Hispanic one said, trying to smile. "Want some coffee or some water?"

Charlie tried to smile himself. Right away, there were four warning signs. The first was that the detectives made no move to shake hands. That would have signaled that they were equals, and an interrogator has to be in command. Second, they were not going to introduce themselves. Again, it helps them to be superior to the suspect—they know who you are but you do not know who they are. Third, this guy was calling him by his first name—standard way of establishing familiarity with a suspect while at the same time remaining his superior. Fourth, the coffee meant they intended to take their time.

So Charlie put his hand out, and the Hispanic officer shook it somewhat reluctantly.

"Charlie Binder."

"Detective Ruez, and this is my partner, Detective Pool."

Charlie forced a handshake on the other detective. Now they knew he knew how to play the game.

"I was a detective here, you know, back when." Charlie wistfully scanned the institutional room, table, chairs, and mirrored wall. "Interrogated quite a few people in this very room. I'll take that coffee light and sweet."

The two detectives shared a look but did not move to go get the coffee. Which meant that someone behind the mirror was going to get it. Which meant that they were probably video recording the interrogation, too. Charlie knew this was serious, and the detectives were not doing anything to make him think otherwise.

What crime had he committed, after all? Well, he knew about stolen money, Danny's treasure, the money I had recovered. To plan to steal for his own purposes might be conspiracy, but he knew it was very unlikely the DA would ever seek an indictment on something with so little hard evidence. Finding the dead guy in the motel room—he did not believe that they could be positive Charlie went in the room. He had been careful to wipe the doorknobs and light switch. Unless they talked to that maid, the one who keyed the room for him. That could get him in trouble under some new Good Samaritan laws, if not an obstruction of justice statute—clearly he went there seeking Danny for a reason, which led into the conspiracy charge.

Charlie had to know if they talked to the maid. So he cut to the chase.

"We don't need to wait for the coffee to start, fellahs. First, do you guys have any proof I went in that room?"

Ruez looked at his partner. Pool shrugged.

"The maid," Ruez said.

"Right. I need a lawyer."

This meant, of course, that even though the police were at least beginning to see what had happened, Charlie was going to tell them as little as possible. This would not make it easy for the cops to figure out what was going on. Or to figure out why so many dead—or nearly dead—bodies were showing up in their precinct.

Even in East Brooklyn, three bodies in twenty-four hours was a lot of bodies.

They would not find Pete's body, victim number four, anytime soon. Even while Ruez and Pool were interrogating Charlie, Danny was busy at the house on Vanderhoosen Drive dragging Pete down the stairs by his feet, the head clunking on each step.

Until the last step, where Pete's head hit the cement with a sound not unlike a coconut falling from a palm tree onto a California patio.

FORTY-ONE

"WHERE IS FANNY?"

A mousy woman in a pink tank top and clear plastic smock, with suspicious button eyes, stood before me. Her hands were in clear plastic gloves that massaged black gooey hair dye into the head of an old Italian woman in a salon chair. It looked like the mousy hairdresser was making a mud pie with a cow patty.

Beyond these two was the majesty of Tangles. A row of pink salon chairs and mirrors lined the right wall, and turquoise pedicure thrones lined the left. Women were seated in some of these chairs in various stages of transformation. Faces were smeared with bright green beauty ointments, hair was spiked in tinfoil for streaking, feet were boiling in blue liquid, and hands were inserted into buzzing electric nail dryers. The attendants were prodding, poking, smearing, filing, and rubbing body parts. I tell you, it looked more like the lair—not the *liar*—of some mad scientist than a beauty salon. If I simply say "Bride of Frankenstein" you will understand what I am talking about.

"She ain't here," said the woman with the black gooey dripping plastic hands.

"Have you seen her?"

"Who are you?" She stopped massaging, and I was glad, because it made me slightly queasy.

"Me? I am an . . . associate of Fanny's."

"If you were really an *associate* of Fanny's, you'd know where she was, wouldn't you?"

I did not care for her snide grin.

"My name is Morty, and you are?"

"Silvia." Now her grin turned slightly furtive, and she began smooshing the black cow patty again, but with more force.

From snide to furtive in a mere moment. Their minds work on so many levels at once. I believed it was time for some heavy flirting.

"*Silvia.* What a pretty name." I smiled, smiling the smile I reserve for the girls, and sometimes for my landlord. "Fanny never said there was someone as charming as you working here."

I know, you are groaning from my obviousness, but as I told you before, it is my considered opinion that with women it often pays to be obvious.

She suppressed a giggle, looking sideways at me like she did not believe a word of it, but wanted to. "What's the emergency, Morty?" She looked down at the black squishy hair, smiling to herself coyly.

How long would I have to keep up my flirtations? I wanted to strangle her, make her mind just work on one level. Mine.

"It is a long story, Silvia, and I would not want to bore you with it. What I would want would be to meet you some night at Octavio, yes? But I would not bore you."

Color came to her cheek, but her gaze remained on the *squish squish squish* of the cow patty in front of her.

"Octavio. Hmm. I go there sometimes. Saturdays."

"Well, I might just see you there. Yes?" I puffed out my chest, my smile turned on full force. "Buy you a daiquiri, perhaps?"

"Promise?"

Oh, for Christ's sake.

"I never joke about drinks with a beautiful girl."

Now the old woman under the black cow patty shot me a glance. Even she could not stand to hear this nonsense.

"Fanny was in first thing but canceled her appointments and took the day."

I tried to contain my anxiousness.

"Silvia, do you dance? It would be a great disappointment if you did not, as I would most look forward to doing so after that daiquiri."

The old woman shot me another look, and I heard her mutter, "Get a room, willyah."

"I dance, and I might dance with you." Silvia wiggled her hips in a way that I think she thought was kittenish. "You talk funny, but I like it."

"I will then be hopeful for the pleasure of a dance. Until Saturday?"

I turned to go, but turned back. She had a dreamy look in her eyes.

"Oh, Silvia, darling, can you tell me where Fanny lives? I really must deliver some important documents to her. It has to do with . . . the estate of a dead relative, and some inheritance." Scammers are always trying that one on me in e-mails, so I figured it must work a lot of the time.

"You mean her uncle?"

"Hmm?"

"Her uncle, the one that lived on Vanderhoosen."

A lightning bolt cracked through my skull.

"Trux?" My voice quavered, and sheer astonishment may have filled my eyes, but Silvia's mind was elsewhere, so I don't think she noticed.

"Well, that is Fanny's name, silly." She batted her eyelashes at me. "I want a strawberry daiquiri."

"Of course, as many as you wish."

"She lives in that white four-story five blocks toward the avenue, on the sunny side."

"Silvia, you are a gem."

I turned to go, my smile replaced with a grimace. I know, because I saw it in one of the mirrors.

I began to make quick work of the five blocks on foot, the lightning bolts splitting my brain every time I spat the words "Fanny Trux."

This goes to show you how important it is to inspect a woman's driver's license on the first date. Usually, I do this to confirm her age and address. The age I need to know because some of them are very good at looking younger than they are, and as a general rule a man desires a woman at least a little younger than himself. You want the address because if she passes out in your car or is impossibly drunk, you want to be able to take her home without going through her purse. A woman can grip her purse with uncommon force even in an unconscious state. In an advanced state of intoxication, they can be idiotically coy and not tell you where they live, and at that point all you want to do is get rid of them because it is likely they will puke on your floor mats—if you are lucky. Do not think less of me for this tactic: the person in the passenger seat is the one who drank eight Fuzzy Navels, not me.

I generally manage to examine a woman's license by showing them mine, pointing to my picture, and saying how bad it is.

Then they say theirs is worse—almost always—and you tease them into finally showing it to you. A furtive and informative little game.

So Fanny was Trux's niece. She seduced me to get at the money. She canceled our date and, once she knew I would be out at Oscar's, came to search the place. When she did not find the money in my apartment, her next move was to sleep with me again and then in the dangerous after-sex conversation ask about the money and try to get some details. Once I was asleep, she snuck out of bed and stole the new key on the ring, the only one that did not fit my car or my apartment.

Perhaps she noticed the new key appear on my key ring after our first date. She would have to be very observant to notice such a trivial thing, but I find women are often keenly perceptive of the little things, sometimes to the exclusion of the big things.

If she knew of the cash in the first place, though, why did she not retrieve it after her uncle died and before I got there? She was not in my industry and would not have had contact with the day laborers to know that I found money in her uncle's house. She must have known about it before I cleaned the house to have followed this so closely, and as soon as I was done cleaning the house, she sought me out to see if I found it.

Ah.

But if she is Trux's niece, then Danny could be her brother or cousin, because it was Danny's uncle's house where the money was. Trux was uncle to both of them.

Ah.

Danny's last name is Kessel, so he cannot be her brother, he must be her cousin. Danny would be Uncle Trux's sister's son.

Did this mean Danny had sent Fanny? That they were working together in this very sneaky way?

Ah.

What made Fanny take the key when she could not possibly know where the locker was? The document under the battery. She may even have found that first. Was taking the key to make me come to her? To make me find her, where Danny would be waiting to make me take them to the locker? Or bargain with me?

Ouch.

My brain hurt, a gray blob bulging with all the treachery and variables. All I wanted to do was find a bar and drink until what was going on somehow became clear. Drinking, of course, is a man's first impulse when he is overwhelmed. A man fights with his girl, walks out, where does he go? A man is fired from his job, where does he go? A man wrecks his sports car, where does he go? Unfortunately, the only thing drinking makes clearer is the futility of not drinking, which is not much help and only results in a bad hangover on top of your other problems. We know this, of course, but do it anyway, much the same way a dog eats grass and vomits.

I pushed on down the boulevard and could see the white building ahead, the one with the furniture store on the ground level.

My phone rang, and it was the giant mouse.

"Morty? Hugo."

"Hugo, I am still rather busy—" I was picturing a squirrel puppet on the other end of the line.

"I'm at the airport," he squeaked.

"The airport?"

"I have a confession."

"Confession? Hugo, what are you talking about?"

"I found Frog. Here, at the airport." When he squeaked the word "airport" it sounded like a rusty screen door opening.

"Really? Where is he going?"

"He's not going anywhere. Now."

"Hugo, you are being very mysterious, and I do not have time for any more mystery in my life at the moment. I will call you—"

There was a noise and the call dropped on his end. I had full bars. Just as well. I hated to hang up on him, but as you know, I was focused on that double-crossing dirty-dealing flimflamming Fanny.

I challenge you to try saying *that* three times fast without saying "Flammy" at the end at least once.

I was approaching the entrance to her building when I saw the door open and Fanny step out. She was looking in her purse, not where I was, so I veered into the furniture store.

Through the front window, over a particleboard bed inset with fake zebra, I watched as she stepped up to the curb next to the hydrant. She was waiting for someone to pick her up.

I circled around to the matching zebra pattern dresser and vanity, further hidden from view. My eyes were glued to her, my mind racing. She was in a short black skirt, a pink tank top, a bright green hoodie, and pink sandals. Her hair was up with one of those big clawlike fasteners, I do not know what they are called.

Her purse dangled from her right elbow. A pink suitcase was in her left hand. *Going somewhere, are we?*

If I confronted her now, would she give me the key? Of course not. Why should she? If I tried to take the key by force—assuming she had it and not Danny by this time—fellow Brooklynites would step in to help her, or the police would. I had the advantage. She did not know whether I knew she had taken the key, or that I was watching. Besides, something told me that whoever it was that came to pick her up would explain a lot about what was going on. Would it be Danny?

But once she was picked up by this mystery person, how would I follow? I had left my car five blocks away. An alternative mode of transportation was what I needed.

"Nice set, isn't it?" A kid about twenty with an aspiring mustache was at my elbow. From his manner, his clip-on tie, and our surroundings, I gathered he was a furniture salesman.

"For your wife?" He gestured at the zebra bedroom set. "You can't put a price on class, am I right?"

I eyed him, sizing him up. Well, he was young, and young people are liable to agree to anything. "Perhaps you would care to make an easy hundred?"

He looked concerned, as if I were suggesting sex or something.

"See that woman? I need to follow her, but my car is five blocks up the boulevard. You have a car here?"

Now the lad looked at Fanny, then at me, then back to where his manager was struggling with a vending machine.

"Motorcycle. But I'm not giving it to you. I dunno you."

I pulled a hundred bucks from my wallet and looked at his name tag. "Scott, do you really think I go around all day stealing motorcycles from furniture salesmen? Here is my driver's license, you can hold onto it."

He looked at Fanny again, then back at his boss, who was banging on the vending machine.

"You know how to drive a bike?" He was staring at the money.

"Yes, of course." That was no lie. My first car was a motorcycle. Well, you know what I mean.

"Two hundred." He was biting his lip but still staring at the money.

"Scott, this is all I have on me. I will give you another hundred when I return with your bike. Then you will have two hundred. Yes?"

"Are you a private detective or something?"

"Not exactly."

"What did she do? Cheat on you?"

"She cheated me, yes. So we have a deal?"

He sighed, still wary. So I took his hand and placed the money in his palm. This technique works a lot of the time to make a deal go through. Has to be cash, though. Checks do not work. "Where's the bike?"

He fished a small set of keys from his pocket and placed them in mine. "Up the block. Green, helmet on the back. I need it back by five. We close at five."

"Got it."

"Better hurry."

"Hmm?"

"There she goes."

I looked out the window and saw an orange car pulling away, Fanny missing.

While haggling with the no-mustache kid, I had missed seeing who picked her up.

I dashed out the door.

FORTY-TWO

IT WAS AT THIS TIME, while waiting for Charlie's lawyer to arrive at the precinct, that the cops finally put out a bulletin to their troops about Danny. The description the Luna Motel clerk had given them. Tall, dark complexioned, turtleneck, sport jacket, white scar on lip, women's sunglasses, possibly dangerous.

It was also at this time that while waiting in the interrogation room, Charlie collapsed and was rushed to the hospital. It seemed his daughter was right, he should have been better at taking his heart medicine every day.

It was also at this time that in Queens, at the airport, Hugo was under arrest for charging through security and assaulting Frog as he awaited his flight. Like Charlie, Frog was in an ambulance on his way to the hospital.

FORTY-THREE

MOTORCYCLES. I DO NOT LIKE them. Yes, I used to ride one, and like all motorcycle riders I have an accident story. Only I am scared straight by my terrifying ordeal, not boastful of it.

It was wet, after a light rain, and I was on the Long Island Expressway, behind a tractor trailer that slammed on its brakes and jackknifed. I swerved around it only to encounter the reason the tractor trailer jackknifed: A pile of construction debris had fallen off the back of a dump truck. I hit the debris, rode over it in a jump like Evel Knievel, and when I landed lost control and skidded on my side. Fortunately I was wearing leathers and was not that torn up.

But as I looked up from where I lay with my bike, I saw the tractor trailer sliding sideways over the debris, right for me. I knew I did not have time to stand the bike up or to scramble away. My number was up. I just covered my face and awaited my doom.

There was a whoosh, a shadow, and the smell of burning rubber.

When I looked up I saw that the trailer had passed over me and that the other cars behind it had stopped.

A miracle.

I never rode a bike again.

Now here I was climbing onto a bright green racing bike, yanking on the matching green helmet.

Well, to me it was like a racing bike, one of those that require the rider to lean forward, legs hiked up like a jockey on a Thoroughbred. It howled when I started it, and kicked forward like a spirited horse out of the gate. I just made the first light and could see the orange sedan that had picked up Fanny. It was stopped two lights ahead. I got stopped at the next light and took a moment to look over the bike's instrumentation. Compared to the Yamaha I rode eighteen years before, this was like piloting an alien spacecraft. All the instruments were glowing orange and digital. I adjusted my helmet, squeezed the brakes a little to get the feel of them a little better, and saw the traffic light change. I continued down the boulevard of three-story brick commercial buildings with residential above, past Tangles. That mousy girl with the black gooey hands would be disappointed Saturday at Octavio when I did not buy her those strawberry daiquiris.

I was trying to throttle back and not get too close, but it was difficult because the driver of the orange car was moving slowly. Its back window was tinted, so I could not make out anything of the occupants.

Then I realized that with my helmet and tinted visor, the occupants would not be able to make me out, either. Speeding up, I maneuvered into the left lane and began to move up alongside the orange sedan. It was an old car, with a growling V-8 and dual exhaust, and the left side had some dings and fiberglass patch work. Whoever Fanny was riding with did not have much money. If they did, they would have at least changed the faded orange primer paint job, to say nothing of fixing the body. Yet it was the kind of car that was common in Brooklyn. The junker muscle car with primer paint job. They were in the Hispanic neighborhood where I grew up, and still are. The hot-rodders who owned them formed clubs based on the models and would park with their hoods up as a group by the park, tinkering with their carburetors. This one would have been part of the Malibu club, because that was the model.

The lights on the boulevard are synchronized, so that we continued without a red light. We passed the street where Mary's real estate place was. If Danny killed her, I hoped he met with a nasty fate.

I was waiting for a red light so that I could pull right up next to the driver's window and get a good look. When you want a red light, one does not come.

There was a beep behind me. A silver BMW was impatient with my slow progress, so I dropped back behind the orange Malibu and let the BMW pass. This was just as the Malibu drifted further right and made a wide right turn. I cut in behind, only looking over my right shoulder as I did so.

A tractor trailer blared its horn—I had cut off a semi, and I heard its brakes lock, smoke billowing from the tires.

I was suddenly back on the pavement on the Long Island Expressway.

This is of course when the orange Malibu came to a stop in front of an old woman with her grocery cart crossing the street.

I swerved around the orange car, out of the path of the semi. There were cars in the oncoming lane of the side street, so I could not go there. The lady with the cart was directly in front of me, and I narrowly made it around her by completing an S-turn out of my swerve.

This racing bike was very nimble. I was not. I reached out

with my foot in a vain attempt to keep from having the bike go down on its side. I say vain because that is exactly what happened. Right in front of the Malibu, which was stopped anyway.

I was not going that fast at all, so I managed to ease the machine down and spin my leg out from under it as I went down. From what I could tell the bike had not sustained any significant damage.

Perhaps I was not meant to ride motorcycles, yes?

I rose to my knees, and the passenger door to the Malibu opened. Fanny stepped out, considering the fallen biker with a mixture of concern and disbelief that I had done what I had done.

"You OK?" A young black man in a suit had approached from the opposite direction, and his hands were on my arms, helping me up.

"Yes, yes . . ." I reached down and began struggling to get the bike up off the pavement. People on the sidewalk had stopped and were staring. I straddled the bike, and as I started it, I looked back at the Malibu. Fanny was standing directly behind me, with no idea who I was.

"You coulda killed that poor woman, asshole." Her arm was outstretched toward me in a derisive gesture.

There in her hand, the one she pointed accusingly at me, was a key. Yes, the key to the locker. We were on the road to the storage facility, and she must have been ready to retrieve my money.

Reversals of fortune such as this do not happen frequently, and require action before thought.

I snatched the key and let out the clutch almost simultaneously. I felt Fanny's hand grapple with the back of my shirt and the material rip, her grasp broken. A hundred yards and three heartbeats down the tree-shaded road, I looked back. The Malibu had only just started to pursue, but it was coming quickly.

It was time for me to become a better biker. Fast.

FORTY-FOUR

AS I WAS FLEEING THE orange rat-rod Malibu, Danny was considering his next move. He had put the body of the man with the two-by-four in the basement. Danny realized the one that escaped—me—was the one he was looking for. When I pulled up, he could see my white rust-bucket Camaro with MARTINEZ HOUSE CLEANING printed on the door. Now it was gone, and I had escaped his grasp. How would he find me? Certainly not by waiting in the house next to his uncle's.

That was another thing that bothered Danny. What was Martinez doing in the house next to his uncle's? From the window of his uncle's house Danny had watched as the two men went around back and broke into the neighbor's vacant house. These certainly were not real estate agents or prospective buyers, and the one with the two-by-four kept prodding the tall, dark, and extremely handsome man like he was forcing him to go with him into the house. What were the two men doing upstairs when he entered?

A careful search of the second floor and attic told Danny nothing.

One thing was for sure: That thief Martinez would not come back to the house knowing Danny might be there.

Which meant he had to go looking for me again.

Yes, but where? How? His only connections to me were Dexter and Mary, and both of them were dead. The other connection was Dexter's cell phone, which had my phone number in it. What use was that? Call that thief Martinez and politely invite him to come to dinner? He could not imagine I was that stupid.

Thief Martinez. The saying "It takes a thief to catch a thief" was not unfamiliar to him, and so he thought his next move should be to consult with another house cleaner to find out where I might be.

So he walked the few blocks to the boulevard of two- and three-story brick buildings, shops on the ground floor and residences above. Some of the windows of those residences had older women in housedresses leaning on pillows on the open windowsills. It is the time-honored pastime of many older Brooklyn women with nothing to do. They perch like magpies surveying their domain, saying hello to people they know on the sidewalk, and monitoring those they do not know. They also talk to each other. Well, not so much talk as yell across the street or down the block or even across the air shaft. What do they discuss? Their poor health. Why are they in such poor health? Because they spend all day perched in windows instead of moving around and keeping their blood moving. And they do not mind sharing their complaints with the entire neighborhood as they shout to each other across the street.

The sight of these old bats shouting and complaining the afternoon away comforted Danny. It was good to see the old women still did this because it meant that some things had not changed while he was in prison. It made him feel that he might just be able to make it on the outside after all. Assuming he got the money. And stopped putting his ice picks in people's chests.

"Excuse me," Danny shouted to a white-haired walrus in one window.

The white walrus leaned farther out to get a better look at Danny. "Yeah?"

"Good morning. I was wondering if you might know where I could find someone who cleans out houses."

"Outhouses?"

Danny actually chuckled. "I'm sorry, what I meant was someone who *clears* out houses, like after someone has died, like that."

The white walrus's button eyes shone a little brighter. "Ooo! Someone died? Who died?"

Danny glanced around him and saw the other magpies—or walruses, or what have you—leaning a little farther out their windows, all ears. I think both walruses and magpies have ears, don't they, Father?

"Nobody you know, I'm sure," Danny said.

"If they live around here, I might," the white walrus shouted.

Danny ignored the question. "Do you know anybody? Or anybody who might know?"

The white walrus looked unhappy but pointed up the boulevard. "Oscar's."

"Oscar's?"

"Yeah."

"Excuse me, but what is Oscar's?"

"A tavern. Some of them feelers hang out there. Like vultures, they are."

All the other magpie walruses clucked in agreement.

She looked down at Danny's confused face. "It's a tavern. Oscar's. That way."

A few minutes later, Danny darkened the doorway to Oscar's. He took off his sunglasses and stepped up to the bar.

"Ooo!" Mim hooted. "It's Danny Kessel!"

Danny squinted and made out her pale, beehived form surrounded by newspapers at the end of the bar.

The only other people there were Oscar and Slim Jim. Oscar was like a marble statue behind the bar, and Slim Jim was like a frozen Butterball turkey at the video poker machine.

"Ooo." Slim Jim backed away from his game. "He must be looking for Morty."

"Shaddap," Mim snapped.

Danny waited to see if any of them made a move. They did not.

"Excuse me, but could any of you tell me where Morty is?"

"See?" Slim Jim sidled closer to Mim, like she might actually be able to protect him.

"We dunno where he is," Mim croaked.

Danny looked at Oscar, who shrugged.

"I know where he lives," Slim Jim said, raising his hand.

"Shaddap!" Mim pushed him away from her.

"For a hundred I'll tell you where."

"Slim Jim!" Mim scolded.

"Well, he's gonna find Morty eventually, am I right? For a hundred I'll tell you where he lives."

"For fifty," Oscar rumbled, "I'll tell you where you can find his foreman, Speedy."

"You rotten bastards," Mim spat. "Danny, I ain't telling you nothing for nothing."

"He's right," Oscar said, gesturing to Slim Jim. "Morty has to face the music sometime, and if Slim is getting something for it, I can, too."

You see, Father? These were my friends. As I pointed out before, New Yorkers have little sympathy and less tolerance for weakness. To their way of thinking, if I was in a jam with Danny, that was my own fault for being vulnerable. They could not make me any more vulnerable than I had made myself, could they? And if they could make themselves stronger at the expense of my weakness, that was the way of the jungle that was East Brooklyn.

"Sorry, but I'll give you both fifty for what you can tell me."

Of course, they began to do just that.

That is when I walked in wheeling the motorcycle.

FORTY-FIVE

I HAD MANAGED TO LOSE the Malibu pretty easily. I took Fedder Alley, made a right on a street, then left into Mucklebust Alley, which is now a pathway where a car cannot travel. Then I went left again on a street, through a side yard, and soon found myself on the boulevard. That primer orange monstrosity was long gone.

Where could I go? Not home. Fanny might have figured out who I was—why else would the mysterious motorcyclist steal the key? And under the helmet I was wearing the clothes she had seen that morning when we left my place and were accosted by my landlord. So I could not see how I could go to the storage locker. Besides, carrying the Scottish suitcase on the bike just seemed a recipe for disaster. The Malibu could pop up anytime.

I wanted to get out of sight as soon as possible, then later go to my car.

Oscar's was nearby.

"Oscar, my friend! Would you mind if I park this inside for a few hours?" I put my helmet on the bar where Buddy would be sitting before long. "I promise there are no leaks or anything. This is an emergency or I would not ask."

They all looked at me as if I were a ghost.

Except for the tall one with the Gap hat and plaid long-sleeved shirt.

He smiled.

Like a puddle in winter, I froze.

It was the man from the house. The man whose testicles I had bashed a few hours before. He was casually tucking two fifty-dollar bills back in his wallet. "We need to talk, if you don't mind."

My eyes met Oscar's, Mim's, and Slim's.

"We didn't tell him anything or anything," Slim stammered.

"Fellahs, if this is going to get messy, could you take it outside?" Oscar: what a pal. "This is my place. Whatever is going on between you fellahs . . ."

No accommodation for the weak.

"Excuse me for interrupting, but there won't be any trouble," Danny said with a calming gesture of his hand. "I just want to talk to Morty. At that table. Can I buy you a drink, Morty?"

To tell you the truth, Father, my legs were shaking so badly both from the motorcycle and fright that if I had tried to run I think I would have ended up on my knees. Then I really would have taken a beating.

Fate, you seem to be forgetting about my promise, about the money to a good cause.

"I am sorry for before," I finally managed to mutter. His blue eyes were looking straight through me. Like ice picks. How appropriate, yes? I saw him squirm slightly with the memory of my knee crushing his scrotum.

"I startled you. It's OK. Can we sit?" He waved a hand at the table, the one where Pete the Prick used to sit before he got an ice pick and a drag down into the Vanderhoosen basement. Where the Balkan Boys used to sit with Pete before they took a thump-ing from Pitu and Mamma.

Well, it did not seem to me at the time like he was going to hurt me. As a matter of fact, I will be brutally honest: I was a little bit relieved. That may surprise you, Father Gomez, but if you have ever expected a bad thing, and then have it finally hap-pen and it is not as bad as you thought it would be, then you will know what I am talking about. It was daylight, and I was in a public space with witnesses. He would not torture the informa-tion from me at Oscar's Grille. He would not kill me in front of witnesses. So what was the worst that could happen? At least I could try to talk myself out of it.

I was relieved that he and Fanny were not of one purpose. If he were driving the primer orange Malibu, how could he be here? And without Fanny? Whoever was with Fanny could not be half as dangerous as this ex-con with the Gap hat and nice manners.

Danny shot a glance at Oscar. "Beer, please. You?"

"I know what he wants." Oscar sighed, no doubt thinking only of the fifty bucks he almost made. "What kind of beer?"

"Ooo, what're you, an idiot?" Mim cackled. "He don't care what kinda beer. He's just here to talk to Morty."

Moving sideways, and not taking our eyes off each other, Danny and I eased into chairs on opposite sides of the table. I felt if I so much as blinked he might do something violent. At the same time, as I said, my brain was telling me that there was no way he would pull something harmful in public.

We waited.

The drinks arrived.

Danny leaned slowly across the table toward me.

So did I. Except, of course, I leaned toward him.

Our faces could not have been more than six inches apart, and I could see the jagged white scar on his lip fairly tremble.

He said, "You found it?"

I shook my head. "I found money. But I do not think it was yours."

He blinked very slowly, and when his eyes were focused on mine again he said, "What makes you think so?"

"I will tell you this much: I did not find five million, not even close. If I may be brutally honest with you, I am doubtful you could fit five million dollars in peanut cans under a couch."

"Peanut cans?"

"Yes. Tight ones."

"Tight ones?"

"A tight one is a short can—usually a Planters nut tin—with a roll of cash squeezed 'tightly' into it. Some would have you believe that such a can of money is called a tight one because it sort of resembles . . . well, an asshole. It is what they call a play on words."

Danny looked away at the wall for a moment, biting his lip. "Under the couch? In cans?"

"This is how I often find money in houses I clean. Old people stash money, then die, and nobody knows it is hidden under the couch, or in the drapery valance . . ."

"Valance?"

"Yes, it is the thing that goes at the top of the drapery, to shield the top. Do you think for a moment I would make up something as idiotic as this?"

His eyes met mine again, but they were squinty. "I don't know. How much did you find, then?"

I figured I had better tell him. "One hundred and ten thousand dollars!" I made my eyes light up like I was excited beyond words. If he made me give him half or even the whole amount I just lied about, I would still be both alive and six hundred and ninety thousand dollars richer. I ask you, Father: Is a hundred and ten thousand dollars too much to pay for one's life? To realize the dream of La Paz free and clear?

"What were you doing in that house I found you in, with that other guy?"

"He was trying to force me to give him the money because he felt cheated that I won the contract to clean the house. I told him I hid it where I found it, in the attic."

Danny's eyes widened.

"Excuse me, but you're saying that you found it—"

"Yes, at 804 Vanderhoosen."

"My uncle lives at 806."

"Yes? But that is next door to . . . is your uncle's name Trux?"

"No. Kessel. My father's brother, Cuddy. That's why you found it under the couch. I didn't put my money in peanut tins." He leaned back in his chair, crestfallen. "You're right, Morty. It wasn't my money that you found."

Could this possibly have gone any better? At that moment I felt so good that I actually felt sorry for him.

"Danny, it is too bad. The cleaner of that house must have—"

His eyes locked back on mine with the speed of a snake on a tiny defenseless mouse.

"Who?"

"Well, it could have been almost anybody, really . . ." At first, I felt alluding to Frog had been a blunder, but all at once, I realized that when Frog was buying me drinks and toasting to my good fortune, he was really toasting to his own. That when he wanted me to keep the cops off, it was for him, not me. That when Hugo called from the airport, the Swiss bank account . . .

Frog had cleaned 806 Vanderhoosen a few weeks back. Frog had the five million and was escaping to Switzerland with it. By that time I figured he was over Greenland somewhere in first class, thinking about how he used me and my legitimate find of eight hundred thousand dollars, my life in jeopardy, as a shield for his escape.

Bastard. No sense protecting him now.

I was not an idiot for the slip about the house cleaner, only for letting Frog pull the sheep over my eyes.

"Frog has your money."

"Frog?"

"Yes, Louie 'Frog' Franco. It was he who cleaned 806 Vanderhoosen Drive two weeks ago, and he was at the airport an hour ago. I got a call from his foreman, who was trying to find him. I fear he is probably over Greenland now, drinking cold duck and eating soft herbal cheeses and laughing, the dirty bastard." I reached out and put my hand on Danny's forearm. "I will tell you where he lived, and you can ask his landlord, and wait, but he will not be returning unless he is a bigger idiot than I am. I will put you in touch with his foreman, who will tell you the same story I just told you. I am sorry, Danny."

At this point our conversation had reached conversational levels. Oscar, Mim, and Slim were agape, meaning their mouths were hanging open with surprise. Of course, it was Mim who spoke first, and quietly for a change.

"Ho-lee shit."

That pretty much said it all.

FORTY-SIX

SO WE WERE SITTING THERE at Oscar's, four of the
five of us agape (not me—I had a sympathetic, sad smile on my
face), when Buddy came barging into the bar talking.

"Ooo: You won't believe it. Hugo beat up Frog at the airport.
Frog is at East Brooklyn Hospital, and Hugo is at a precinct in
Queens. It took a buncha TSA guys and a loada cops just to take
Hugo down, like baboons on an elephant. Whatsamatter?"

Buddy looked at each of us in turn until finally his eyes came
back to Danny, who shot to his feet, put on his sunglasses, and
walked out the door.

"Who wassat?"

"Danny Kessel," Mim barked.

"It was Frog that had his five million!" Slim sank onto a bar
stool, amazed.

Oscar began to tap a beer for Buddy. "I think Danny is headed
to East Brooklyn Hospital to get Frog to tell him where it is."

Buddy pointed at me, cocking his head. "Then it wasn't you
who found his five mil?"

"Idiots." I shook my head wearily. "I kept telling you people
that I did not have the five million, but you did not listen. I

cleaned the place next to Danny's uncle's place. It was Frog that cleaned that house and found the money. Now I'm guessing that Frog tried to make off with the money, part of which was Hugo's, and that made Hugo very angry."

Buddy slid onto a bar stool. "Ho-lee shit."

"That's what I said." Mim chuckled.

I stood, picked up the helmet from the bar, and went over to the motorcycle.

"Where you going?" Mim asked.

"To return the bike, of course."

"Somebody gonna call the cops?"

"About what?" I asked.

"Danny," she said.

"As far as I know he has not done anything wrong. If he has, it is up to the police to catch him. Or that detective who was here. I want nothing more to do with Danny Kessel and that five million." I slid the helmet on my head and wheeled the bike back out into the late-day sun.

It had turned humid as hell, and by the feel of it, we were in for a thunderstorm, the kind we often get on summer afternoons.

I stopped at an ATM for more cash, returned the bike to the furniture store kid, handed him the second hundred, and walked to my car. It had a ticket on my windshield. Expired meter.

I am telling you this very plainly, Father, because I was mentally exhausted, just going through the motions. A great weight had been lifted from me, and my mind was free of knots.

Well, there was the matter of Fanny. Too bad, a very attractive girl, and I liked her, but that bitch had played me for an idiot. But I had the locker key, didn't I? Who was the idiot now?

The most important task was to move the money to a new

location. The reason? Because as soon as I did that, Fanny and whoever was her accomplice in the orange Malibu would no longer know where the new storage locker was.

But how to get my money and not have those two crooks try to take it from me or follow me?

I smiled the big smile I usually reserve for the ladies and occasionally my landlord.

I had an idea.

At a bargain store, I bought a duffel bag.

At a free newspaper box, I transferred the contents into the duffel bag until it was bulging.

At my car, I put the bag into the backseat.

Whistling a merengue to myself, I drove calmly down the boulevard to where the tractor trailer almost ran me down, and where I almost ran down the old woman with the grocery cart. I made the turn and then drove to where the storage facility was. I drove past once, and sure enough, I saw the orange Malibu parked down the block, in an alley. I guess they thought that if I returned I would not think to check to see if their car was nearby. Idiots.

I drove around the block and into the storage facility, through the gate, and parked. I did not see Fanny or anyone else suspicious hanging around. It would not have mattered if I had.

There was a pay phone just inside the entryway, and nobody around. I dialed 911 and got the dispatcher, told her I saw a man and a woman with a gun outside the storage facility, and hung up.

I went to my locker and opened it.

Inside was the Scottish suitcase. I unzipped it a little. The cash was still there. Just checking. After the key had vanished, I felt anything could happen.

I went back downstairs and from inside watched the police arrive. They began to talk with the guard, and he jerked a thumb toward the entrance.

That is when I exited.

One of the cops cocked her head at me. She was a strapping brunette with a French braid and slight mustache. Her hands were on her gun belt. "Hey, you, mister. You call 911?"

"Me? No, officer."

She looked me up and down a moment and then went back to talking to the guard. Nobody could prove I made that call—or let us just say it was not worth the effort. I put the Scottish suitcase with the eight hundred grand in my trunk.

I started the car and drove from the lot. Wherever Fanny and company were, I was sure the police scared them off. They probably did have a gun if they intended to take the money from me.

This would be the tricky part, but I was pretty sure that Fanny and whoever were not hardened criminals like Danny.

I drove by where the orange Malibu had been, and it was gone.

Taking my time, I stopped for a soda at a deli and then made my way home as the skies were getting dark. Not from night, but from storm clouds.

The Camaro tucked into a parking spot up the block, I took the duffel bag from the backseat and headed toward my door.

Footsteps were behind me, and I was sweating but moving slowly and casually.

"Morty!"

I turned.

It was only Speedy.

"Speedy, my friend. *Qué pasa?*"

He smiled and pulled a gun from his pants pocket.

Do not ask me to tell you what kind of gun, Father. It was not a rifle, if that is what you are thinking. It was a revolver, I guess, black.

"*Por favor, amigo.* The bag."

Fanny emerged from the alley up the block but did not come near. Clever girl—staying clear of danger, let Speedy take all the risks.

"Speedy, what are you doing . . . do you mean to tell me *you* and Fanny . . ." Of course. I am an idiot. It was he who knew to look under my battery for the paperwork to the storage locker. Remember? His father in Central America somewhere used to keep the family's meager savings under the battery of a Ford Fairlane. The lipstick on his neck at the chica bar would have been Fanny's pink lipstick, and that would have been her waiting for him, her shadow on his window, when I dropped him off. While I went to see Dexter, she left Speedy to go search my place and then wait for me. "You do not drive a Malibu."

"My car broke, so I borrowed this one from my cousin." Speedy shrugged, looking cheerful. Cheerful probably because Fanny had serviced him in the car to build his courage.

"She came to the house on Vanderhoosen as we were working, after you took the tight ones away. It was her uncle's money. He used to tell her about it to torment her, even though she—his only surviving relative—brought him food. He even showed her a tight one once to prove it. He hated Fanny and would not let her in the house after a while because he knew she was looking around for the money. It was a sick game. Even after he died, there were instructions that she receive nothing and have no access to the house. She tried breaking into the house once after he died and the neighbors saw her and the cops came and the estate lawyer had a restraining order put on her to stay away from the house. The lawyers were giving everything the old man had to the Catholic Church, but they didn't know about the tight ones, though Fanny didn't know if they had found them or not." He shrugged apologetically, smiling. "Give me the bag."

"You are my friend, Speedy. I cannot believe . . ." Now *my* mouth was agape. There were tears in my eyes—partially genuine, I must tell you. Even though he was stealing a duffel full of free newspapers, it hurt me that he would do such a thing. Yet I told you before that his trustworthiness was untested.

He held his hand out. "The bag."

Slowly, I slipped it off my shoulder and handed it to him.

"Speedy, you fucking bastard. I will get you for this."

"No, I do not think you will. We are going away together, just me and Fanny."

"You better go far and fast, old friend." I was acting real mad, you know, like Clint Eastwood, my eyes all squinty, my jaw working, my hands flexing at my sides like I was ready to draw my six-shooter. My imaginary six-shooter, of course.

"I am sorry, but it is rightfully her money." He backed away, and the two of them went around the corner into the alley.

I backtracked to my car and drove to a pay phone. I called 911 again and told them that I had seen a Hispanic male in a straw hat and flannel shirt with a taller woman with great tits and elegant nose in an orange Malibu rat-rod with a gun, and they drove off onto the Belt Parkway. How did I know they would be on the Belt Parkway? Because it is the nearest highway. If they were to go far and fast, that would be the way, and it is near enough that I hoped they would wait that long before opening the bag.

But it did not matter. I drove west, inland, on back streets, away from the Belt Parkway, until I found a smaller storage facility called Storage Hut on a corner a few blocks from East Brooklyn Hospital. There was a Sudanese security guard who showed me to my new rental locker.

The money was once again secure. Next time I needed the bag, when I left town, I would hire a security guard or private detective to accompany me.

This Storage Hut key was smaller, and so I wrapped it in the paperwork, stuffed it in an envelope, and mailed it to my business P.O. box. It could sit safely and comfortably in my box under the watchful and protective eye of the U.S. Postal Service.

I was clever, wasn't I, Father? I think I saw something like this in a movie once, so I am only really clever for having remembered it.

And it was idiotically easy, yes? You see, Speedy and Fanny were amateurs, and they thought that the element of surprise was all they needed. I am quite certain that any professional criminal would have had me open the bag and show them the money.

Yes, of course, Fanny and Speedy could come back at me, but the element of surprise was gone, their trap sprung, and the rat now wise to the danger of cheese. In the mind of the amateur criminal, I think there is a big difference between trickery and robbery, even though both can land you in jail. If they are going to commit a felony like any common criminal by pulling a gun on me and making me take them to money, then why not go to Manhattan and hold up Donald Trump? Or kidnap Oprah for ransom? The effort is essentially the same, the reward greater with millionaires.

I will be brutally honest, and please do not think less of me, Father: I still get a great deal of satisfaction thinking about those two opening the bag, and Fanny giving Speedy an earful about how it was all his fault somehow, and the subsequent gloom in the Malibu. Perhaps they would pull over to a rest area on the Belt Parkway to try to think of their next move; maybe they would pull over next to the Verrazano Bridge. You would not have to hear a word that was said to understand their defeat. Just watch them from afar, Speedy downcast, Fanny pacing and flailing her hands around, the approaching storm clouds roiling the sky over the giant expanse of the bridge over the narrows.

Devastation and defeat. What a glorious sight.

I sigh contentedly every time I imagine it.

Never saw either of them again outside of my mind.

FORTY-SEVEN

I HOPE YOU ARE SITTING down, Father. I was not when I heard this next part, but fortunately I was at Oscar's, so a bar stool and a stiff drink were at hand. Mim was reading aloud from her paper, and Slim and Buddy and Buddy Dyke and Oscar were riveted.

I could give you the straight newspaper account Mim read to us from the *Daily News,* but it does not do the story justice, so I will tell it to you my way, the way I imagine it all happened, knowing the people involved, painting you a picture. It is for dramatic effect, yes? Any idiot can read the *Daily News* account. They did not even mention the storm.

Lightning flashed and crackled across the sky as Danny entered the white hospital corridors by way of the delivery entrance. There were too many cops standing around the emergency room entrance. After killing four people, Danny figured there might just be a description of him if one of the bodies had been discovered, and no criminal enjoys the company of cops under any circumstances.

He passed between two oxygen supply trucks loaded with canisters. Both were idling, and nobody in them. Even in his tense and eager mood, Danny reflected how it was nefarious that oxygen suppliers would leave their engines running. Perhaps in an effort to reduce the amount of free, unpaid-for oxygen?

Climbing the stairs to the loading bay, he went through the swinging doors, past a room where the oxygen supply men were drinking coffee and chewing the fat, past the doorway to the shipping and receiving room crowded with boxes, and through more swinging doors into the main corridor of the hospital, next to the elevators. He pushed the up button, and it lit up.

Danny waited with hands folded before him, Mr. Manners in his brown plaid shirt, brown jacket, brown Gap ball cap, and brown Donna Karan sunglasses.

Some nurses came and stood next to him. They smiled at him, and he nodded.

See, Father, these are the details the newspaper would not supply. Isn't this much better? I think so.

So Danny is standing with these nurses, waiting, and an elevator arrives with someone on a gurney and an IV. They exit, Danny and the nurses enter, and a doctor arrives at the last second. So there are four of them.

"I'm sorry," Danny began, smiling sadly at the nurses and doctor. "The nurse told me which floor to go to, and I'm so worried that I forgot what floor she said. A friend of mine was assaulted. I don't know how bad he is. Could you tell me which floor I should go to for someone like that?"

Danny exited at the fourth floor and went to the nurse's station. There was a large black woman in a white uniform cradling a telephone between her jowl and prodigious shoulder.

"Excuse me, sorry to bother you, but my brother is here. Louie Franco."

She held up a finger. *Wait.*

She muttered something about how they needed more oxygen tanks for someone and hung up. Then she flipped through some computer printouts.

"Room 404." She pointed a thick finger down the hall. "Visiting hours are almost over. You have fifteen minutes."

Room 404? That was the number of the motel room at the thump and bump where he had beaten Dexter's face into a bloody pulp with the telephone. Danny smiled at the absurdity of the coincidence. It was coincidence, wasn't it? "Thank you. I won't be long."

He strode down the corridor and pushed through the partially open door. There were two beds, one left, one right, separated by a curtain. On either side was a dark window splashed with rain and vibrating with the storm's thunder.

In the bed on the right was an older gentleman with ginger hair on his head and a lot more covering his arms and the one leg that was out of the sheets. He was watching television and looked at Danny.

Danny removed his sunglasses and hat out of politeness. "Sorry," he said to the man, who stared at him as if he had intruded. Or was it something else? "Are you Louie?"

The man stared blankly and jerked his thumb toward the other side of the curtain.

Against the wall was a bed and one of those tables that swings over the bed so that the patient can eat and drink. In the bed was a man with slicked-back long blond hair. His eyes were closed. His face was badly bruised on one side, and his left arm was in a fresh white cast.

There was a chair next to the bed, and Danny sat in it. He leaned in close to the man's ear.

"Excuse me. Louie?"

Frog awoke with a start. "Hmm?" He turned his head and looked at Danny with confusion. "Yeah? Who are you?"

Danny smiled serenely. He suddenly felt he would get the five million dollars after all.

"We need to go."

"Go? What d'you mean?" Frog held up his cast, as if to demonstrate that he was injured.

"We need to go. Now. To get my five million."

Frog looked confused a moment, narrowing his eyes, and then he suddenly understood what was about to transpire.

Danny had an ice pick to Frog's throat.

"Please, let's go," he whispered, securing the Gap hat back on his head.

"But . . . but . . ."

Danny just shook his head sadly. *No buts*. He threw back the covers and put a finger to his lips. *Quiet*.

Frog slid to his feet, looking feeble in his flimsy hospital gown. Danny put his arm around Frog as if to help him walk and led him past the partition. Charlie Binder was in the next bed frantically pushing the nurse call button under the sheets.

Danny led Frog out of the room, the point of the ice pick dimpling the captive's flank. Right where the kidney was. If the shiv plunged four inches it would penetrate the kidney and Frog would be dead within minutes. Well, they were in a hospital, they might be able to save him, but Danny did not know or care. The way he had his arm around the patient, it looked like he was helping him walk. The large nurse was just leaving her nurse's station as they approached the elevators.

"Where are you taking him?" she demanded.

Danny smiled politely. "He wanted to get some circulation to his legs. Just down and back, is all."

She did not look happy about it but continued on her way to answer Charlie's frantic call.

The elevator doors opened as they approached. Two policemen inside. The cops stopped talking and looked at Danny, who decided he had better go ahead and get in with them.

Frog goggled at the police, trying to ask for help with his eyes, but they continued their conversation, not looking at him.

On the ground floor, the police turned one way, Danny and Frog the other. The policemen's radios squelched with some excited chatter as Danny led Frog through the doors marked LOADING DOCK.

They passed by an oxygen deliveryman going the other way, rolling a tank, a delivery for the big nurse on the fourth floor. The man looked back at the duo curiously, but Danny saw no need to explain anything to a deliveryman. They passed the storage area, and there was a redheaded hospital worker with tinted glasses and a clipboard. He looked up and said, "Hey!"

Danny walked a little faster, even though Frog was stiffening his legs.

"Please don't," Danny warned, breaking the skin over Frog's kidney with the point of the ice pick.

In the loading bay were the two oxygen trucks, still idling, rain pounding their roofs. Danny opened the driver's door to the one at the bottom of the stairs.

"You drive."

Frog, his long blond hair already sopping wet, held up his cast pitifully. "I can't, I . . . Danny, listen, the money . . ."

Danny backhanded Frog hard across the mouth. "Please get in and slide over."

The red-haired hospital worker with the clipboard was standing on the loading platform.

"What the fuck do you think you're doing?" he yelled over a clap of thunder. Curling his lip with resolve, he added, "I'm calling the cops." He pulled a radio from his back pocket and began speaking into it rapidly. By the time he got a response, Danny was in the driver's seat, and Frog was shoved to the opposite side fumbling for the door handle to get out. The door was locked, but in his panic he did not notice.

Danny threw the truck in reverse and cut to one side, clipping a brick wall. It had been a long time since he drove. He slammed the truck into drive, and the oxygen bottles in back rattled as he roared from the hospital loading zone onto the street.

Frog was still fumbling with the door, so Danny took the ice pick and lanced him through the cheek, right into the teeth. Frog howled with pain and left the door alone to massage the searing pain in his injured cheek and gums.

Danny came to a halt at a light. He began feeling the dashboard for the switch to the windshield wipers, and his forearm rubbed the indicator handle, turning them on. He did not know what he did to make that happen, but as long as it happened he could not be bothered to think about what caused it.

In the side mirror, he saw police cars with their blue flashing lights, and they swung into the loading dock area. Before him, car headlights flashed by in both directions on the avenue, the angry black skies beyond rippling and flickering with electricity.

The traffic light was still red. Danny peered through the downpour both ways on the avenue, inching the truck forward. Rain thrummed the truck's roof.

He checked the side mirror again.

"The money's not here," Frog sobbed from behind where he held his bleeding cheek. "We can't get it now, it already went."

Danny put his finger to his lips again, holding up the ice pick as a warning that made Frog cower. In the side mirror, the rain-blurred image of flashing police cars returned. They were backing out of the loading bay.

Foot on the gas, Danny ran the light and swung the truck out into traffic on a wide right turn. He sideswiped a minivan, which jumped the divider and crashed onto its side. Sparks flew from the minivan's wheel rims as it scuttered and rumbled on its side into an oncoming cement truck. The cement truck fishtailed only slightly as it rammed the front of the van, air brakes locked. The van crumpled and bucked as it reversed course and was pushed into the intersection.

Danny sped down the avenue, the lights now against him, but he paused at the next light long enough to sneak through. Blue from police lights flashed on his face. He didn't even need to look in the side mirror to know the cops were gaining on him.

Frog saw the blue light dancing in the side mirror and had a glimmer of hope. Then Danny surged the truck through another intersection, car brakes screeching around them. But they made it to the other side, the sound of cars punching into each other on both sides.

Frog stared at Danny's ice blue eyes fixed on the road ahead, which were pulsing with the blue police lights throbbing in the mirrors. Jaw fixed, Danny clasped the ice pick in his right hand against the steering wheel.

He's going to get us killed. Frog realized that he must do something or he would not survive the encounter. Danny was insane.

At the next intersection, Danny stopped and looked left.

Frog lurched forward, swinging his cast at Danny.

But not before Danny stepped on the gas.

Lightning bristled across the sky, thunder rumbling like a bowling ball approaching the pins.

Danny's head slammed the driver's window. The truck veered left across the intersection. It clipped and spun a Mini Cooper, veered farther left, and just missed a light pole as it jumped the curb. Oxygen bottles jumped from their racks.

The front entrance of a brick building proved no match for the truck, which punched through the glass and metal frame and plowed into the guard station. Barreling right into the metal security counter, the truck's front end pushed the elderly Sudanese security guard behind it up against an inner brick wall, cutting him in half at the waist like a butcher knife through a sausage.

The brick wall gave and, as it came down, chipped the top off of two oxygen cylinders.

There was a spark.

It took the fire department all night to put out that fire, even in the rain. They had to be careful because oxygen canisters were still exploding hours later. Two firemen were injured by shrapnel.

Yes, East Brooklyn will long remember the night Storage Hut burned to the ground.

I know I will.

FORTY-EIGHT

WELL, AT LEAST I DID not get killed in that fiery truck crash on a stormy night in East Brooklyn. I think you have to try to look on the bright side of things. But when eight hundred grand in tax-free money is incinerated at the Storage Hut by an idiot like Frog? Yes, I blame him for this disaster. Why did he have to choose that particular intersection to clobber Danny? Perhaps fate chose it for him. Perhaps the fate was as much mine as his.

As you might imagine, Father Gomez, my dismay at what had occurred resulted in a malaise for a few days. I thought perhaps opening the envelope from Genealogy Consultants LLC would cheer me up. According to them, my last name is French, not Spanish, and my family originally came from Marseille. I did not want to be French. Who does? Perhaps the French, and only the French.

Still, it was interesting that my father had actually spent part of his childhood in La Paz. I will reveal more on this at the end of this confession, because it explains the big package.

Anyway, other than the fact that my father was from La Paz, it was clear to me that Genealogy Consultants LLC were idiots, and I had wasted my money. They somehow missed the entire conquistador part of my family history.

The only good news I heard that week was that Dexter had regained consciousness and was expected to live. I could only imagine what he would have to go through to rehabilitate, and what he would look like. Could they reconstruct his face? Now he would be a clubfoot and facially disfigured. I truly felt sorry for him and wondered if dying might have been easier.

So I watched TV for a few days and groaned. I did muster the energy to go to Octavio on Saturday night, where I filled that mousy girl from Tangles, Silvia, with daiquiris. Not so many that she puked on my floor mats, but enough that we went back to her place and mated on her couch.

That gave me enough energy to go to the library on Monday and look at my e-mail.

The real estate people in La Paz had sent me a JPEG file. I clicked on the attachment and had to wait for it to open. This would be of the fountain. This would be the Martinez family crest emblazoned in bronze.

But it was not. The fountain was only embossed with curlicues and leaves and such.

I told them I wanted the place anyway and wired the down payment.

I will be brutally honest: Danny Kessel had taught me that you cannot wait forever to make your dreams come true. Sometimes, if you wait too long, it is too late. Then you end up burned alive by an oxygen truck in Storage Hut.

The down payment I could do, and some of the rest, but I did not have enough to live on the rest of my life. How would I make a living in La Paz? I had no idea. I just knew it was now or never, as they say.

Then, believe it or not, I got a call from a real estate agent to clean out an apartment. This agent used to work closely with Frog, because it was Frog who used to specialize in cleaning out apartments. Now this agent needed somebody new to replace Frog. Of course, we were also short another local feeler because Pete the Prick's putrefied body was in a stainless steel drawer at the morgue.

To tell you the truth, I had completely lost any interest in being a feeler, but the agent basically begged me. I had two weeks to kill before my passport arrived, and I had to admit to myself that the cash would prove useful for my four-thousand-mile drive to Baja. Also, if I watched any more television I think I would have gone insane. Have you watched daytime television, Father? It's all about complaining people.

So I accepted the job and arranged for a container.

On the clean-out day, I grabbed three day laborers, making sure one could speak at least some English.

We went to the building. I recognized it.

"No," I told myself. "It cannot be."

But it was.

I had been hired to clean out Frog's apartment.

The hand of fate can be a dirty dealer, let me tell you.

No, there were no tight ones under the couch. There was no hidden money. I knew there would not be; I felt it as soon as I entered.

The laborers were carrying the couch down the stairs to the Dumpster, and I was watching the front door to make sure the idiots did not damage the vestibule in a way that would make the landlord angry.

A delivery truck squeaked to a stop at the curb, and a Pakistani man in shorts, T-shirt, and lifting belt approached the front door. The couch was just coming out, and he had to wait. After the careful exit of the sofa, the grunting laborers weaved down across the sidewalk with it toward the Dumpster.

"I'm looking for Franco," the Pakistani said to me. I think he thought I was the landlord.

I looked at the delivery van, and a sign on the cab door read AIR FREIGHT EXPRESS SERVICES.

You know how I have told you, Father, that I have a feeling when there is money in a house? Even though there was no money in Frog's apartment, I suddenly got that feeling.

I smiled at the deliveryman and said, "I am Franco."

"We got a return."

"A return?"

"You paid for guaranteed delivery or return."

"Yes, of course."

"Sorry, but it wasn't picked up at the Zurich depot, point of delivery. Sign here."

I signed and followed him back to the van, where another Pakistani man had lined up four wooden crates, each big enough to hold a television. The five crates had customs stickers on them.

Swiss and U.S. customs stickers.

You are not an idiot, Father Gomez. You know what was in those crates, buried under used paperbacks.

FORTY-NINE

IT TOOK ME TWO DAYS to take care of business, tie up loose ends, and pack up the Camaro with a few essential belongings. One thing you learn as a feeler: People have way too much crap. As you know, I did not have much, and most of that I did not care about. I had bought four suitcases to hold the valuable belongings. You'll find it funny to learn, Father, that the four suitcases I bought were the cheapest I could find, plaid ones, like the one with the eight hundred thousand. Fate and irony share the same bed.

I cleaned out my own apartment in two hours with three laborers.

One final visit to the monster toad under the stairs was necessary. I needed to give him the keys; he needed to give me my deposit.

I did not even knock on his door—the landlord was waiting for me at the bottom of the stairs.

"You never did learn to sort your recyclables, Martinez."

He stepped aside as I approached, a garment bag over my shoulder. "Here is your key. The deposit?"

As though trying to think of some last-minute reason not to

give it to me, the landlord pulled a wad of bills reluctantly from his pocket. "That the only key? What about that Jersey girl, or that other one, the stomper?"

I dropped the key in his hand and turned mine over for the cash. "No copies."

Instead of putting the money in my hand, he made me take it from his. I laughed at the last idiotic gesture. Done with his games, my mind was somewhere on an interstate headed west.

"Lemme guess," he said to my back. "You're movin' to Jersey."

As the vestibule door closed, I gave him a thumbs-up, a smile, and a final remark.

"Bayonne is the new Brooklyn."

I knew that would upset him for days, perhaps even weeks. A parting gift from me to the monster toad.

Happy to be leaving, I was also nervous. Yes, the prospect of a new life in a strange place was one reason. The other was that I was anticipating something going wrong. Fanny and Speedy could be in the car behind me, or perhaps Hugo had escaped and was closing in, or even just some crazy tractor trailer would plow into my car and stop my trip at the start.

Or was I was sensing something else?

From the very beginning of this story, Father, I have more than once mentioned fate, and what a strange thing it can be. If I had to ascribe meaning to my tale? One often hears the phrase "tempting fate." But you see, I do not believe we as humans have much sway with that old bastard fate. He can no more be tempted than he can be avoided or dissuaded. What I wonder is when does fate let you go and destiny take you in hand? Was I at just such a juncture? I drove toward the traffic light at the avenue.

Left turn: the Belt Parkway, Verrazano Bridge, Staten Island, the four-thousand-mile expanse of gas stations and shopping malls and my birthright.

Right turn: deepest, darkest Brooklyn, my homeland.

Of course, I am not sure what you feel about fate, Father. Since you spend a lot of time praying and talking to God, I guess you must believe there is a way of influencing how things turn out. Like many, I wish I felt that were true. Like many, I wanted to try to make it true.

I made a right turn, and in ten minutes I was at East Brooklyn Hospital.

Dexter's room was filled with flowers from all of Brooklyn's most notables, various unions, the borough president, and even the mayor of all New York City. It was quite touching, really. How much of it was sentiment directed toward keeping Dexter from any deathbed confessions about dirty business? It would have been interesting to know.

Dexter had a room to himself, one with a view much like the view from his office at the *Brooklyn Gazette*. Through the window I could see the distant Wonder Wheel twinkling in the Coney Island sunshine. In front of that window was a one-eyed mummy, on his back, on a bed. Dexter's head was completely wrapped in bandages—all except for a slit for his mouth and a hole for the left eye. As I approached, the eye turned my way.

"Dexter . . . hello, I came to see how you are."

A purple eyelid blinked slowly. The rest of him was completely motionless.

"I guess that was a stupid thing to say. Obviously, you are not well. And in some small way, I feel it is my fault. I never should have come to see you at the *Gazette* that night."

His left hand rose slowly, and he waved it at a pad of paper and pen on the sheets next to him. I stepped closer.

"You want to write something?"

The left hand gave me a thumbs-up. Gingerly, I put the pen in his hand and held the pad for him to write. He did so, slowly.

"You know, Dexter, this whole mess was like the hand of ill fate was at every turn. But I was glad for your help, and I wanted you to know I appreciated it very much, and that if there's anything I can do to help you now, that you should tell me, and you can consider it done. We may not be able to control what happens all the time, to influence our own fate, but I am thinking that perhaps we can influence other people's fate. Does that make some sort of sense?"

He stopped writing and lowered the pen. I turned the pad toward me. Scrawled on the pad were the words:

TRUX ATLAS

I did not understand.

"You mean Mr. Trux. I cleaned his house. It was the house next door to the Trux house, the one Frog cleaned, that had the Atlas armored car heist money in it."

He waved the pen impatiently and scrawled once more. I turned the pad, and it was one word, underlined:

DRIVER

"Driver? I don't understand." I was an idiot, and once more he waved his pen and scribbled impatiently:

TRUX INSIDE MAN

I blinked at the words, then looked at the mummy's blood-shot, watery eye.

"Trux was the Atlas armored car driver?"

Dexter gave me a thumbs-up and let his exhausted hand drop.

"The money I found, in the tight ones under the couch, that was the inside man's money?" That was why Dexter wanted to meet me at the Trux house on Vanderhoosen, to explain that. "The armored car driver was Trux."

His thumb flicked yes.

"Ah, so that explains it." It also explained why Fanny was so sure the money was there. She knew the old fart was holding out on her, that he was in on the heist, and she was just waiting to swoop in once he died and grab it at the first opportunity. Only her timing was off. "And . . . do the police know this?"

His thumb flicked.

"Ah. Well, I guess you warned me that you might have to spill the beans. But they have not come to see me."

The first and middle finger of Dexter's left hand mimicked legs running across his sheets. The mummy's watery eye beheld me, unblinking.

FIFTY

I HURRIED DOWN TO THE car and revved her up. I was glad to have stopped in and said my piece and expressed my regrets on Dexter's unfortunate incident with Danny, but the mummy was right. This was no time to sit still. I had containers stuffed with cash waiting for me. Better to get a move on before the cops or anybody else found me and tried to take my destiny away.

I made a left on the avenue and then a right on the parkway, angling away from my former residence and toward the highway.

I stopped at a light.

An orange car pulled up on the left, and I shivered.

Thankfully, it was not Fanny and Speedy but a Rastafarian.

My breathing was uneven, and my grip on the steering wheel sweaty. Something bad was going to happen, one more shot across the bow of my galleon from fate.

At the next light, the orange car was again on my left, the music from its stereo system so loud that my whole car vibrated. That is when he suddenly turned the music way down. That is when I noticed a police car pull up on my right.

The officer was looking at me. A small two-finger salute and a fragile smile was my response to his stare. The light turned green, and the orange car and I moved forward at exactly the same speed, not wanting to excite the police. The Rasta and I exchanged a glance. Then I checked my rearview mirror. The cop was following, slowly.

Morty, you are being paranoid. The entrance to the Belt Parkway is five blocks ahead. You can even see the big green highway sign from here. From the ramp to the Verrazano is maybe ten minutes, and in a half hour you'll be in New Jersey. Four or five days after that we'll be on the veranda of your new home.

I could hardly wait to walk through the gate of the new house, into the area enclosed by stone walls overflowing with bougainvillea. The front door's iron knob cold in my hand, I would twist it, feel the heavy old latch lift, and the giant oaken door would slowly swing open. Sun would be spilling in the windows at the far side of the room, the air cool, dark, and smelling of old leather and stone. Softly, in the distance, would be the strum of a street musician's guitar. Turning to my right I would see the large array of French doors leading to the veranda. Halfway to those doors, I would stop and turn slowly to see the courtyard. And the fountain.

The big green sign sailed overhead. My blinker was on for the ramp.

The ramp was blocked.

By a police car.

The Rasta was still next to me, his eyes wide, and he continued straight past the ramp, unhindered. I signaled left to follow the Rasta, but another police car was suddenly on my left.

The officer was pointing for me to pull over.

I brought the Camaro to a stop, my heart bucking. Was entering my new home all some fantasy? It felt so real that it must be something that would happen.

Yet looking at the police car blocking the highway entrance and the other police car that slid in behind me, I felt like I would never leave Brooklyn, that I had been an idiot to think that I could escape with the money. At the same time, I was beginning to feel indignant. You know, Father Gomez, I found that money fair and square. Well, at least the first batch of money. That was legally mine. The entire contents of the home had been turned over to me in a legally binding document. Inasmuch as those idiots crashed into Storage Hut and burned my money, they were liable for my money. True, there was a lot more money now, but at least eight hundred grand of it I should be allowed to keep.

I should never have gone to see Dexter. Had I not, I would be in New Jersey, and home free.

A plain brown sedan pulled in front of the Camaro, a police light flashing on the dash.

I opened my door and rose slowly from the Camaro. I could hear all my joints creaking with dread. Two men in wrinkled suits emerged from the brown car.

Ruez came from the passenger side. He wore a grin on his face and a badge on his belt.

Pool slouched on the driver's side of the sedan, looking like a prep school truant. He was holding a piece of paper. "We have a warrant to search your apartment and car."

Someone said, and I think it was me: "Can I ask why, officer?"

"You can ask." Ruez raised an eyebrow doubtfully. "We already went to your apartment. Landlord said you're moving out. Can we ask why?"

I narrowed my eyes, feeling indignant again, tempted to be a smart-ass and answer as he had. "It is a free country. I am tired of Brooklyn, especially after all the bad things that have happened to my friends. Like Dexter, and Frog and Hugo and Pete the Prick."

"We saw the apartment. Empty." Ruez nodded at the Camaro. "Now let's see the car."

I did not move.

Pool waved the warrant. "We can smash the car windows to gain access if you want."

"It is not locked," I said, but I think his idea was that if I gave them any trouble they would smash the windows to punish me.

The two detectives pulled all my pathetic belongings out onto the hot roadway shoulder, between our two cars. The patrolmen from the other two cars were directing traffic. After Ruez and Pool finished pawing through each bag, each box, each container, I put them back in the car.

"Now here." Ruez tapped the car's trunk.

Mechanically, I slid the key in the lock, and the trunk popped open.

Ruez and Pool exchanged a glance when they saw the four matching Scottish suitcases, and then looked at me. My expression was blank. Nothing for me to do except stand by and watch.

They groaned as they pulled all four out and laid them on the macadam. Ruez and Pool each knelt next to a suitcase and unzipped them.

Then they opened them.

"What's this?" Ruez's eyebrows were raised.

Pool's brow was knit. "You wanna explain this, Mr. Martinez?"

"What is there to explain? You see what is there. Is it a crime?"

Ruez held up one of the books and read the spine. *"History of Spain, 1300–1600?"*

Pool dug through the books in his suitcase. "These are all Spanish history books."

Ruez unzipped another bag. "You have four suitcases of history books?"

"You can see that for yourself, officer." I was careful not to smile. Cops can get angry when they look foolish; no percentage in making them more so. "Was there something you were looking for?"

They stood, both of them with hands on hips, their guns visible at their sides.

Ruez heaved a sigh of frustration. "You cleaned the Trux place. Word is out you found money there. The money was likely stolen."

"In this business, there are many rumors. I did not find any money there. I just cleaned the house."

They were squinting at me, waiting.

I wanted to turn suspicion away from me, somehow. I needed them to let me go so I could drive up that ramp onto the Belt Parkway and vanish forever.

The Belt Parkway. The route Fanny and Speedy were going to use to escape, the idiots.

Then, the dark clouds on my brain were parted by a promising, sparkling idea, like a beam of sunshine in a thunderstorm.

"I do not know what you want me to tell you, officers, but I am happy to help in any way that I can. If there was money in the Trux house, I would likely have found it . . . well, I suppose my foreman Gonzales could have found it. I left him alone in the Trux house to run an errand. When I returned to the house there was a woman, Trux's niece, Fanny Trux. But she was just there to collect some boxes of old clothes."

Ruez and Pool exchanged a glance.

"Did you look in the boxes?"

"Well, no, the house was full of junk. The more I did not have to haul away, the better. Are you trying to tell me the boxes were . . . that it could have been the stolen money in there? Or that perhaps Gonzales and this Fanny Trux could have been working in concert? No, Gonzales would not double-cross me. He is my friend."

I did not know if they knew about the 911 call I had put in to the cops to have Fanny and Speedy picked up on the Belt Parkway or not, or whether they found the gun on them and had them in custody. By the lopsided grins that sprouted on their faces, it seemed possible. They turned and walked back to their car, pulled a fast U-turn, and sped away. The other two cars turned off their lights and followed.

They did not even say thank you or good-bye or apologize or anything.

I stood on the shoulder of the parkway looking at the four open Scottish suitcases, the sun beating down on my collection of history books.

Hey, I am not an idiot. If my bags were searched at the border, and I had four million two hundred thousand dollars along for the ride, I would have been in deep trouble. I nailed those four Swiss crates shut and shipped the paperbacks and money to La Paz.

FIFTY-ONE

WHICH BRINGS US TO MY father's youth in La Paz. The Genealogy Consultants report told me my father's early childhood was spent at Nuestra Señora de Cortés, at your orphanage. He was adopted by American parents when he was eight and taken to Newark, New Jersey. The hundred grand in the large package is yours to spend to improve the fate of orphans like my father.

I am here in La Paz, like a retired conquistador, writing you this note. I am on my veranda, enjoying a nice breeze and a glass of a red wine called nebbiolo. (Oddly, they do not sell cold duck here.) I can just see the topaz blue waters of the Sea of Cortés above the two houses across the street. Sorry: *a través de la calle.*

You might well ask how my father—if he grew up in your orphanage—knew of this house in which I sit. Your church and buildings are quite close by, and I can see them where I sit if I turn around. Perhaps he could see this house from his window. Perhaps he imagined himself here, with the children and parents that once happily lived here. Perhaps it is all he ever wanted for himself and his family, his legacy to me.

I can also see my fountain from here, in my courtyard. I had my family crest made by some local artisans, and they have attached it to the front. I have not found my little Mexican wife yet, but I am working on it.

Father Gomez, I hope you do not feel it necessary to reject the money in any way. Yes, the money was taken by bad men under worse circumstances—but let the money now go to a good cause, to the children of your facility. Giving money to the government or to a bank is like handing a cup of water to a whale. Besides, when things got hairy there a couple times, I promised fate that if I were spared I would give some of the money to a good cause. And what better cause than that of La Paz's orphans, so that like my father, they may dream of and find better things in this life. I admit, my father never found himself here on this veranda, as he would have wished it. Just the same he would be very pleased with the way things have turned out. Sometimes, I think, the ends justify the dreams.